TAKE THE BULL BY THE HORNS

CYNTHIA TERELST

ISBN: 978-0-648729464

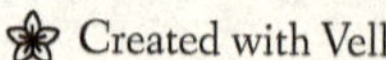 Created with Vellum

*Thank you to my family, friends, followers and fellow
writers, who support and encourage me.
You help me keep inspired.*

CHAPTER ONE

Peyton

I SAT in my Audi in the four-car garage, staring at the wall. There was no point in putting it off any longer. I needed to face my family. I needed to tell them the thing they least wanted to hear. And after that, I would hit them with what they least expected to hear.

I stepped out of the car. Fourteen months ago, driving a car had been impossible. Ten months ago, it had been a goal I set out to achieve, among many others. Eight months ago, I ticked it off the list. There'd been so many achievements except the one my parents wanted.

I took a deep breath and went inside. Mom stood at the marble counter, serving up dinner, her long blonde hair tied at the nape of her neck. Before the accident, my hair was long like hers. But the fire had burnt that, as well as my skin. Dad came from the living room, the remote control in his hand. Both looked at me expectantly. My stomach somersaulted.

I looked down at my feet, took a breath, and raised my eyes. "Dr. Mendez doesn't think I will get full functionality of my hand back."

Mom sucked a breath in.

Dad shook his head. "That's not an acceptable outcome. We need to consult another specialist."

Mom nodded. She grabbed her phone off the counter. "I've compiled a list."

I sighed. We'd already been through this, multiple times. "Dr. Mendez is one of the most renowned specialists in the United States. He warned us from the outset that this could be the outcome."

Dad's lips tightened. His face set in determination. I'm sure they would escort me to as many doctors as it would take for them to hear what they wanted—that I could resume my career as a surgeon.

I was so tired. Tired of the pressure I put on myself to recover. Tired of their expectations and resulting disappointment. Tired of fighting for a career they wanted for me. It felt like their love and support hinged on that one thing—me following in their footsteps just like my sister had.

I needed to get away. But could I do it? I'd already accepted a job in another country, in a totally non-medical related field, without consulting my parents first. But why did I need to consult them? I was twenty-six years old. But in those twenty-six years, I'd never once made a decision for myself. I'd never done anything for myself without considering what they would think or say, whether they'd approve or not.

The accident had made me stronger in many ways. It had given me a small amount of separation from them. I needed to believe in my capabilities. I needed to believe in myself. I needed to say the words.

"I've accepted a job in Australia as a nanny," I blurted out.

Dad placed the TV remote on the counter slowly, deliberately. "I beg your pardon?"

"I'm going to Australia."

Mom's face was ashen. "To be a nanny?"

"Yes."

"You can't just run away from this. You need to face it head-on," Dad said. His face was obstinate, and his shoulders rigid.

What did he think I'd been doing?

"I've been facing it head-on for fourteen months."

Was that too brazen? My heart hammered in my chest. I wanted to step back and look anywhere but at them. But I rooted my feet to the floor and held my head high.

Their eyes widened. Good little Peyton had never spoken up to them before. My stomach clenched. I was really doing this. Holy hell. Mom stood beside Dad, standing tall, her chin elevated. A pose I knew well. Sweat pooled under my arms.

"Is this where you see your life heading? Being a nanny? There are other worthy careers you can strive for," she said.

My car keys dug into my palm. They were ready to continue making my life choices. I shrunk under their unrelenting stares. I guess they were right. Maybe there were other options I could consider. Maybe...

"What about David?" Mom asked.

The audacity. Bringing David, my so-called fiancé, into this was uncalled for. I brought myself to my full height.

"David has no bearing on my decision."

"He should. He is your fiancé," Dad said.

"My fiancé? He has not visited for the last two months unless it was because you invited him to dinner."

"He just started his residency at Massachusetts General," Mom said. "You know he works long hours. He's under a lot of pressure to secure a spot at the hospital."

I let out an exasperated breath. I didn't want to have this conversation with them. I would never win. David could do no wrong in their eyes. I'm sure they'd prefer him as a child rather than me.

I couldn't help myself. "They've banned all phones, too, have they?"

"He's very busy."

This was ridiculous. I clutched my keys harder. "The only reason David hasn't broken off the engagement is because of you. He doesn't care about me."

"That's not true," Mom said; agitation filled her voice.

"Yes, Mom, it is true. It's all about status. Your status. His family's status."

I'd given this a lot of thought over the past fourteen months. We'd drifted further and further apart since the accident. If I were to be honest, we hadn't been that close to start with. Not in a relationship sense. We moved in the same circles, but there was no true intimacy between us, nothing deep.

"He can hide behind his busy career all he likes, but it's been over for months."

"You need to speak to him. You cannot make this decision alone."

"I will speak to him." And that would be giving him more than he had given me. "When I tell him I've accepted a job in Australia."

He would be nothing but relieved.

Unlike my parents. This wouldn't be the last conversation we had about this. I needed to stay strong and stand my ground.

Australia sounded more inviting by the minute.

CHAPTER TWO

Lachlan

I DROVE INTO MY CARPORT. Jane's car was in its old spot, almost like it still belonged there. Like she hadn't moved out three years ago. Scarlet and Thomas's squeals of delight floated through the open car window. What were they doing? I got out of my car and walked toward the back of the house. My eight-year-old daughter and five-year-old son were chasing each other under the sprinkler.

"Daddy," Scarlet yelled when she saw me.

Thomas's eyes were like automatic target trackers. He spotted me within a millisecond. He broke out into a wide grin as he ran towards me. Scarlet was right behind him. They launched themselves at me, soaking me with their drenched clothes. They didn't care that I was covered in dirt from a day of work on the farm. I swung them around.

That's when I noticed Jane and my mother watching us, matching smiles on their faces. What was my mother doing here?

"Kids, we're just going inside for a few minutes to talk to Dad," Jane said.

Felt like an ambush.

I followed Jane and Mum inside. That saying about Plain Jane never applied to my ex-wife. She was tall with flowing blonde hair. Scarlet definitely took after her in the looks department. No matter; I had a gun to keep horny boys away when she became a teenager.

Jane and Mum sat at the table. It was a beautiful old wooden table passed down through the generations. It was made in this house and would stay here until the house no longer existed. I went into the kitchen and stood behind the counter, facing them both.

"We've hired a new nanny. She starts next week," Jane said.

I looked between them. Trying to keep my voice calm, I said, "You did what?"

Mum gave me her 'don't you start shit' stare. "Lachlan, the last one quit two months ago. School holidays start next week. We need someone to look after the children when they're here with you. You can't drag them all over the farm while you work."

True, but that wasn't the point.

"You chose a nanny without consulting me?"

Mum still had that strict look on her face. "Let's be honest, Lachlan, your previous choices didn't go very well."

True again.

"What experience does this nanny have?"

Mum and Jane glanced at each other. Jane shifted in her seat.

"She doesn't have experience being a nanny, as such."

I placed my hands flat on the counter. "Define, *as such.*"

"She has a niece and nephew she's looked after," Mum said.

Jane smiled, almost letting out a laugh, before composing herself. I focused my attention on her, raising my eyebrows.

"Nothing," she said, lifting her shoulders.

"That was more than nothing." The almost-laughter had me suspicious.

"I think she said something like, 'I've dealt with a lot of male surgeons, and they may as well be children.'"

I sighed. She was a nurse. Ten points there. Thomas always got cuts and scrapes. "A nurse is a good choice."

Mum and Jane shared another look. What now?

Mum used her calm, reasonable voice. "Technically, she's a doctor."

"Like a paediatrician?"

"No, not exactly," Mum said.

"She's either a paediatrician or she isn't."

What were they hiding?

"She was training to be a surgeon."

"And now she's going to be our nanny?"

"Yep," Jane said, a little too brightly.

I drove my palms into the bench. "So, you've hired someone who was training to be a surgeon but isn't now, for some reason you haven't explained, who has basically no experience with children, to look after our kids, one of whom has already sent four nannies packing?"

"Yep," Jane said. I'm sure she was being dismissive just to irritate me.

I doubt male surgeons had anything on Thomas. Some days it was a struggle to keep him still. And Scarlet could give as good as she got. If she didn't like you from the beginning, it was hard to win her over.

The kids were going to have a field day.

I LAY ON THE BENCH, doing chest presses. My arms struggled on the last rep. I put the bar back in the cradle before staring up at the ceiling. What were Mum and Jane thinking? Surely there were better choices out there for a nanny, like someone with actual nanny experience. As disturbed as I was, I knew they wouldn't have made a careless choice. There was no point arguing with them. They'd already hired her. And I didn't need the aggravation of them ganging up on me.

And the fact that school holidays started next week, and I hadn't hired anyone, gave them more reason to make a choice without me. Mum had her own life, and I couldn't expect her to look after them again. But this nanny would live on the farm, both when the kids were here and when the kids weren't. I should have been the one to choose who that would be. Except I wasn't making a choice fast enough.

I huffed. I'd be using the gym a lot more. It would be a good place to work out my nanny frustration and help me reset. How long would this one last?

Bruce's car pulled into the driveway. His heavy steps approached the shed. As he leant against the door frame, his wide shoulders blocked out the moonlight.

"Hear you've got a new nanny coming," my brother said.

News travels fast on the farm.

I sat up and turned to him.

He gave me a lopsided grin. "She's a bit of a looker too."

I narrowed my eyes. "How would you know?"

"Mum showed me pictures."

They didn't show *me* pictures.

"I doubt they hired her for her looks," I said.

"It's good for you, though. Those other nannies weren't much to look at."

I shook my head. "She's here to care for the children. That's it."

He shrugged. "Yeah, but when the kids are with Jane, she can keep you company."

I stood up and went to the dumbbell rack. I grabbed some weights and started bicep curls. She wasn't even here yet and I had nanny frustration to work out. I was not going to entertain Bruce. I was too busy to worry about his shit talk. I had obligations—my family and the farm were at the top of that list.

He smirked. "Come on, she'll be a cure for your loneliness."

I gave him a firm stare. There was no reason for me to interact with the new nanny when the children weren't with me. "Some people are happy to be alone. Being alone doesn't make someone lonely."

The glint in his eyes told me he wasn't going to give up. "Do you think your big muscles will impress her?"

"Fuck off, idiot."

Bruce could joke as much as he liked. It didn't matter how good-looking she was. She was here to do a job. I was effectively her employer, even if I wasn't the one to hire her. And I was not interested in anything more than that.

CHAPTER THREE

Peyton

A GREEN LANDSCAPE spread out as far as the eye could see from the plane window. Trees dotted the ground; sometimes, they grew thick like a forest until bare land took over again. Hills occasionally broke the flatness. From here, they looked like bumps on the land, like the scars that ran the full length of my arm. The scene was beautiful, but my arm? Not so much.

The plane circled the town, or was it a city? No skyscrapers here. Just lots of buildings and houses spread out in a small geographical area before the land took over again. The hospital I'd worked in was bigger than any building I could see from the sky.

The small aircraft landed with a soft thud. I watched the passengers around me. They were much more relaxed than those I'd normally see on flights. In America, they'd be up out of their seats collecting their baggage from the overhead lockers before the doors had even opened. Most of the people on this plane stayed seated.

We disembarked onto the tarmac. The heat radiating off the black tar reminded me I was far from Boston, where frosts were browning the grass. I followed the others into the building and to the arrivals area of the Tamworth Airport, searching for Jane, who was meeting me. A smiling blonde headed in my direction. She was wearing shorts and a T-shirt. My stomach tightened. I was overdressed in wide-leg pants and a three-quarter-sleeve cotton shirt with a collar. I could have worn jeans, but the flight was long, and there was no need to be uncomfortable.

"Peyton?" she said when she reached me.

"Yes." I returned her smile.

"I'm Jane." She stuck her hand out.

I hesitated for a moment before reaching my hand out to meet hers, conscious of how my sleeve rode up my arm. How would she react? She took my hand firmly and shook it. She didn't even give it a second glance. I'd stopped wearing the compression garment after my last appointment with the occupational therapist. It meant that my scars were visible to everyone twenty-four hours a day.

"Nice to meet you," I said.

"Scarlet and Thomas are at the farm this week with Lachlan. They're both very excited to meet you."

Jane and Ann, the children's grandmother, had told me all about them. They sounded very active and a lot of fun. It would be quite enjoyable to be exposed to something other than hospital treatment rooms and my parents' scrutiny.

"I'm excited to meet them too."

"Let's get your suitcase," she said, heading to the luggage carousel. "Like I mentioned, the farm is an hour from town. The children live with me one week in Tamworth, and the following week they're with Lachlan."

I nodded. Lachlan was an unknown to me. He hadn't

been involved in any of the interviews. Did that mean he wasn't interested in who looked after his children? Was he too busy for mundane things like my father was?

"Ann lives on the farm too. Lachlan is in the main house now. Ann has a smaller house. Bruce, Lachlan's brother, also has a house there with his wife." The farm sounded bigger than I'd imagined. I hadn't spent much time in the country, but when I was watching renovation shows during my recovery, they would sometimes feature farmhouses on a few acres. If Lachlan's farm had multiple houses, it would be bigger than a few acres.

I stepped forward when I saw my bright turquoise suitcase and pulled it off the carousel.

"I don't know how you manage to fit all you need in just one case," Jane said, moving toward the doors. "Since I became a mum, I seem to overpack for every occasion."

"To be honest, I didn't know what to pack. I'll probably need to go shopping."

"Depending on what you want, there are a few shops in Tamworth. Otherwise, you can shop online. But deliveries can take a while out here."

I followed Jane to her car and put the suitcase in the trunk.

"Hot tip—write a list whenever you think of something you need. The one-hour drive can be a pain in the arse."

"Is there a town closer?"

"Yes, Lilli Lilli is twenty minutes from the farm. They have limited shopping."

She continued to chat as we drove. I forced myself to stay awake, listening to Jane and watching the scenery. This was a totally different world from Boston, with its mixture of old buildings, grand houses, luxury apartments and outdoor cafes. The further we drove, the fewer houses we passed. The land here stretched to the horizon, with very little except trees to disturb the bareness. Wire fences straddled each side of the road, sometimes interrupted by long driveways that presumably led to houses I couldn't see.

Finally, we slowed and turned into one of those long driveways. The car vibrated as we drove over bars of steel stretched across the road.

"That's a cattle grid," Jane explained. "The cattle won't cross it."

"Why?"

"Their legs get caught between the steel bars. Cows are scared of falling and hurting themselves, so they don't risk crossing them."

I had so much to learn.

"The farm has been in Lachlan's family for generations. They raise beef cattle here—all Angus."

We drove past a paddock full of red cows. Red Angus? I thought they'd be black. I had a lot of research to do. I could do that while the children were with Jane. I hadn't decided what else I'd do during that quiet time. Lots of reading and maybe a course online. But on what?

A single-storey house came into view. A wide verandah circled the limestone building and shaded the large windows. Lush lawn surrounded the house with beautiful gardens and large shade trees.

Jane stopped the car in the driveway, and we hopped out. Two children came running from around the side of the house. Must be Scarlet and Thomas. Scarlet's blonde hair was in two pigtails, and Thomas had a mass of messy brown hair. Their grins were identical.

Two figures made their way down the stairs. I knew Ann instantly from our video calls.

The man beside her was striking. Sunlight glinted off

his thick golden-brown hair like surgical blades would shine under focused lighting. He was tanned and muscular with tattoos down one arm, a mixture of black and white and colour, indistinct at this distance. Wowsers, I didn't know farmers looked like that. I blushed. While Ann oozed warmth, he oozed stoic resignation.

I tore my attention away from him and settled it on the two children in front of me. I knew exactly what it was like to be the youngest child and always addressed last. So, I spoke to Thomas first.

"You must be Thomas," I said, giving him a big smile.

He nodded with such intensity it was a wonder he didn't give himself whiplash. Then, as if controlled by a remote, he stopped and stared at my arm. I watched as his gaze went from the tips of my fingers to the cuff of my sleeve.

Jane shifted beside me. "Thom—"

"Does it go all the way up?" he asked.

"Thomas," Lachlan said, his voice firm.

"I'm so sorry, Peyton," Jane said.

"It's OK."

I had to answer their questions sooner or later. Kids were always curious. They'd often ask questions adults were too afraid to. I crouched down, so I was on Thomas's level.

"Yes, it goes all the way up." I pulled my collar down to show him the scars at the bottom of my neck.

Thomas's eyes widened. "Does it hurt?"

"Not as much as it did."

I turned to Scarlet. "It's nice to meet you, Scarlet."

"It's nice to meet you, Peyton." She stuck out her hand, not even glancing at mine.

I shook it.

I stood back up and turned my attention to Ann and Lachlan. Ann approached and wrapped her arms around me. Her warmth was comforting and gone all too soon when she let go.

"It's great to have you here at last."

Anyone would think they'd been waiting for me for months rather than three weeks. That's all it had taken to apply for the job and make the move half a world away. I could make a life for myself here, couldn't I?

I glanced at Lachlan. His expression hadn't changed, except now he was watching my every move. My stomach tightened. I raised my eyes to his. Chocolate and amber. Silk and fire.

Was he going to say something?

"Peyton, this is Lachlan," Jane said, breaking the silence.

"Nice to meet you." I massaged my right hand as I waited for him to say something or do something.

"Likewise." Lachlan reached out to take my hand.

As I placed my hand in his, a surge of energy ran through it. His engulfed mine. The buzz that came off it directly contrasted with the reserved man who stood in front of me. Now that he was closer, I could see his tattoos clearer. It was a delicate balance, a well-woven mixture of flowers, machinery, musical notes and names.

"Don't mind, Dad," Scarlet said, looking between us. "He's pissed that he didn't have a say in our new nanny."

"Scarlet," Jane said in a warning tone. I'm not sure if it was because of the language Scarlet had used or what she had divulged. What she'd revealed certainly explained Lachlan's behaviour.

Lachlan's lips twitched. Oh, so he had a sense of humour. Good to know.

"I think your choice is perfect, Mummy." She gave me a sweet smile.

"Yeah." Thomas nodded with gusto.

"We are going to have so much fun," Scarlet said.

"You're not the fun police, are you?" Thomas asked, his round, boyish face serious. "The last nanny didn't let us do anything."

I held my laughter in. I couldn't begin to imagine what *anything* included. I had a feeling these two would keep me on my toes. Constantly.

Keep them alive. Keep them entertained. Have fun with them. I could manage that...surely.

"No," I said. "I'm not the fun police."

Thomas clapped and ran off. I smiled after him. I needed to find a way to work with that energy.

"Peyton's had a long trip. I'm sure she would like to rest now," Jane said to Scarlet.

"Maybe you can come for dinner later. And tomorrow we can give you a tour of the farm and introduce you to everyone. Maybe Dad can put on a special lunch for us all. And—"

"There will be no fraternising on this farm," Lachlan said.

CHAPTER FOUR

Lachlan

Four females turned in my direction. Scarlet cocked her head. Mum's eyes were wide. Peyton's mouth dropped open. But the most disconcerting was the small smirk from Jane.

What was she smirking for?

My little outburst was obviously not my best moment. I widened my stance. If we were being honest, I hadn't had any good moments since Peyton had stepped out of the car. I'd only managed to say a few words, and they weren't exactly enlightening.

Everything about Peyton had me on edge, even the way she'd reacted when she saw me. She'd measured me up in an instant. What she thought of me, I couldn't tell. Why did I care? She was here to look after my children. Liking me had nothing to do with it. All I knew was that I felt a pull towards her, and I didn't like it.

"Right, OK," Mum said, breaking the silence. "Let's show Peyton to her unit."

Mum walked off with Peyton and Scarlet. Jane and I followed while Thomas played in the sandpit. Scarlet chatted incessantly. Mum interrupted only when something needed to be clarified.

What on earth were they thinking hiring someone like Peyton? Her clothes alone told me about the comfortable life she lived. A farm was no place for her.

She had some sort of pull with each of them. Mum and Jane had treated her like she was an old friend. Scarlet was drawn to her like a magnet. But what struck me the most was Thomas's reaction. He was genuinely happy to have her here. He hadn't given two shits about any of the other nannies.

"What was that all about?" Jane asked as the distance increased between us and the others.

"What?"

"That no fraternising crap."

"She's here to do a job, that's it."

Jane rolled her eyes. "So, we can't be friends with her?"

"And when she leaves, then what?"

Jane regarded me. "Why would she leave?"

"Look at her, Jane. She doesn't belong on a farm."

I shouldn't have looked. Fuck. Her beauty wasn't just in her face, with clear skin and bright honey-brown eyes. Even her short sandy brown hair, tousled from her flight, was charming. Most of us would have looked like shit after travelling across the world, but not Peyton. And it wasn't just about her curves. She had this grace about her in the way she walked and silently observed. There was confidence in her but also hints of uncertainty.

I frowned. Why was I looking? Evaluating? She wasn't a bull in the sales ring. She was the nanny for my children. *That's* the only reason I noticed these things about her.

Jane gave me a sidelong look. "You don't get to choose where Peyton belongs—farm, city, north pole—it's her choice."

What was going on here? Was Scarlet right? Was I pissed because I didn't get to choose the new nanny?

I sighed. "I know. But living on a farm is tough. It's isolating."

"She's tougher than you think."

Her scars. Was that what Jane was referring to? Peyton was nervous about them, or maybe the right word was conscious, like the small flicker of surprise on her face when Scarlet offered her hand so freely or the tiny jerk of her hand when mine took hers.

"She handled Thomas well," I conceded.

Jane nodded. "I liked the way she got down to his level to speak to him."

"And when he ran off, she didn't give any indication that she thought it was rude."

Jane laughed. "My God, remember Mildred? She always insisted that he stay until he asked to be dismissed."

Yeah, she wasn't one of my best choices. She'd lasted a month. We'd see if Peyton could outlast her. Probably not.

When we reached the unit, the other three were waiting at the top of the stairs for us.

Mum was speaking to Peyton. "The unit is close to the house for those early starts but also private enough that the children shouldn't disturb you."

Scarlet opened the door and stepped in. "This is your kitchen. It's not very big. But it has an oven and fridge." She looked around the space proudly as if she were a real estate agent. Too much reality TV? Or maybe she'd inherited Jane's flair for selling.

Peyton's honey-brown eyes studied the area and then

rested on Scarlet. She smiled at her—genuine, wide and toothy. "It has everything I need. It even has a table where I can eat."

Scarlet took the few steps to the lounge area. The sliding door at the other end of the room opened, and Thomas came running in, flinging himself onto the couch. He patted the seat beside him, and Peyton sat.

I'd need to remind him about this being Peyton's home, not his.

"Comfy?" Thomas asked.

"Oh, yes, very comfortable."

"The TV in the house is bigger. You can come watch movies there."

"What movie do you suggest?" she asked.

Thomas leant in close to give his whispered answer.

Jane nudged me in the ribs. "There goes your no fraternising rule."

I grunted. Smart arse. Of course, she'd watch movies in the main house when she was looking after the kids. Looking after them wasn't fraternising. Everything else Scarlet had suggested was. How the hell was I going to set ground rules when they seemed so enchanted by her? I don't even know why they were so enthralled. Was it because she spoke *with* them instead of *to* them? The other nannies hadn't done that. Or was it because she was friendly and open?

"Scarlet, let's show Peyton the rest of the unit, and then we can leave her to get some rest," Mum said.

Jane and I waited on the back verandah. The unit was roomy for one person but stifling for six.

"Looks like Ben is interested in Peyton too," Jane said.

I followed her gaze. The bull was at the fence, watching everything.

"Make sure you tell him not to fraternise too."

Was I ever going to live that comment down? It didn't matter. Separation was important, and I was going to maintain it. I wanted to live a simple, uncomplicated life where I could do what I do best—look after my family and the farm. Having a friendship with the nanny didn't sound uncomplicated.

CHAPTER FIVE

Peyton

I LAY IN BED, willing sleep to come. I was beyond
exhausted. It had taken over twenty-four hours to arrive at
the farm. I'd tried to sleep on Australian time, hoping that it
would reduce the jet lag.

I'd watched Lachlan and his family walk away from me
an hour ago. Even his butt had an attitude. It certainly
looked good in his work shorts. I giggled. I was definitely
beyond tired now, thinking about a virtual stranger's butt.

The way he interacted with his family as they walked
away was enlightening. It was like he was a different person
from the one who'd presented himself to me. He was full of
energy, laughing as Thomas rode on his back. He and Jane
may not have been married anymore, but they were still
close.

I'd never be close like that with David. The moment the
accident happened, he'd started drifting away. At first, I
thought it was because he didn't know what to do. The
extent of my injuries had been a shock to everyone. But it

hadn't been that at all. I didn't meet his needs anymore. I couldn't be what he wanted me to be. And if I couldn't be a surgeon, the perfect wife, the person by his side, supporting him, then I wasn't worth his time or effort. Even our last encounter showed that.

WE STOOD in my father's study. You couldn't get much more impersonal. David looked every part of upper-class America with his designer jeans and long-sleeved polo.

"What do you mean you can't be a surgeon?"

"My hand doesn't have the fine motor skills I need to perform surgeries."

He glanced at my hand. He tried to hide his disgust. But it was clear to me. I'd worn a long sleeve top for that reason. Any doubts I'd had about taking the job in Australia were eliminated at that moment.

"You're a doctor. If you're not a surgeon, there are other specialisations you can pursue."

He was just like my parents. Being a doctor alone wasn't enough for them.

"I'm not going to pursue another specialty. I'm leaving medicine."

"What? What about our future?"

I sighed. He was going to make me say it. He didn't want to be the one to put an end to our relationship. This had to be turned around onto me so that he didn't look like the bad guy. It was all about his reputation.

My hands shook. I needed to say the words. This would be the second time I'd spoken up for myself in two days. Probably more than I'd done in my whole life. Because disappointing people and risking their love was not something I did. But I didn't have his love anymore. I wondered if I ever had.

"David, if our future is dependent on me being in the medical field, then there is no future."

"What are you saying?"

Something he was too afraid to say. I wasn't going to unpack this with him. He didn't deserve that. I rubbed my right hand. Six years was a lot to throw away. Should I explain it all to him? Try to get him to understand? No. Because it was all about him. It would always be about him.

"I've accepted a job in Australia. I'm leaving in four days."

I studied his face. Surprise. Comprehension. And finally, relief. No words trying to change my mind. No reassurances about our relationship.

"You'll be an excellent surgeon, David." I kissed him on the cheek and walked away.

My parents went to him as I walked up the stairs. Their voices were low, but I knew they were consoling him, offering him the support they didn't offer me.

EVERYONE'S LOVE for me was conditional.

I didn't need a relationship like that, or any relationship for that matter. I didn't need to feel that I wasn't good enough for someone because I couldn't meet their ideal. And I didn't need to feel like my scars were a barrier to love.

I couldn't let it bother me. I had a new future here. There were two beautiful children to look after. Jane and Ann were ready to embrace me. And Lachlan? Well, Lachlan, I'd just have to figure out as we went along. I didn't have to worry about being anything for him except a carer for his children. If I could prove to him that I could perform that duty, surely, he'd be more accepting of my presence.

My eyes sprang open. Grunting. Soft but insistent. Scratching? Was that scratching? The bull? No, it was coming from under the unit. The bull, who'd watched my every move through the windows after the family left, wouldn't be under the unit.

It was dark outside. The clock read four in the morning. I must have fallen asleep at some point; I wasn't going out into the dark to investigate. How much longer until the sun rose? I grabbed my phone and checked the weather app for sunrise. First light would be in one and a half hours. OK. At least it would be daylight when I walked over to the house for the 6:00 a.m. start. More movement. Then silence.

I tried in vain to go back to sleep. Not even meditation worked. All I could see was me walking down the steps and some weird Australian animal launching at me. The silence stretched out and out until my alarm went off. I hadn't heard anything below me since those sounds that had woken me. I swung out of bed, trying to be light on my feet. I didn't want to disturb whatever it was. Then I realised the water from the shower would wake it anyway.

At ten to six, I poked my head out the door, surveying the verandah. Nothing was lying in wait. I stepped out and made my way to the stairs. I glanced around. No movement. I made my way down the stairs and strode across the lawn, constantly glancing from side to side.

By the time I got to the back door I was so amped up I would have broken into a sprint if a leaf rustled behind me.

Lachlan was there waiting for me. His eyes narrowed. "Is something wrong?"

I looked back over my shoulder. "No."

What would he think if I told him I was frightened by

some unfamiliar noise? I'm sure there were lots of noises I wouldn't know on a farm. He raised his eyebrows as he glanced over my shoulder. When he found nothing, he shook his head and stepped aside, letting me in.

The kitchen was huge, matching the size of the kitchen at home. But where the one at home was sleek lines, hidden appliances, and marble, this one was shaker doors, wooden bench tops, natural light and warmth. Ha, those home renovation shows I watched while recovering paid off.

"The children are still asleep. They probably won't be awake for another hour."

"OK." That's all I could manage. I was transfixed by those brown eyes of his, the fire in them duller this morning but no less captivating. I swallowed and moved my attention to my surroundings. "What do they have for breakfast?"

"Toast, cereal, whatever they want. But not ice cream."

"Ice cream?"

"Scarlet will tell you it's calcium and a legitimate breakfast food."

I laughed. "She has a good point."

And the stern look returned. My stomach tightened as I averted my eyes. Why on earth did this man have such an effect on me?

"Well, obviously, I won't be giving her ice cream for breakfast."

He gave me a curt nod. "What do you have planned for today?"

"I think Scarlet and Thomas want to show me around the farm."

"The keys for the Land Cruiser are beside the door."

Small feet thundered through the dining room and into

the kitchen. Thomas's freckled face grinned up at me. So much for sleeping for another hour.

"I'm off now. I'll be back for morning tea." Lachlan made his way to the door.

"Morning tea?"

He rubbed his chin. "Mid-morning break, where we have a bite to eat."

Did he come back for morning tea every day or was he keeping an eye on me?

I watched as he sat on the bench outside to put on his boots.

"Are you still tired?" Thomas asked.

What gave me away? "Some strange noises woke me up."

Lachlan's boots were on, but he remained seated.

"What sort of noises?" Thomas asked, his eyes wide as he perched himself on a stool at the counter.

"Scratching and grunting."

"Oh, that's probably Mr Harrison."

"Who?" What would a man be doing under my unit?

A light chuckle came from the bench outside.

"Mr Harrison. The wombat," Thomas said.

A wombat, right. What was a wombat? "Are they dangerous?"

"Mr Harrison won't hurt you. He's used to us."

"OK." He wasn't used to *me*.

I blushed. Lachlan must think I was crazy or stupid. He could have tried to be reassuring instead of just sitting on the bench, not saying a word. Everyone knew half the animals in Australia wanted to kill you. So much for speaking up for myself. I sighed. This was going to be harder for me to learn than I imagined. Being in a new place didn't automatically mean I was this wonderful new me who could put twenty-six years of oppression behind me.

Scarlet walked in, rubbing her eyes. "It's the snakes you need to worry about."

"The snakes?" My voice came out higher than I intended.

Lachlan chuckled as he stood up. Without a glance back, he walked to his car. He was a snake in the grass, lying in wait. But for what? And what exactly was I supposed to do with a snake of the human variety?

CHAPTER SIX

Lachlan

I shook my head as I sat in the car. Scarlet was such a shit-stirrer. And I was a dick. I should have gone back inside and spoken to Peyton about snakes. She came from the big smoke. She'd have no idea what to do if she saw a snake. Would she know what to do if someone was bitten by one? She'd probably never dealt with a snake bite before. Would it happen? Unlikely, but still.

Bruce was in the machinery shed when I parked. He gave me a shit-eating grin as I entered. "How's your morning been?"

Why was he asking?

"Fine."

"Been doing some early morning fraternising?"

For fuck's sake. Who told him? If he knew, everyone on the farm would know by now.

He watched me closely, the grin growing wider. "Who even uses that word? Maybe a seventy-year-old."

"Ha ha. You're such a comedian."

"You're the one who said it...old man."

And it seemed I was going to be reminded about it for a very long time.

"Are you finished? We've got work to do," I said.

We needed to move cows from the river paddock. The feed in there was getting low.

"Is she as pretty in real life?" he asked.

Nope, he wasn't finished.

"She's alright."

She was more than alright. Her ready smile lit up her face. And her composure was in direct contrast to that. It was like she was one person with Scarlet and Thomas and a different one with me. I guess that was to be expected after my behaviour.

I walked over to my quad, checked my helmet for unwanted eight-legged visitors, and then put it on.

Bruce followed. "Just alright? I guess her social media lied."

"You'll meet her soon enough. The kids are going to give her a farm tour."

Bruce put on his helmet and hopped onto the quad parked beside me.

"So what was with the fraternising comment?" He was serious this time.

"I don't know. She's here to do a job. That's it. Just like I have a job to do."

"So, that's it. She looks after the kids, and then you live totally separate lives?"

"Precisely. I don't have time for relationships."

Bruce's eyes nearly popped out of his head. "Relationships? How did we go from keeping you company to relationships? She's your nanny, and you're acting like she wants to jump your bones."

"That's not what I meant." I certainly didn't want to fucking jump hers.

"I hate to break it to you, but you're not irresistible."

I sighed.

"Don't sigh at me. I swear, sometimes you have the IQ of a Vegemite sandwich."

He started the quad and headed to the river paddock. I followed. What he said did have some merit. Our lives would be intertwined because of the children. The least I could be was friendly as well as professional.

I didn't need to worry about a relationship other than friendship. I was good at friendships. Just look at Jane and me. We were always better as friends. Trying to be more than that didn't work. It certainly wouldn't work with someone like Peyton—a reserved city girl.

As we moved the cows along the laneway, opening and closing gates so there could be no backtracking, I looked out for the Land Cruiser. I didn't see it once. Maybe they'd changed their mind.

I PULLED into the driveway at morning tea. Peyton, Scarlet and Thomas were near the vegetable garden. It wasn't exactly a garden, more like an area vegetables once grew that was now full of weeds. Ben was at the fence watching them. What was with that bull?

I approached them. Scarlet and Thomas's faces glowed.

"Daddy, we're going to plant a vegetable garden," Scarlet said.

"Peyton said we will need to use Google to see what's good to plant now," Thomas said.

That was a good idea. They'd be able to see how much effort went into the food we eat. Not just on our farm but vegetable growers as well. A lot of people thought farming was passive. You plant some seeds and come back later to collect the vegetables. But farming is far from passive. An important lesson for all children. Is that why Peyton was doing it? Or was she just trying to keep them busy? Probably the latter; I'm not sure too many city people think about how their food is grown.

"That's great. There are some gardening books in the house that might help," I said. "You'll need to find a way to keep Mr Harrison out of the garden."

This was my chance to redeem myself. I turned to Peyton. "His burrow is under your unit. He comes out at night to feed. He won't bother you."

She nodded and gave me a small smile. I guess that's all I deserved. I could have eased her mind hours ago.

"Will he eat the vegetables we plant?" she asked.

"It's hard to say. They don't normally eat garden plants and crops. But they like to dig."

"OK. We'll add that to our list of things to investigate."

"Did the kids talk to you about snakes?"

"Yes."

"We told her there were venomous ones and non-venomous," Scarlet said.

Thomas nodded vigorously. "But we don't want to get close enough to find out."

"And if we see a snake, we should stand still and let it go on its way."

"Or move away slowly," Thomas said, stepping back to show us exactly how slowly.

I ruffled his hair. "That's right. Most snakes are shy. They don't want to be near you as much as you don't want to be near them. They usually only attack if they feel threatened."

"And we told her what to do if someone is bitten," Scarlet said.

Peyton smiled at them. "Keep the patient still. Call an ambulance. Apply a bandage over the bite. And then an elasticised one as high up the limb as you can get," Peyton said, confidence in her voice.

"Perfect," I said.

She must have looked that up or remembered it from her training. The kids wouldn't have given her that much detail.

"Don't worry," I said. "Snake bites are rare. But it's good to be prepared."

She nodded.

I was doing good at this redeeming shit. I didn't want her to feel that we couldn't be friends or at least friendly. It wouldn't be the end of the world if we were.

"Let's have morning tea." I started walking toward the house. "Are you going for your farm tour before lunch? We'll be out by the central crush."

"Where is the central crush exactly?"

"Turn left when you leave the house, turn right at the old dead tree, cross the bridge, turn left at the old pumphouse, keep going for a couple of Ks..." I trailed off.

Peyton stared, her brows furrowed in concentration. "I'm sorry. I don't follow."

"The directions?"

She nodded. "Is the crush on the farm?"

"Yes. We have five thousand acres here."

"Of course, sorry. The directions made it seem..."

"That's how we give directions out in the country. We don't have street signs."

"OK. I guess I need to write them down then." She paused. "There's one other problem."

Problem?

CHAPTER SEVEN

Peyton

WELL, I might as well admit it. Hopefully, Lachlan's grace would persist. He did talk to me about Mr Harrison rather than allowing my concern to continue. And he did discuss snakes. Although it felt like a test. Let's see how he'd feel about this revelation.

"I don't know how to drive a stick shift."

He stopped walking and turned toward me. My stomach twisted as I looked up into his face, not knowing what expression I'd see.

His eyes widened, but he didn't look angry or condescending. "You don't know how to drive a manual?"

Why was he so surprised? Because we lived in two different worlds, that's why.

"Most cars in America are automatics."

"Oh, right. OK." He ran his hand through his thick hair. "Um, do you want to have a lesson?"

"Yes, please."

I didn't really have a choice. If I didn't know how to

drive the car, I could never leave the farm. But besides that, it would be fun to learn something new. That's one reason I found surgery so fascinating. There was always something different. Some procedures were ordinary, but others were unique and seen rarely.

"We can start during my lunch break. The fourby is pretty easy to drive."

"The what?"

"The Landcruiser is a four-wheel drive—a fourby."

Wombats under houses, no street signs, and weird names for cars. Was this a farm thing? Or an Australian thing?

We followed him into the house. I imagined he wouldn't have long for morning tea, so we'd prepared a fruit platter before he returned. Nothing fancy, just cut up apples, oranges and watermelon.

"Scarlet and Thomas helped with the fruit," I said.

Lachlan's eyes narrowed. Had I done something wrong?

"I thought it was a good idea for them to choose the fruit and arrange the platter."

He nodded. Did that mean he approved?

"I bet I know who chose what," he said to the children.

The kids grinned. Thomas looked like him, although he smiled a lot more than his father.

"Guess," Scarlet said.

"You chose the watermelon, Thomas the oranges and Peyton the apples."

"How did you know?" Thomas asked.

"Dad's intuition."

Scarlet screwed up her face.

"As your father, it's my job to know your favourite things."

I smiled. He was proving my assumption wrong again. He was more involved with his children than I first thought.

———

"READY FOR YOUR LESSON?" Lachlan asked as he walked through the kitchen door.

"Do you want to eat first? We've made sandwiches, your favourite, according to Scarlet."

He nodded and sat down at the table. Lachlan's mouth lifted on one side as he examined the sandwiches on his plate. He gazed at Scarlet, his eyebrows raised. "Peanut butter, honey and banana?"

She shrugged. Thomas was giggling so hard that he was at risk of falling off his chair.

"Isn't it your favourite?" I asked.

"Not even close." His voice was hard.

I looked down at my hands. Would I ever be able to do anything right in his eyes? I couldn't even make him a simple sandwich.

"You shouldn't believe everything these kids tell you," he said. There was a lightness to his voice. As I looked up, he was swapping plates with Scarlet.

My pulse slowed. I'd overreacted and jumped to conclusions. He wasn't angry with me. I needed to remember I wasn't in Boston with my parents anymore. Thomas's giggles should have told me it was all a joke. I needed to lighten up.

Scarlet was laughing too. "You should have seen the look on your face, Daddy."

"I'm sure it will match the look on yours when I tell you I've already told Peyton no ice cream for breakfast."

She pouted.

I sat in my designated chair to eat my sandwich. The same as Scarlet's because the combination sounded interesting, and being here was about being open to trying new things.

Lachlan glanced at my plate but didn't say a word.

The dynamics in this family were totally different from what I was accustomed to. There were serious moments, but those were mixed with lightness and laughter. The Lachlan I saw today was the opposite of the man who I'd met the day before. I liked this Lachlan better.

As soon as we all finished eating, Lachlan asked, "Ready?"

I stood up. "As ready as I'll ever be."

We went outside. Lachlan had already moved the Landcruiser, or fourby as the kids liked to call it, onto the road. I went to the car and opened the door. Wrong side. Not a great start.

"Whoops," I said, stepping backwards right into Lachlan. I bounced off his chest, and he reached out to steady me. Big hands. Strong hands. Gentle hands. A flush crept across my cheeks. He let me go and made space for me to pass him.

I walked to the driver's side and pulled the door open. The car was much higher than I was used to. How was I going to get in without embarrassing myself? I watched Scarlet, who opened the door behind me. She stepped onto the sidestep, so I grabbed onto the handrail and followed suit. We all put our seat belts on. I noticed that Thomas sat in a booster seat.

"OK." Lachlan indicated to the gear stick. "There's neutral, where no gears are engaged, five forward gears and reverse. You start in the lowest gear, and as your speed increases, you go up in gear. The sound the car makes will tell you when to change gears."

I had no idea what that meant, but nodded anyway.

"To change gear, you need to put the clutch in."

Clutch? This was beyond foreign. Lachlan must have seen my lack of comprehension. He pointed down at my feet. There were three pedals there. "The one on the right is the accelerator, the brake is in the middle and the clutch is on the left."

OK. That wasn't so hard.

"Press the clutch in, and I'll show you the gears."

I did as he asked and watched as he changed the gear shift into different positions.

"Your turn."

I followed his example through all five gears, then returned it to first and took my foot off the clutch.

"Good. Now start the car."

I did what he said. The car lurched forward and stalled. Small grunts came from the back seat. I broke out into a sweat.

"When you start a manual, it needs to be in neutral, not in any gears, or if it's in a gear, you need to have the clutch pressed in."

"OK."

"Whenever you change gears, you need to engage the clutch."

How was I going to remember all this? We hadn't even started moving yet. I pressed the clutch in and turned the key. The car started and stayed stationary.

"Good. Now take the handbrake off."

I looked for the handbrake button and couldn't find it. Lachlan pointed to the lever behind the gear stick.

I released the handbrake. "Thanks. My car has a button."

"To move forward, you need to disengage the clutch and, at the same time, engage the accelerator." He put his hands up and showed me the actions my feet would take.

I followed his instruction. The car did a jerk, and the engine stalled. Sweat pooled in my underarms.

"You let the clutch out too quickly. Let's try again."

Two more attempts, and I was no better.

"I'm sorry. I'm nervous. I just need a minute."

I pulled up the handbrake, got out of the car and stood in front of it, trying to control my breathing and nerves. A few seconds later, Lachlan was standing beside me. I continued staring at the road, not even glancing at Lachlan.

"The car makes me nervous," I said. "It's bigger than anything I've ever driven."

I massaged my right hand.

"You'll get used to it."

I nodded, keeping my eyes straight ahead. He was much more patient than I expected him to be. My parents and peers at the hospital would sneer at this sort of failure. My thumb made circles on my wrist. I needed to own up to all of my feelings. What was the point of moving halfway across the world to learn to be myself and make my own decisions if I hid my thoughts and feelings? It was how he would react that held me back. No one had ever allowed me to express myself before without dismissing me.

I gave Lachlan a skittish glance. "You make me nervous, too."

CHAPTER EIGHT

Lachlan

"WHAT DO YOU MEAN?" I asked.

Peyton turned to me. She swallowed. "I know that you don't want me here. I'm trying to show you that Ann and Jane made a good choice, but I can't do anything right."

What was I going to say? I don't think you're cut out for farm life? I don't think you're going to last? I had no right to say any of those things. She'd been here for one day, and this perception I had of her wasn't based on fact.

"Mum and Jane making a decision without me has nothing to do with you."

She continued watching me with those observant brown eyes. I shifted from foot to foot. She expected more. Was I willing to give more?

"You're good for Scarlet and Thomas." I looked back at the car. "They've never been this relaxed with any of the nannies I chose."

Her shoulders slackened. I hadn't realised she'd been so tense.

"I feel so stupid about Mr Harrison."

"To be fair, we should have told you there was a wombat living under your unit."

This was bad. I'd done nothing to help Peyton settle in. I'd just set her up to fail. Why had I done that? Just because I was *pissy*? That was a stupid reason and an unfair one. I don't even know why I was so upset that they'd chosen without me. Was it because they had taken my choice away or because they thought they could choose better? Probably a mixture of both. There were two things I was good at—looking after the farm and caring for my family. And the thought that I couldn't choose a good nanny for my children pointed to failure. And I didn't want to fail them.

She looked down at her feet and then back at me. "What about the bull?"

"Ben?"

She nodded.

I let out a surprised laugh. "To be honest, I have no idea what's going on with that bull."

"Should I be worried?" She glanced towards Ben's paddock.

"No. Ben is friendly. Even the kids can lead him around."

She turned her attention to the car. "I don't know if I'll ever get it."

I waited for her to face me again. "When you're performing a surgery, you use two hands, right?"

She nodded.

"So now you're going to use two feet instead."

"OK." She rubbed her hand. She'd done that a few times since we'd met. Was it a comfort thing?

"You don't need to learn it all today. No one learns to drive a car in one day."

A little crease appeared between her eyes. And then, in an instant, she smiled. It was like a switch had been turned on.

"Well, I better learn quickly. I told Scarlet and Thomas we'd go into town to get supplies for our vegetable garden."

And with that, she turned and strode back to the car. I shook my head and followed her. She was a puzzle. I buckled myself in and waited.

"Ready?" she asked me.

"Whenever you are."

She turned the car on and followed my previous instructions to a T. We were soon driving along the road slowly. The kids cheered from the back. Peyton smiled broadly. She was getting the hang of it but still needed more practice.

"I'll take you all into town after work," I said.

What the hell was I getting myself into? Nothing. It was a one-off thing. I was only doing it to keep them all safe.

***

"WE'LL NEED to drive to Tamworth to get everything you need," I said as I walked out into the backyard after my shower. They were standing in the vegetable garden, deep in conversation.

Peyton gave me a smile. Finally, a real smile for me. "Thank you for taking us in. I know you must be tired after work."

"No problem." I would do anything for my children, but her genuine gratitude warmed me. "How about you drive to the gate to get some practice?"

"Sure."

She practically bounced to the car. Her cheerfulness

extended to the children. It was wonderful seeing them so carefree. The drive to the gate was uneventful. Peyton was picking it up quickly.

Scarlet and Thomas chatted all the way to Tamworth, telling Peyton about the different farms and what they liked about living in town and on the farm. Peyton listened intently the whole way, asking questions. I don't know how she had the energy to be so focused after spending the day with them. Some days their constant energy and chatter left me exhausted.

We pulled into the surprisingly busy carpark. "This is Bunnings. It's an Australian institution. They sell just about anything here for home and garden."

"And they have the best sausage sizzle on weekends," Scarlet said.

Peyton's eyes narrowed. "A what?"

"Don't you have sizzling sausages in America?" I asked.

"Do you mean sizzling hot?"

I laughed. Americans had no idea. "A sausage sizzle is where sausages and onions are cooked on a barbeque. They put them on a slice of bread with a sauce of your choice. You pay a couple of bucks, which goes to charity."

"Sort of like a hot dog," she said.

"Yes, but a hot dog is a different type of sausage and is usually served in a bun."

"Dad, we'll have to come back on a weekend so Peyton can have one," Scarlet said.

I nodded. I didn't want to commit to another outing with Peyton. There was a reason behind this one. It wasn't just an outing for the sake of an outing.

We walked into the big green building and grabbed a couple of trolleys before heading to the garden section.

"What do we need?" I asked.

Peyton pulled out her phone and opened a list. I read the contents.

"Chicken manure?"

"A website said it was good to keep wombats away," Peyton said. "And if we build a small fence around the garden, it will be a double deterrent."

Hopefully, that would be enough, as long as Mr Harrison didn't decide to use his tunnelling skills.

"You'll need to look out for square poo," I said.

Peyton's eyes widened. "What?"

"Wombat poo is shaped like a cube. Something to do with its intestines."

"Interesting. We'll be sure to keep an eye out for cubed poo."

Peyton, with the two kids in tow, approached one of the gardening attendants. "Hi, we'd like to start a vegetable garden. Can you show us to the seedlings, please?"

The man kept glancing at Peyton's hands on the trolley. She was wearing a long sleeve shirt that hid most of her scarring. Scarlet had noticed the way he was looking too. She was frowning at him. If Peyton noticed, she was good at ignoring it. My jaw clenched. He led them to the seedlings. Peyton and Thomas started choosing some punnets, but Scarlet hung back and waited for the man to pass her.

"It's rude to stare," she told him.

The man blushed and nodded before scampering away.

My heart swelled. She was such a thoughtful kid, not afraid to speak her mind. I thought back to the conversation Peyton and I had at the car at lunchtime. The way she would look at me before speaking showed how hesitant she was to speak up. Was it because of her burns or something else?

CHAPTER NINE

Peyton

WE'D BEEN WORKING on the vegetable garden for the past few days, weeding it, turning the soil, and then planting. It was a morning job. Afternoons were just too hot. We were finishing the last plantings as Lachlan pulled into the driveway at lunchtime. We'd worked later than usual because the kids wanted to show their mom the garden when she picked them up this afternoon.

Lachlan came over to inspect our handiwork.

"What do you think, Daddy?" Scarlet asked.

"Fantastic. Who's going to look after it while you're not here?"

"Peyton will," Thomas declared.

"Will she just," Lachlan said, giving me a half smirk.

I knew that signal. It's one I'd mastered reading over the last few days. Funny how a few days ago, the man didn't even want to be near me, and now I could read signals from him like you would with a friend.

"I didn't agree to that," I said, shaking my head.

Thomas's eyes grew wide. "But the plants will die if you don't water them."

Scarlet stood next to her brother. "You can't let them die. We worked so hard."

I couldn't continue the charade. I couldn't break their little hearts. "I—"

"Maybe if you ask Peyton nicely," Lachlan suggested.

"Will you look after our vegetables, Peyton, please," Thomas implored.

"Well, since you asked so nicely."

They both ran to me and wrapped their arms around me. "Thank you," they said in unison. It reminded me of patients' families who were grateful to hear good news after surgery. Their feelings would sometimes get the better of them, and they'd hug me while they cried. A lot of surgeons are wary of the contact. But I always embraced it, knowing that we would continue to be involved in the patient's care, and it was a joint effort. Relationships were important. David never thought so. He was a get-in, get-out sort of surgeon, never welcoming the good or dwelling on the bad but always accepting the accolades.

Lachlan and I smiled at each other.

"Let's go and have lunch," I said.

We all walked to the house together. I stretched my arms over my head. It had been a long time since I'd done so much manual labour.

"I look forward to a nice long bath tonight."

Lachlan opened the door for us. The corners of his lips were upturned as his warm brown eyes drifted down my body. My taut muscles became even tighter. Heat flushed my cheeks as I lowered my arms. Why was he looking at me like that?

Thomas turned around and started off toward the garden.

"What are you doing?" Lachlan asked.

"I forgot something."

Lachlan shook his head as we all entered.

"How was your morning?" I asked.

"We were flat out like a lizard drinking."

I narrowed my eyes at him as I thought about lizards drinking.

Lachlan laughed. "Lizards drink fast. We worked hard and fast like a lizard does when he's drinking."

I nodded. That made sense, I guess.

Lachlan turned to Scarlet. "You kids will need a shower before your mum gets here."

"Yes, Daddy," she said as she washed her hands covered in dirt and chicken manure in the kitchen sink.

"You know we have a bathroom for that," Lachlan said.

Scarlet shrugged her shoulders and dried her hands. Thomas came in, and I ushered him to the bathroom so we could wash our hands together. By the time we got out, Lachlan had started making our sandwiches.

After lunch, I insisted the kids shower, and then we went outside to read *Because of Winn Dixie* on a blanket in the shade. The children lay on their backs with their eyes closed. They interrupted every now and then with questions or comments. About an hour in, Thomas started kicking his legs around. He'd had enough quiet time. He got up and went to the sandpit, and I closed the book before laying down next to Scarlet.

"Peyton, how did you get hurt?" she asked, her voice quiet, almost as if she was afraid to ask.

I opened my eyes. She was sitting up, so I mirrored her pose and took a deep breath. My scars weren't something I chose to speak about. But it was important enough to her to ask, so I should answer.

"There was a car accident. A mom and two girls were trapped in the car."

The night had been dead silent except for the girls' cry for help. They'd been yelling for their mother to wake up.

"I went to help them, and the car caught on fire."

Scarlet wrung her hands together.

"Did they die?"

"No. I got them out."

"What about their mum?"

"She was able to get out before the fire was too bad."

"Are the girls OK? Did they get burnt too?"

"No, they didn't get burnt."

I'd shielded them with my body.

Scarlet's shoulders relaxed.

I looked for Thomas. He wasn't in the sandpit. There was dripping water in the distance. Where was he? I jumped to my feet and ran towards the sound. Thomas was standing near my back verandah, water puddling around his feet.

"Thomas?"

He turned to me, panic on his face. But he didn't say a word. He looked alright. I couldn't see what was causing the water until I looked toward my sliding door. There was water flowing out of it.

"Thomas, come here."

He ran to me and sunk his face into my stomach. "I forgot to turn off the bath."

"The bath?"

Oh crap. "Stay here."

I made my way to the stairs. "Scarlet, go and get the

walkie-talkie. Ask your dad to come home now." I reached the door. "Tell him we're all OK. I don't want to scare him."

I opened the door, and water gushed out.

CHAPTER TEN

Lachlan

"Daddy, are you on channel," Scarlet's voice said through the two-way.

"Yeah, kiddo."

"Can you come home, please? We've got a bit of a problem."

I threw my tools down. Bruce did the same. He was right on my heels as I headed for the car.

"Peyton said to tell you we're all OK."

And yet it was Scarlet who'd called me. I jumped in the car and put my belt on.

"She doesn't want you to be scared. None of us are hurt."

Bruce and I shared a glance. He spoke into the two-way as I sped towards the house. "Scarlet, can you tell me what's happening?"

"There is water coming out of the unit, Uncle Bru."

"Water?" he said.

None of this made sense.

"Yeah, it's all over the grass."

She was out of breath. Was she running? I was out of breath, and all I was doing was driving the car. Peyton's forethought to tell us everyone was fine helped ease some of my panic. We drove straight to the unit and ran around the back. Peyton was hugging Thomas, who was crying.

"Thomas left the bath on, and water has gone through the unit." Her voice was calm, reassuring as she stroked his back. "I've turned the tap off," she said as I made the way to the stairs. Water squelched under my feet. If I didn't have my steel caps on, my feet would be soaked.

"Lachlan." There was alarm in her voice this time.

I spun around, and she was right there, grabbing my arm. "What about Mr Harrison? His burrow is under the house."

Bruce was just about to step into the unit but turned back around. "I'll go get the pump."

Peyton was staring under the house, and the children clung to her. They were both crying now.

"I'm sorry, Lachlan. He was only gone for fifteen minutes. I should have kept a closer eye on him." Peyton's eyes filled with tears.

"This much water didn't just appear in fifteen minutes." I looked at Thomas. "When did you turn the bath on?"

He was sobbing. "When we went in for lunch."

It must have been when he ran off when we were going in to eat. That was hours ago.

"Daddy, will Mr Harrison be OK?" Scarlet asked.

"Wombats are smart. He would have dug a tunnel higher to get out of the water."

"That's a lot of water," Peyton said, her voice quiet.

"He'll be fine." I hoped my voice was reassuring.

Peyton continued to stare at the space under the unit

and comfort the children. She showed no concern about her unit or about whether her belongings had been destroyed. All her concern centred on a wombat that had scared her the first night she was here and the children. Bruce was still a few minutes away. I needed to distract them.

"Scarlet, Thomas, go up to the road and let me know when you see Uncle Bruce."

They held each other's hand and headed off.

I turned my attention to Peyton. "Let's go inside and check the damage."

She nodded. The tears welled up again. She followed me in. There was water all through the unit. The carpet in the bedroom was soaked.

"Fuck, what a mess."

"I'm so sorry, Lachlan." Her voice broke.

I wanted to hug her, but that was inappropriate. Instead, I gently squeezed her upper arm. "Peyton, this is not your fault. Thomas does shit like this all the time."

She nodded. It was feeble.

"Once we pump out the burrow, we can get rid of all the water that is left and dry it out."

It would need a lot more than that, but she didn't need to know that.

"Uncle Bruce is back, Daddy," Scarlet yelled.

We went outside, and I helped Bruce set up the pump. I didn't turn it to full power as I didn't want to risk hurting Mr Harrison even if he was at least twenty solid kilos. I crawled under the house, mud covering me from head to foot and stuck the hose into the burrow. It was stuffy under there.

If Mr Harrison charged at me in this cramped space, I'd have nowhere to go.

"OK, turn it on," I called out.

Within seconds I could feel the water being sucked through the hose. As the pressure eased, I moved the hose around to make sure I got into all the tunnels and crannies. I had no idea how far the tunnels ran or how many there were, so I just poked around blindly. Finally, there was nothing but air.

"Turn it off," I yelled.

I retreated from the cramped space backwards with my shirt riding up and mud covering my stomach and chest. When I stood up, I saw Jane had arrived. Scarlet and Thomas stood between her and Peyton.

"Did you see Mr Harrison, Daddy?" Scarlet asked.

"No, he was tucked away tight."

"How will we know if he's safe?" she asked.

"I will keep an eye out for him," Peyton said.

"All night?" Scarlet asked, her face turning up to Peyton's.

"If I have to. I'll message your Mum tomorrow so you can all know he's safe."

Scarlet nodded.

"How bad is the unit?" Jane asked.

"Bad. Everything is waterlogged."

Jane nodded slowly, then said, "Peyton can't stay in there."

Fuck. I hadn't thought that far ahead. There weren't many options for where she could stay.

CHAPTER ELEVEN

Peyton

I CAN'T STAY in the unit? Well, obviously, but it hadn't registered until now. Where would I go?

"There's the farmers' quarters," Bruce offered.

Jane tapped her lips. "No one's been in there for a year. I'm not sure it would be habitable."

"That's too far away," Scarlet said. "Can't she stay in the house, Daddy?"

Lachlan's eyes widened, and his jaw went slack. My face probably mirrored his. It was one thing looking after his children when I had my own space at night and something completely different living with them all.

"That would break the no fraternising rule, Scar," Bruce said.

He and Jane shared a look and laughed.

"Wasn't that broken days ago when they all went to Tamworth?" Jane asked.

Another round of laughter.

It was fine for them. They'd known Lachlan forever. He

was virtually a stranger to me. To be fair, after I'd told him he made me nervous, he'd been much friendlier. I glanced at him. It was hard to read his face.

"Seriously, Lachy, the house is big enough," Bruce said.

"Yeah, I guess."

Did I get a say in this? I shook my head. It didn't matter. Staying with him in the house didn't have to be forever. It was just until the unit was repaired. How long would be the deciding factor.

"How long will the unit take to repair?" I asked.

Lachlan looked back at the unit. "It depends on the extent of the damage. We will need to dry it out. Rip the carpet up. See how much water damage there is. Could be days, could be a couple of weeks."

That didn't sound too long. Maybe I should look at the farmer's quarters. But that might create more work for everyone if we need to get it ready. And I'd created enough work already.

"Don't worry, Peyton," Bruce said. "Lachy lives a good, quiet bachelor life. If he's not working, he's watching some crap on TV, reading or working out."

Bruce looked a lot like Lachlan, except he wore his thick hair longer so that it curled at his ears. His brown eyes didn't have the same amber flecks, and they always had a mischievous glint. I liked him. He gave off an approachable vibe.

Lachlan looked between the unit and me.

"It's only for a couple of weeks," Jane said.

Maybe I needed to reassure him. "I'm sure I can stay out of your way."

I meant it. I'd do my best to give him his privacy.

He said nothing.

"Or we can go check out the other place if you prefer," I added.

"No, the house is the best solution," he finally said. "We won't be in each other's faces all the time. I'll be at work."

I smiled to myself. It felt good to be involved in a decision that affected me.

"OK, that's settled." Jane clapped her hands. "Let's go get your stuff."

IT WAS quiet without the children. Everyone had left after dinner, and I was alone with Lachlan. I missed the seclusion of my own unit.

"I'm going out to wait for Mr Harrison," I said.

"Do you mind if I join you?" Lachlan asked.

He *wanted* to spend time with me? No, he probably wanted to make sure Mr Harrison was alright. That made more sense. It wouldn't be bad to have him for company. Over the past week, I'd seen a different side to him. He joked with the kids and would talk about his days at work with Bruce. He never excluded me from the conversation and was always open to my questions. There was no reason to exclude him now.

"No, that's fine." I walked out of the house.

He followed, grabbing two wooden chairs off the veran-dah. "We'll sit under the tree by the sandpit. That way we can see him when he comes out, but we won't disturb him."

We walked to the tree and sat together in silence for a while.

For someone who seemed to like his privacy, it was strange that he was giving it up so easily.

Lachlan looked up at the midnight blue sky and spoke

softly. "When we first started our week on, week off with the kids, I hated it when they went back to Jane."

Why was he telling me this?

If it was hard for me, it had to be a thousand times harder for him. "It sure is quiet without them," I said.

"After a while, I got used to my alone time. Bruce doesn't understand. He thinks I'm lonely."

Was the darkness making him brave? We'd never discussed anything this intimate before, or anything personal, really.

If he could be brave, so could I. "I think it's a strong person who can enjoy their own company."

"Do you enjoy yours?" he asked.

"Yes." How brave could I be? "Growing up, my parents were always busy. They're both surgeons. My sister is a few years older than me. We aren't very close."

"It was different for me. Our family was always close."

"I can see that. Bruce likes to tease you a lot."

"He's a shit head."

I never really knew what I was missing until I moved here. I liked the way they talked things through. Everyone showed each other love and respect. At home, respect was given to me only when I achieved something they thought important.

"You're close to Jane," I said.

"We were friends for many years before we became parents. We'll always love each other, just not in the way you should to spend forever together."

I turned my head towards a rustling by the fence. On the moonlit night, I could see the outline of the bull. He always seemed to be watching me.

"I like it here," I said. "It's so peaceful. I never knew so many night sounds existed." It sounded stupid coming from an adult, and I was embarrassed to say it out loud. "In the city, all you hear are cars, sirens, people or domestic animals."

We were silent. I basked in it. It wasn't uncomfortable. I thought it would be strange being alone with Lachlan. In a way, it was. But it another way, it was liberating. I didn't have to pretend to be what he wanted, beyond someone to care for his children. And I'd done a good job of that until today.

"I'm sorry about the unit, Lachlan."

He turned to face me.

"It wasn't your fault. Thomas gets these ideas into his head. You never know what he's going to do next."

"He does get distracted sometimes." I laughed.

"He's only five." Lachlan's voice was hard. His hands pressed down on his legs.

"I wasn't saying it's a bad thing. I give him one instruction at a time and then keep him focused."

"He starts school next year. I'm worried about how he'll settle in."

"I'm sure the teachers deal with all types of children. They'll know what to do."

My first thoughts about Lachlan not caring about his children or who looked after them couldn't have been further from the truth. He would do anything for them, including sitting outside with the nanny, waiting for a wombat to emerge.

A shadow moved near the unit. I grabbed Lachlan's arm. His muscles flexed under my touch.

"Mr Harrison," I whispered.

The wombat moved quickly, despite his short legs, under the fence and into the paddock. Lightness spread through me as I smiled at Lachlan. He smiled back. That smile made him even more beautiful. I sucked a breath in as the truth of my thought spread through me. I withdrew my hand. This was too intimate.

"Is it too late to text Jane?" I asked.

"No, I'm sure the kids will want to know."

He pulled out his phone and gave them the good news.

I stood, taking hold of my chair. "Thank you for sitting with me."

Lachlan rose. "Thanks for the chat. I hope you don't feel lonely here. I know not everyone is like me."

I didn't understand where this was coming from. Was he suggesting we be friends? Or was he saying that he needed space and he hoped I understood?

"I don't think I will be." I didn't know what else to say. "I'm heading off to bed."

Alone. In his house. Both thrilled and apprehensive about the time we'd just spent together.

CHAPTER TWELVE

Lachlan

Peyton kept her word about staying out of my way. When I got up the next morning, I half expected her to come out to have breakfast with me. She didn't. I couldn't even hear movement in her room. Maybe she was sleeping in on her first day without Scarlet and Thomas.

Not that I was listening for her.

I pulled into the carport for morning tea. Had she emerged yet? I was earlier than usual as we needed to drench and vaccinate the cows before lunch, and we needed to allow enough time to finish the job. There was a light on in the shed. I was sure I hadn't left it on when I'd finished my weights last night. I'd been distracted by Peyton and the fact that she was now living in my house, but not *that* distracted.

I strode over to the door and reached my hand in to switch off the light. Peyton was lying on the bench with a dumbbell in her hand.

"Peyton?"

She jumped up, her eyes wide. In an instant, she wrapped her towel around her shoulders. "Sorry, I didn't expect you back yet."

I stood, staring.

"I'll just put this away. I'll come back later."

"What are you doing?"

I never knew anyone who could make me say such stupid things. What was she doing? Well, she wasn't reading a book, was she?

"I use the weights to help me with contractures." She hurried to the dumbbell stand to put the one she was holding away. Her hamstrings tensed as she bent forward to place it on the stand. I'd never taken notice of how shapely her legs were before. Why was I looking now? I shook my head.

The towel slipped off her shoulder, showing her scarring. She pulled it back into place.

"Contractures?"

"Burn scars thicken and tighten. It makes it hard to bend your joints. Hands can become deformed."

"And doing weights helps stop that?"

She made her way to the door. "Yes. At first, I could hardly move. I had surgeries where the scar tissue was removed and replaced with healthy tissue. That's because as you heal, the skin starts to grow back together and pulls the edges of the wound together. This is known as contracting. It makes the skin tight, and it's hard to move."

She flexed her hand and wrist. "If I didn't have those skin grafts, I wouldn't be able to do this."

I watched as she did it again. She wasn't able to form a tight fist, but it was a fist just the same.

"After the surgeries, I wore a pressure garment twenty-three hours a day. It helps prevent scars from becoming raised and hard. I wore it for twelve months. Once the scars mature, it can come off."

I stood there, still staring.

Her eyes widened. "Oh, I didn't really answer your question. Sorry." She tugged on the towel as if checking it was still in place. "When I could start moving, the aim was for my skin to be stretched. A good option was to use weights to add to the resistance when stretching."

"So, what sort of exercises do you do?"

"Anything that bends a joint—triceps extensions, bicep curls. I do these other ones that push my fingers back and hold it for thirty to sixty seconds."

She stood in front of me. "Doing weights helps in two ways. When your body is burnt like mine was, it goes into overdrive to repair itself. You lose a lot of muscle mass. Doing weights helped me regain that. I found I enjoyed it too. It was therapeutic. I didn't just stick to exercises that worked my arms and shoulders. I worked the whole body."

I nodded. No wonder her arse looked so good. What the fuck? I needed to keep that thought to myself.

"Sorry again. I should have asked if it was OK to use your weights," she said.

"No problem."

"I notice you usually come out at night. I'll try to work around that."

"It's OK. You can use them whenever you need to." Wow, I could actually show I was a gentleman and be accommodating for once.

I moved out of the doorway, and she left without saying another word, the towel still wrapped around her shoulders. There was so much about burns I had no idea about. When I was sure she was gone, I sat down on the bench and googled skin grafts. The most I knew about them was that they took skin from one part of the body and put it on another.

I watched as a doctor got a small machine, sort of like a cheese slicer and peeled the skin off a lady's leg. I sucked in a breath. Just like that, a whole section of skin was removed. It was all bunched up until he stretched it out into a rectangular piece to place over the burn site. He then spoke about putting mesh over the wound and attaching the skin graft to that. But that can increase contracting and cause alligator-looking skin. In some places, Peyton's skin was smooth, so they probably hadn't used the mesh on all of her grafts. He sewed the graft on like he was sewing a patch on a piece of clothing. He said that sometimes glue was used instead of stitches.

Once he finished sewing, he syringed saline under the graft and squeezed it out between the stitches to wash away any blood because the blood would stop the graft from sticking. I shook my head. The whole thing was mind-boggling.

Wow, that lady only had a small section repaired, and it was one skin graft. Peyton said she'd had *surgeries*. Multiple. I couldn't imagine going through that time and time again. It would add trauma to trauma. Fuck.

And then the recovery on top of that. And cleaning of wounds. I cringed as I watched someone showering and cleaning the wound with a cloth. They had to debride the wound as well. That's what the video called it. I called it torture. It seemed to be a fancy name for removing dead tissue. It was mind-blowing.

Jane's words returned to me: *She's tougher than you think.* She wasn't wrong.

Peyton had strength, determination and tenacity.

What other misconceptions of mine would Peyton prove wrong?

CHAPTER THIRTEEN

Peyton

I NEEDED to face my fear of the chickens. To say that I was scared of something that didn't even reach the height of my knees was ridiculous, but I was sure that these chickens could smell my fear and would make me pay for it. I stood outside of the coop and stared at them. They were all going about their business, some on their nests, others walking around pecking the ground, others just lying in the sun. Not one of them paid any attention to me.

I took a deep breath and opened the door. I made my steps as light as I could as I entered. Heads turned towards me. But no one charged. That was positive. I took another step towards the nesting boxes, careful not to get in anyone's way. Scanning the area with each step, I was conscious of every chicken. My foot connected with something solid. My eyes darted to my feet to see that I'd knocked a water bowl just as wild flapping occurred to my right.

I froze. A chicken ran towards me with loud clucks, flapping its wings furiously. Scarlet had told me to wave my hands at them to shoo them away if I needed to. Big brave movements, she'd said, not little waves which could aggravate them more. That's what I did. The chicken turned around and went in the opposite direction. Prickles spread across my skin. I sighed.

I stretched my fingers out, releasing tension. I needed to show these chickens that I had no fear. No more tentative steps. I needed to move with purpose. I strode to the nesting boxes. Most of them were empty. I placed the eggs in the basket I carried.

Then I got to Goliath. She intimidated the hell out of me. She sat there staring at me with her beady eyes, never once taking those eyes off me. I stared her down. I mean, if I could stare down a body in front of me before I began a difficult surgery, surely I could stare down a chicken. I took a step closer. It was tentative. What happened to my brave, determined steps? Goliath happened, that's what.

She growled. Actually growled. I didn't even know that was a sound chickens could make. I needed to collect these eggs. Scarlet told me the eggs needed to be collected every day to prevent them from being broken.

I took a step closer, so I stood directly in front of her. Maybe I needed to stop staring. Maybe that was a threat to her. I looked to the side. She still growled.

I couldn't stand there forever worrying about this chicken. I reached my shaking hand forward. Her beak darted towards me. I snatched my hand back. Movement sounded behind me. My heart raced, and I braced myself for an attack.

"Peyton, do you want some help?" Lachlan asked.

I gave the chicken one last stern look before I turned around, resigned to the fact that I needed Lachlan's help just to collect some eggs.

Bruce was standing beside him. "That chicken really needs to be on a dinner plate."

Lachlan glanced at him sideways. "Don't speak about Goliath like that."

"She's mean."

"She's broody."

Was there a difference?

Bruce grunted.

I looked between them. "Whatever she is, I can't get her eggs."

Bruce nudged Lachlan. "Well, go on then. Show us your magic."

Lachlan entered the coop and stood beside me. We weren't touching, but a current ran between us like we were swapping electrons and creating a static charge. If I touched him, would I get a shock? My heart jolted. Touching Lachlan, even for the sake of an experiment, was not acceptable, professional behaviour between employee and employer.

He moved forward towards Goliath, and I followed him. As he reached his hand out, she pecked him.

"It doesn't really hurt. It's like a pinch, and it doesn't break the skin." He moved his hand away.

It might not hurt, but I wasn't volunteering my hand to find out.

"Hand me that spade," he said, pointing to a spade with no handle leaning against the wall.

I handed it to him. He placed the spade beneath Goliath and tilted her up. She gave it a couple of pecks, her beak twanging on the metal.

"By doing it this way, she can't see your hand reaching under her to get the eggs, and if she did, she wouldn't be able to peck you."

He didn't take the eggs, just demonstrated and then removed the spade.

"Your turn."

I copied exactly what he did and had the same result. Goliath didn't attack me at all, and I was able to retrieve the eggs safely. I placed them in the basket.

"How did you learn how to do that?" I asked him.

"YouTube can help with just about anything."

Bruce laughed as we left the coop. "Goliath lives for another day."

"She's a good layer. There's no need to resort to drastic measures just because she's a bit broody," Lachlan said.

Bruce gave me a wink. "Yeah, I mean, you're more than a bit broody, and we still let you live."

Lachlan shot him a glare.

Bruce smirked. "What do you think, Peyton? You live with the man. How broody is he?"

I held up my hands. "Leave me out of this."

"I think that means a lot broody."

Lachlan considered me.

It's not like I'd said he was *a lot broody* straight out. But the man *was* moody. I didn't know how to take him sometimes. One minute he was chatty, like the night we watched Mr Harrison, and then he was virtually mute, like when he found me in his gym.

"I'm going to put the eggs away," I said, heading towards the house.

"Good idea. We're heading off to do men's work," Bruce said as he walked towards the unit.

He didn't just say that, did he?

I spun around. "I hope you're not insinuating that a woman's place is in the kitchen."

Lachlan's lips quirked. He turned towards his brother and raised his eyebrows.

Bruce took a tiny step back. "Well, um, Kayley is better in the kitchen than I am, and you know..." His voice drifted off.

"No, actually, I don't know," I said.

"Bruce doesn't do any domestic chores," Lachlan said dryly.

"Any?" I asked.

Bruce shuffled from foot to foot.

"You're one lucky man, Bruce. Not many women would put up with that."

"That's what I tell him. I tell him he shouldn't take Kayley for granted. One day she'll lay down the law, and he won't know how to step up."

Bruce shrugged.

"You should listen to your brother more. He might be broody, but he knows what he's talking about," I said.

Bruce lifted his head and smirked. Lachlan rolled his eyes even as his smile escaped. I turned around and walked away. I didn't want to believe Bruce was sexist and domineering like many of the surgeons I'd worked with. He was too nice for that.

"Step up, Bruce. That's what a man would do," I called over my shoulder.

CHAPTER FOURTEEN

Lachlan

I STOOD IN THE KITCHEN. The early morning sunlight shone through the windows, casting geometric patterns across the floor. Peyton was awake. I could hear movement in her room. She'd been awake for at least ten minutes. She hadn't joined me in the kitchen before I headed to work since the kids left.

Probably not a bad idea. Sitting with her while waiting for Mr Harrison, telling her things very few other people knew, was dangerous. It insinuated that there was more to our relationship than there should be. I was her employer. She was our nanny. I had responsibilities that I couldn't forget or avoid. Getting distracted by Peyton did not fit into that.

Then why was I disappointed that she hadn't come out of her room yet?

Peyton's door opened. My heart rate quickened. She rubbed her eyes as she walked into the kitchen. Her short hair was standing in all different directions. It was the complete opposite to how she normally looked in the morning—fresh, neat, and composed. Maybe she hadn't slept well. It had taken me a while to fall asleep. It was summer, but she still had a long sleeve top on. I doubt she slept in it. That would be suffocating.

"Good morning," I said. "Would you like some coffee?"

"Yes, please."

I poured her a cup and pushed it across the counter to her. If I had known her better, I would have made a joke about her appearance. But that could go completely wrong.

She peered at me over the top of her cup. "I was avoiding you. But I decided that was childish."

What was I going to say to that? "Avoiding me?"

She gave me a half smile. "You like your privacy. I respect that. And now you have me living in your space. So I thought I'd give you some."

Fuck. Nothing like being candid so early in the morning. Nothing like making a guy feel like a dick. Those first impressions are hard to live down.

"You don't need to hide away. This is your house too."

She nodded. "That's what I told myself in the end. What was I going to do, hide in my room every time you're home?"

"I'd rather you not."

She gave me a smile. It seemed like I'd delivered the message she'd wanted to hear.

"What are your plans for today?" I asked.

"I'd like to go out this afternoon to take some photos of the farm. There's this site online that gives out assignments every week. It sounded like fun, so I joined their newsletter. After that, I thought I'd come and help you and Bruce with the unit. Show him a woman can do *men's* work."

Was she saying she wanted out already?

"We'll be there after morning tea."

"I'll make sure I perform my vegetable garden duties by then." She laughed.

"That should take all of five minutes."

She nodded. "I have a book to read to keep me entertained."

"What are you reading?"

"I've just started *Tomorrow, When the War Began*."

"Good series. There's a movie, too, based on the first book."

"Ooh, good, best I finish it then."

I was tempted to say we could watch it together. It was a good movie; I'd seen it more than once. But I needed to keep my distance. Being friendly was fine, but doing things together took it to another level.

***

"HAS Lachlan scared you out of the Bach Shack already?" Bruce asked Peyton as she entered the unit. She was in shorts, a T-shirt and a light cardigan.

"The what?" she asked.

"The Bach Shack—bachelor house."

Was there no limit to his stupidity?

Peyton laughed. We were all in trouble if she found him funny. "It's not what I ever imagined a Bach Shack would look like."

Seriously, she was going to use the phrase too?

"Yeah, I guess he's too clean for that," Bruce remarked.

"I don't see a problem with a man being clean or a man who cooks. And does his own washing," Peyton said.

"Ask him if he's stepped up at home yet," I said.

"I'm working up to it. Not sure I need to though; I make the place look magnificent just by being present."

Peyton stared at him like he couldn't be serious; Bruce puffed his chest out and posed. She burst out laughing. Maybe I needed to try to be funnier, like Bruce.

"If you're done being an idiot," I grumbled, "we've got work to do."

"You're no fun," Bruce said and headed into the bedroom.

"I'll strip the bed for you. I'd hate for you to do a domestic chore," Peyton said.

He gave her a smirk. I chuckled. It seemed like this city girl could give as good as she got.

As she headed to the main house to put the sheets in the washing machine, Bruce remarked, "I like her."

I nodded. There were lots of things I liked about Peyton Carter. Her honesty and bravery to speak openly were at the top of that list. And each time she did, it was delivered with more confidence.

Would she feel comfortable enough to remove the long sleeves one day soon? Would she be confident enough to show us?

CHAPTER FIFTEEN

Peyton

"What are you watching?" Lachlan asked as he walked into the lounge room. He rested his arms on the back of the couch while staring at the TV screen.

"Just a medical show."

He studied it closer. "I've seen this. Jane enjoyed watching it."

He made his way to the front of the couch and sat next to me. Two interns had just snuck into an on-call room and were going at it. I shifted in my seat. Couldn't he have walked in when they were performing some elaborate medical procedure?

"Does this shit really happen?"

I snuck a look at him. He was blushing. From the heat on my skin, I knew I was too.

"No. No one has time for that."

"Right, because you're meant to be doctoring, not—" He waved his hand at the TV.

I nearly laughed at his inability to say sex or fuck. I'd

heard that word come out of his mouth plenty. But not here on the couch with me.

"These two are supposed to be interns. Their supervisors would watch them so closely they'd never have a chance to sneak off to have *sex*."

He put his feet up on the coffee table in what I'd come to recognize as his relaxed mode. I'd seen it emerge more and more over the past few days. I liked it much more than the scowl he had the first two days I was here. If I thought back, it was hard to see it clearly. I hadn't seen it since we'd done our vegetable hunting in Tamworth. No, more like since I'd moved in.

"What about the hours they work? They never seem to leave the place."

"It is pretty insane. Especially during intern."

"Do you miss it?"

Oh, that was a good segue. It was time to take a ride on the honesty train again.

"Yes and no. I liked helping people get well. But there was a lot of pressure." More honesty needed. "Especially from my family. They all wanted me to be like them."

He stopped watching the TV and watched me instead. "You didn't want to be like them?"

"I don't know what I wanted to be. They're all surgeons. I was never given a chance to be anything else."

His mouth twisted. How could I explain this to him? He'd always wanted to be a farmer. He was born into it. Wait, I shouldn't be so presumptuous. I was born into being a surgeon, but it didn't mean that's what I wanted to be.

"Did you always want to be a farmer?" I asked.

His eyes shifted. What was that? Doubt? Guilt? "Farming was my life. I knew this was where I was going to be, and I was happy about that." He took a deep breath.

"But I also wanted to experience more. So, when I finished high school Jane and I travelled for a bit. I sang our way through towns." Another deep breath. "When Dad died, I came straight back."

There was too much information there for me to unpack.

"Your dad died not long after you left high school?"

He swallowed. "Yeah, a brain aneurysm."

He was so young. I waited for him to say more. When he didn't, I said, "You're a singer?"

"I sang, and I wrote songs."

That explained the musical notes in his tattoo.

"Do you still sing?"

"Only for the children or my family. Or in the shower and at work."

In the shower? As water ran down that torso I'd caught a glimpse of when he came out from under the unit covered in mud? I shook my head and reined in my imagination.

I'd never heard him sing. But why would I? We'd lived in two separate houses when the children were here. And he wrote songs. I was almost desperate to hear one now. But it was inappropriate to ask him. It was a boundary I wasn't ready to cross. Lachlan turned his attention back to the television. Two of the residents were ogling their superior. They were the best bedroom eyes I'd ever seen.

"Did you have the hots for your superiors?"

Was he fishing?

"Definitely not. But some interns had this worshipping thing going on."

"But not you?"

"Bit hard when you work with your fiancé."

He swung his head to me.

"Fiancé?" I had his full attention again.

"Yes, David and I went to college together and then completed our internship and started our residency at the same hospital."

"Where's David now?"

He *was* fishing. Butterflies floated in my stomach.

"He's still finishing his residency."

"And you're here?"

"David and I broke up. Things changed after the accident."

I massaged my right hand, starting with my fingers. Lachlan watched, quiet, not pushing me, letting me open up at my own pace. Was I ready to say the words? I'd never said them out loud before. To anyone. Who was I going to say them to? My parents always defended David, and my sister just dismissed my thoughts.

"If Jane was in the hospital, would you visit her?"

"Every day. "

I had no doubt his words were true. And they weren't even married anymore.

"I was in the hospital for months. David visited ten times."

Lachlan sucked a breath in. I lifted my eyes to his. I needed to say the words to him. I needed to feel him listening. I needed to be heard.

"What about if she needed surgery?"

"I'd be in that waiting room going out of my damn mind."

"And if she had to go to treatment week after week, month after month?"

"I'd go with her as much as I could."

"David did none of that. He may have turned up for a few, but it was out of obligation rather than caring."

"Fuck wit." Lachlan's jaw tensed.

I needed to tell him the rest. I needed to share the resentment, the shame, the pain. Not all of it. I couldn't do that. Just the David part. But why was I telling him? Why was I sharing such intense information with him? Maybe because I was just the nanny, and there was no pressure like I'd feel if he was someone pursuing me. In that case, I'd think about measuring my words. But I didn't want to do that. I wanted to be honest with myself and others. I wanted them to accept me and what I had to say. I never wanted to hide myself away again. And that would always be a risk.

I took a deep breath. Time to open up a little more. "David and I were in a car accident. While I ran to save the other family, he stood beside his car."

Lachlan's eyes didn't leave my face. He rested his hand on my leg, encouraging me to go on. It was the weight of it, the comfort of it, that kept me talking.

"I always felt like he blamed me for my injuries. Once he told me I shouldn't have gone to that car."

Lachlan's face turned red. Yet he stayed quiet. His hand remained.

"And the way he looked at me, Lachlan, at my scars ... he was repulsed. I repulsed him." I took a shaky breath. "He wouldn't even touch me to comfort me."

Lachlan's face contorted, and his nostrils flared. But his eyes didn't leave my face. "What a fucking knob."

His hand left my leg, and he took both of my hands. "Peyton, that man is a fucking loser. He didn't deserve you."

Those words and his vehemence were a vindication to my heart and mind.

This man, who I barely knew, had listened to every word I'd said. He'd *heard* every word I'd said. And even though I had no idea why I'd shared all that I had, I was glad that I did.

"I bet that's the last time you sit with me to watch TV." I gave a little laugh. "I'm sure you didn't expect me to download all that on you."

I held my breath, waiting for his reply.

"It's not like I haven't shared personal things with you."

I nodded. Our relationship was no longer strictly professional. Was this wise?

"Let's have dinner," Lachlan said, letting go of my hand. That was a quick change of subject. Did he feel the shift too?

I nodded and stood up. "Do you need help?"

"If you can make a salad while I cook the steak, that'd be great."

We went into the kitchen together. I'd been this close to him before, but this time it felt different like we were experiencing another level of intimacy. Maybe it was because of what I'd just shared. Maybe it was because of his kindness.

He brushed against me as he made his way to the drawers to grab the frypan. Waves of heat radiated through me. Just from that small innocent touch. Imagine if he'd stood behind me, touching me deliberately. Tingles spread across my skin. I took a deep breath to recentre myself.

Every interaction between us felt deeper, driving us closer. But did I want closer? It had never worked in my favour before. It was different here, though. I was different. I had control over myself. Control over my feelings was something else entirely. And having feelings for my boss probably wasn't that smart. Even so, I wasn't sure if I could stop them.

CHAPTER SIXTEEN

Lachlan

A HURRICANE in the form of my two children came crashing through the front door.

"Daddy, did you miss us?" Scarlet said as she threw her arms around me.

"Every single day."

"I missed you too."

I hugged her tighter. Even though we lived apart, we still had open communication. She could call or message me any time she wanted. Same with Thomas. But he wasn't as talkative on the phone.

He'd bypassed me and gone straight to Peyton. He was telling her a story about his scraped knee. She listened, nodding and using lots of facial expressions.

He stuck his knee up in the air. "Does it look OK?"

She knelt to inspect it. "In my professional opinion, amputation is not necessary."

He gave her a small, unsure smile.

"Good news, bud, we don't need to chop your leg off," I said.

"Good." He ran to his room.

"I'm not sure having only one leg would slow him down," Jane said.

I shook my head. "Probably not."

"Scarlet, why don't you check on the vegetable garden with Peyton," Jane said.

Peyton took the cue. "Oh yes, you should see how the plants have grown."

I watched as they left the house. Peyton's legs were browning up.

"So, how was it?" Jane asked.

"How was what?"

"Sharing a house with Peyton."

Surely she wasn't serious. *That's* what she wanted to talk about? How much did she already know? The talk on this farm reached her in Tamworth as if she still lived here.

"Peyton is respectful of my time and space. I appreciate that."

"Right, so you didn't eat meals together?"

"We live in the same house. It only makes sense that we eat together."

"And you didn't watch TV together?"

Mum or Bruce? Could have been Mum. She'd dropped around one night, and we were on the couch watching what I refer to as Peyton's medical show.

"I wanted her to feel comfortable, to treat the place as her own."

Jane smirked. "Right, and the way you watch her, is that to make her feel comfortable too?"

"What the fuck are you talking about?"

Jane's smirk grew. She was baiting me. "Oh, nothing."

"I do *not* watch Peyton. "

I didn't. I didn't notice the way she carried herself or how nice her legs were or the way she laughed at Bruce's poor attempts at comedy or how she was deep in thought when they were assessing a patient on TV. I did think about what she told me about how her fiancé had treated her so badly. No one deserved to be treated like that, especially Peyton.

"Tell yourself whatever you like," Jane said. She shut off my next denial by turning in the direction of Thomas's bedroom. "Thomas, Mummy's going now."

He came running out to give her a hug, and then we all went outside. I made an effort not to watch Peyton as she spoke to Scarlet.

"Hmm," Jane said as she walked away.

"GET YOUR PJS ON, and we can play a game before you go to bed," I said as I piled the dishes on the kitchen bench.

"OK," Scarlet and Thomas said in unison, running off.

They could get changed quickly when it suited them.

"I'll help with the dishes and then head to bed," Peyton said, coming to stand beside me.

"You can join us if you like." What was I doing?

"No. You haven't seen them all week. I'm sure you'd like some alone time with them."

She got it, and that made me respect her more, which made it even easier to want to spend time with her. I didn't see a problem with that. Housemates spend time together all the time. It was normal.

"You don't need to make yourself scarce because the kids are at home."

"Let's see what they want to do. Maybe they want some alone time with you."

She held out her hand for the dish cloth. "Is it OK if I wash today?"

"Sure." I handed the dish cloth over and grabbed the tea towel instead.

"Sometimes my hand feels stiff, and the warm water helps."

Thomas came running back in. "I'm ready."

"We need to finish the dishes first." I ruffled his hair.

He sat at the table.

Scarlet came in and sat opposite him. "Can we play the mystery game?"

"I don't like that game," Thomas said.

"Only because you never win."

"It's too hard."

"What game are they talking about?" Peyton asked.

"The *Who Done It* game. It's hard for a five-year-old to think strategy."

Peyton finished the last of the dishes. "Maybe we can play in teams."

The pair considered each other and then us. Their faces turned serious. I could see an argument starting any second about who was going to be on what team.

"We'll toss a coin," I said before either of them could say a word.

Peyton gave a small laugh. "Good save."

Point one for me.

"I like that you don't take advantage of your position and make choices for everyone," she said.

I'm sure that's what would have happened if her parents or her ex had been involved. To know that she thought I was different to them was heartening.

"Don't think you can disarm me with your compliments," I said, even though she had done just that.

"I'm sure I can find other ways to disarm you." She smiled over her shoulder as she walked to the table.

My chest constricted. Was she flirting with me? No. She was just using strategy. Well enough to keep me dumbfounded. Point two to Peyton.

I grabbed a coin from my wallet on the bench. "OK. Heads means Scarlet is with me. Tails, she goes with Peyton." I flipped the coin. Heads. Winning Scarlet should have been a point for me. She was an ace at this game. But I didn't know how good Peyton was. She took her seat next to Thomas. He beamed up at her.

"We've got this, Daddy," Scarlet said as I sat down beside her.

"We sure do."

Peyton gave me a sly smile. I shifted in my seat. You should never underestimate the opposition. I'd already underestimated how easy it would be to like her.

We started the game. Whenever it was their turn, Peyton would ask Thomas what he thought. It was hard to hear them, but I could see how hard Thomas was concentrating as she guided him. It looked like she was giving him the positives and negatives of his suggestion and would then ask him again. Then they would go with whatever he said.

I liked that. She never dismissed his ideas. She helped him but never took over. Is this what she had wanted growing up? To make her own decisions like this? If she could have made her own decisions, she may have chosen a different career or a boyfriend who wasn't an arsehole. I needed to learn from her. I needed to let my children make their own decisions. I couldn't expect them to take over the farm. They needed to choose that.

"Daddy, it's our turn."

Another point to Peyton. I was distracted.

"What's wrong, Daddy? Running out of ideas?" Peyton asked across the table.

"No. Just thinking."

The game was close. They matched us move for move. Peyton stared me down from across the table. She licked her lips. Her lips glistened. I couldn't stop staring at them.

Was that deliberate? An act of sabotage? A blush rose on her cheeks. No, it was an innocent move until she realised what effect it had on me.

Thomas called out an answer. The right answer. We'd lost. Peyton and Thomas high-fived each other. He couldn't stop grinning.

Scarlet sat back in her chair and crossed her arms.

I gave her a nudge. "That was a good game. Very close."

She nodded. "The closest we've ever had."

I reached my arm out to circle her shoulders in a side hug. It would have been easy for her to be a sore loser seeing as she'd never lost to Thomas before.

"Well, off to bed. I'll be in in a minute to read to you."

They gave Peyton a hug.

She stood up and started packing the game away. "You go. I can manage this."

I started for Scarlet's room but stopped, turning back towards Peyton. She lifted her honey-brown eyes to mine, and I was lost. I bet if I got close enough, she'd smell as sweet as honey, maybe even taste as sweet as honey. I swallowed. This wasn't why I'd stopped.

"Thank you for helping Thomas," I said, my voice thick.

She lifted a shoulder. "That's what I'm here for."

"Don't depreciate what you do for this family."

She blushed. "Thank you."

She was our fifth nanny. She'd be our last if I had anything to do with it. It wasn't just that she was great with the children, she was great *for* them. And as far as company went, she wasn't bad company at all. She made the place feel different.

Yes, I'd keep her here as long as bigger and better things didn't steal her away.

CHAPTER SEVENTEEN

Peyton

"WHAT ARE YOUR PLANS FOR TODAY?" Lachlan asked as I entered the kitchen, showered and prepared for the day ahead. The way he looked at me when he asked questions made me believe he wasn't just doing it to be polite. He was interested.

"I thought Scarlet and Thomas could show me around town."

"There's not much to it."

"That's OK. I'm sure we'll have fun."

We could make anything fun if we tried hard enough. I'd never really visited a small town before. I imagined quaint buildings, tree-lined streets and friendly people.

Lachlan walked to the back door.

"Have a good day at work," I said. "Don't let Bruce off the hook. I want to know what domestic chore he did last night."

Lachlan laughed. "It's nice to see someone else busting his balls."

And I would keep busting them. He needed to stop relying on his wife to do everything.

Half an hour later, the kids wandered in, their PJs still on. I started to get their breakfast ready.

"Would you like to take a drive into town today? You can show me around."

Scarlet's face lit up. "Can we visit Pop?"

Pop? Did she mean Jane's dad? I didn't feel like we could just turn up at his house unannounced. I didn't even know him.

Scarlet pulled the cereal toward her. "The cemetery is on the way."

Oh, she meant Lachlan's dad. Maybe that's something country kids did, go to the cemetery to visit relatives that had passed away. I'd never visited a cemetery after we'd buried someone. Would Lachlan feel like I was invading his privacy? Maybe I should ask him about it first.

My phone pinged. I picked it up. It looked like I had been added to the farm group chat. I skimmed the names. All of Lachlan's family was listed, including Bruce's wife, Kaley, his sister Lydia and her partner, who lived in Sydney.

Lachlan - *I would like to report, for the first time in history, Bruce put his own washing away last night.*

Way to go Bruce. We'll make a domestic goddess out of him yet.

Lydia - *did you get it on video?*

Kayley - *I saw it with my own two eyes. I nearly fainted.*

Ann - *impossible.*

Bruce - *I've put my own washing away before.*

Ann - *when?*

Lydia - *putting it in a pile on your chair is not putting it away.*

Bruce - *it was away from the table.*

Ann - *Bruce dear, did you put your washing away last night or not?*

I could imagine Ann's mum voice in my head.

Bruce - *yes, Mum, in drawers and on shelves.*

Ann - *wonders will never cease.*

Lachlan - *how did you even know where to put them?*

Kayley- *because that's where he finds them after I put them away.*

Lachlan- *five stars to Peyton. We might make an adult out of him yet.*

Ann - *Peyton?*

Lachlan - *she's challenged him to do one domestic task a day.*

Lydia - *the pretty American babysitter?*

I reread that last statement and blushed.

Lachlan- *she's on this group chat, you know.*

Lydia- *oh. Hi Peyton.*

Laughing faces all around.

She called me pretty. Did Lachlan tell her that?

Me - *Hi, everyone.*

Lydia - *thanks for making Bruce pull up his socks. And for making Lachlan happy.*

Happy? As in being a good nanny?

Lachlan - *OK, work's calling.*

Bruce - *did Lydia embarrass you?*
Silence.
Silence.

Lydia - *I guess that means yes.*
This family was crazy. Fun. Loveable. But crazy.

I read back over the messages, and my cheeks continued to heat. Had they been speaking about me? I could have scrolled higher to read the previous messages, but that felt like invading their privacy. And I'm not sure I wanted to see what they'd been saying about me. I imagined those first messages wouldn't use words like pretty or happy.

Had he told anyone about what I'd shared with him? It was the truth, and it was good to speak it, even if it was to Lachlan. His words had comforted me as much as I imagined his strong arms would. The man who was the father of the children I looked after. He hadn't brought it up the next day, and I was grateful for that. No, I don't think he would have told anyone. Bruce hadn't said anything or treated me differently.

I needed to message Lachlan, whether he was embarrassed or not.

Me - *Scarlet has asked me to take them to the cemetery to visit Pop. Is that OK?*

Lachlan - *thank you for asking. Yes, that's OK.*

That was a bit formal. Maybe he was embarrassed. What could I text to make him feel better?

What about, Bruce shouldn't tell people I'm pretty. They'll be disappointed when they meet me. No. That sounded like I was fishing for a compliment.

Me - *you better tell Bruce using words like pretty to describe me won't get him out of domestic tasks.*

Lachlan- *lol. With the whole female contingent in this family ganging up on him, I don't think anything would get him out of it.*

That's better. I smiled.

Lachlan- *would you mind asking Mum if she wants to*

go with you? She might like to have some company at the cemetery.

Me - *sure.*

I put the phone down. Scarlet and Thomas had finished their breakfast and placed their bowls in the sink. I can't believe I missed that. I should have been paying attention to them instead of thinking about compliments. I went to wash the dishes. Just as I finished, the kids came out. Scarlet was in a cornflower blue dress. She looked so sweet.

"It's Pop's favourite colour."

"Perfect for a visit to him then. We're going to drop into Nan's on the way to see if she wants to join us."

"Yay!" Thomas ran out the door.

Scarlet and I followed. I was much more confident in the car after practising. I wouldn't embarrass myself or put anyone in danger. I'd driven the ten minutes to the mailbox each Monday, Wednesday and Friday—mail delivery days. It was a ten-minute drive compared to a thirty-second walk in the city. Mail delivered three times a week compared to every day in the city. There were so many differences in this new life I was living.

"Can you play Daddy's playlist?" Scarlet asked. "You just need to stick the USB in."

"OK."

I headed off to Ann's, listening to some rock song I'd never heard.

"No way!" The kids yelled during a pause in the chorus. "Get fucked. Fuck off."

What on earth? I swung around so quickly I yanked the car to the right. I straightened the car before looking in the mirror to see their gleeful faces looking back at me. They had no qualms about swearing. The chorus came on again, and they yelled out the same thing.

"It's part of the song," Scarlet said.

"It doesn't sound like part of the song to me."

They giggled, and I pulled into Ann's driveway and turned off the car. "Let's see if Nan wants to come."

Scarlet and Thomas ran ahead. By the time I'd gotten to the door, they'd already asked Ann if she wanted to join us.

She smiled at me as I approached. "Just let me get ready. I'll be out soon."

I nodded and herded the kids back to the car. When Ann joined us, she'd changed out of her T-shirt and old jeans and was wearing a navy polka dot blouse and newer jeans. My navy linen shorts and long-sleeved striped top wouldn't be out of place. I started the car. The song that had been playing started again at the beginning. The chorus hit, and all three of them sang, "No way. Get fucked. Fuck off."

I tried to hide my surprise.

"See, we told you it's part of the song; even Nan sang it," Scarlet said.

"Australians like to add their own spin to songs," Ann explained.

I just nodded. What more was there to say? The longer I lived here, the more I learned how different and down-to-earth this country was.

"Can we put up the Christmas decorations when we get home?" Scarlet asked from the back seat.

Christmas was only weeks away. The time had flown since my arrival, and I hadn't had much opportunity to think about the coming holiday. As fun as putting up decorations sounded, I didn't feel it was my place to do so. It wasn't my home. And I wasn't part of their family.

"You will need to ask your dad when he gets home from work," I said.

Scarlet clapped her hands. "We won't be spending

Christmas week with Daddy this year, but that doesn't mean we shouldn't decorate the house."

I hadn't thought of them not being with Lachlan for Christmas. Would that make him sad? Would he rather spend it alone without me in the house?

CHAPTER EIGHTEEN

Lachlan

"You know, you've been happier since Peyton's been here," Bruce said as we drove to one of the back paddocks to do some fencing.

"Maybe because Scarlet and Thomas are happy," I said pointedly.

"Scar and Thomas weren't here last week."

"For fucks sake. Peyton's nice. I like her. She's good company. So what?"

"Ooh, three compliments in a row. You forgot to add pretty."

I sighed. He wasn't going to let this go. "They're Mum's words."

"What would you say then?"

I kept my eyes on the road. "Attractive."

"Bullshit, you've never used that word in your life."

"I just did."

I couldn't help but notice Bruce's shit-eating grin in my peripheral vision. "Are you too afraid to say the word?"

He poked me. The man was a fucking child.

"I just gave her three compliments in a row," I said. "What else do you want?"

"For you to say what you actually think of her looks."

I gripped the steering wheel. "What does it matter?"

"Because I want to know."

He was not going to let up. If he wasn't so big, I'd think about pushing him out of the car.

"I think she's fucking beautiful, OK?"

"Was it that hard?"

I glared at him. "If you ever repeat it, I'll cut your balls off."

"Now, now, there's no need to resort to violence."

I could tell him more. I wanted to tell him more. And if he knew I was serious, I'm sure he'd never repeat it. But saying things out loud made them real. And I wasn't ready to be real. Not in that kind of way. The only real things I knew were my family and the farm.

I'd thought Jane and I were real. We were real good at playing happy family. But Jane never wanted to be on the farm. Her family had nearly gone to ruins trying to save theirs. She did it for me. For us. But in the end, she couldn't pretend anymore. I don't blame her. She gave it a good try. For me. For us. When she'd left, I had to face my failure head-on. It was hard knowing that you weren't enough for someone.

She'd say it was just about the farm, but it wasn't. It was also about me. And that nearly broke me. I was ashamed that I couldn't keep my family together. Depression hit hard. If it wasn't for the kids, my family and the farm, I might still be there now. My family fed me when they saw I was losing weight. They made sure I stayed connected, having me over for dinner and popping over for a chat. Hell,

Bruce even started doing weights with me because he read it helped with stress, moods and sleep. I knew I was better when he stopped coming over.

It took months for me to forgive myself, for me to know that it wasn't all about me and my failure. But in the quietest moments, when you least expect it, those thoughts try to appear, and you need the strength to push them back. I had that now. The strength. And losing it could risk losing it all.

"I think she'll last longer than a month," Bruce said.

He was right. My earlier prediction was way off. She was in her third week now. The kids loved her. My family loved her. Hell, even Jane loved her. Peyton seemed content. She didn't act like she was bored. But would it last? I doubted it.

"The novelty of all of this"—I indicated to all the emptiness around us—"will wear off soon."

"Why? It hasn't worn off for you."

"We were born into it."

I drove through a gate and took the bumpy track to the back fence. I was glad to be out here today, far from the house. Going home for lunch with no one there would have been strange. The truth was I enjoyed having lunch with Peyton while the kids were away. We'd have quiet conversations about the farm and farm life. Peyton was always eager to learn more. She didn't talk much about her life before she got here. I didn't know whether she was trying to forget or if she just didn't like talking about herself.

What I said about her being beautiful was the truth. She had a beautiful soul. And face. And body. Fuck I needed to stop thinking about her.

"How do you think she got those scars?" Bruce asked. His voice was soft. I'm sure it was a question a lot of people asked. But for him, it wasn't a morbid fascination. I knew him as well as I knew myself.

"There was a car accident. Some kids were trapped in a car. She saved them."

He nodded. "Do you think she's here hiding away?"

"I think she's here trying to learn how to be herself."

And I would help her any way I could.

But once she figured it out, she'd be gone. And that is something I needed to remember every time I felt the strange pull towards her. It wasn't a matter of *if* she would leave but when.

And if I got too close, if I tried to have something more with her than a working relationship or friendship, I'd have to face all over again that I wasn't enough for someone.

CHAPTER NINETEEN

Peyton

I PARKED where Ann told me to. We hopped out of the car, and Scarlet and Thomas set out in front of us.

"Lachlan is a lot like his dad," Ann said. "His family always comes first."

"I can see how much he loves you all."

"He doesn't let much else into his life."

He'd let me into his home, and we'd been spending a lot of time together. He and Bruce spent what time they could working on the unit, but farm work had to come first. I didn't feel uncomfortable in the house or like I was in the way. Even with the kids home, he didn't exclude me. It was a privilege I hadn't given much consideration to.

The children stopped at a grave. Scarlet sat down on the grass and started talking.

"They never got to meet Lance. He passed before they were born."

Thomas and Scarlet were both talking now. He wasn't as sure of himself as Scarlet. It was something I often saw in him in his quieter moments. I stood back, watching them, not wanting to interrupt. Scarlet turned and beckoned us over.

"Pop, this is Peyton. She's our new nanny," Scarlet said.

I stood awkwardly beside her. Was I supposed to say something?

"She's the best nanny we've had," Thomas said.

"By far," Ann said. "We didn't let Lachlan choose this time."

Scarlet giggled. "Daddy was so pissed. But I think he likes her now."

"I think so too," Ann said.

"He used to be grouchy, but he smiles a lot more," Scarlet said.

Thomas nodded in that energetic way of his. "Yeah, he didn't even yell at me when I let the bath overflow."

"You should have seen it, Pop. There was water everywhere."

"And Mr Harrison's burrow got flooded."

"But Daddy and Uncle Bru saved him." It was as if Scarlet expected nothing less.

"And now Peyton's moved into the house." Thomas smiled up at me. "It's the best."

"I think so too," Ann said.

It was pretty good. I blushed. Could Pop hear my thoughts? Did he know how much I liked Lachlan's smile? Or how I could get lost in his eyes? Or how he gave me comfort and security just by being himself? Or how I thought his arse looked good in anything?

My eyes widened. Oh crap, I hoped Pop didn't know any of those things.

"Why don't we let Nan have a few quiet moments with Pop," I suggested.

Scarlet nodded, stood up and blew her pop a kiss. We walked back to the car in silence. As we waited for Ann, I watched her. She would glance back at us as she was talking. At one point, she nodded to herself. And then her laughter reached our ears. This is what true love was. There was no till death do us part for Ann and Lance.

"WHERE SHALL WE GO FIRST?" I asked after we parked the car in the centre parking strip.

"The general store," Scarlet said. She took my hand, and we crossed the road. I turned to make sure Thomas was with Ann.

The building had a wide awning and big windows that looked out onto the sidewalk. Scarlet opened the door and strode in with confidence, never letting go of my hand.

The lady behind the counter placed her palms on her cheeks. "Scarlet, darling, you're so grown up." She turned her attention to Thomas. "Thomas, look at you. You're such a big boy." Then she faced Ann. "He's the spitting image of Lachlan." Finally, her gaze rested on me. My face. My hand. Back to my face. Quick. Not wanting to be rude.

"This is Peyton. She's our nanny," Scarlet said like I was a prize bull.

The lady came out from behind the counter. Her bright, flowery dress appeared out of place in the organised store. "Peyton, it's lovely to meet you. I've heard so much about you."

How?

"Are you enjoying being out on the farm?" she asked. "It must be very different for a city girl like you."

She did know something about me.

"It would be so nice for Lachlan to have company. He needs a good woman in his life."

A good woman. Could I be referred to as a good woman? The right woman for Lachlan?

"He is always so busy," she continued.

Was she even going to let me speak?

"He is such a dedicated family man. He gave up his singing career to come back after Lance passed away."

"I wouldn't call it a singing career," Ann interrupted.

The lady gave a small huff.

"You're much younger than the other nannies he's hired. It's better to have someone closer to his age. You would have more in common."

Silence. Was she finished? I'd never had a stranger say so much to me in mere minutes. I barely had time to think. She was still silent. Must be my turn to talk.

"I'm sorry," I said, "I didn't catch your name."

"I'm Agnes. Ann and I go way back. We went to school together."

I glanced at Ann. She gave a non-committal nod. I needed to think of my words here. They, no, she, did not need more to speak about.

"I love the peace and quiet out at the farm," I finally said.

She nodded, eager for more.

"Lachlan is very dedicated to his children." How was I going to get away? "So much so that I thought we could bake him a cake. Which way to the flour, please?"

"Oh, that's lovely. Food is the way to a man's heart. Everything you need is in that second aisle."

"Thank you." I pulled Scarlet along. When we got to the flour, I pulled out my phone.

"What are you doing?" Scarlet asked.

"I'm looking up a recipe for a cake."

"Daddy likes chocolate best."

I nodded and grabbed the ingredients we needed. Better bake an excellent cake if food was the way to a man's heart. I giggled. Lachlan was likely more complex than most men. Scarlet looked up at me. I managed to give her a smile without laughing out loud.

As soon as we left the shop, I said to Ann, "You could have warned me."

She laughed. "I wanted to see how you'd handle the small-town gossip train."

I gave her a sidelong glance. "You would have saved me though?"

"Peyton, you don't need saving. You're as smart as they come."

That was the second nicest thing someone had ever said to me. The first was Lachlan saying David didn't deserve me as he held my hands.

We stopped in front of the next building—bricks painted a dark blue, white trimmings and posts. "This is the post office, bank, business centre and a small information centre for tourists."

"Wow."

"Not like the city, huh?"

"No. There, post offices are just post offices."

The next building was the rural supplies. Lachlan had told me he tried to buy as much as he could through them. So did all the other local farms. He said without local support, they would close.

"This is the doctor surgery and chemist."

"A surgery?" I asked, looking at the old building. "Do they perform surgeries here?"

"No, it's where the doctor works from...his office, I

suppose. We call GPs doctors, and the place where they work can be called a medical centre, surgery or clinic."

I nodded. That made more sense now.

"They're open once a week, a Tuesday here and other days in other towns."

Once a week? At Massachusetts General Hospital, they would see as many patients in a day in the emergency room as this surgery would see in a year.

"Is once a week enough for the community?"

"Not even close. This is the only surgery in a hundred-kilometre radius. Just to see a doctor here, you need to wait weeks. Or make the drive into Tamworth. Most people don't bother. They just suffer in silence."

We continued to walk along the main street, past small houses and a quaint wooden church. It was nothing like Trinity Church in Boston in Copley Square. There the stone church stood its ground, proud and regal, while the concrete and glass skyscrapers towered above it. Some people became members of the church just so they could be married there.

"Why is the doctor's surgery only open once a week?"

"Getting doctors to work in rural areas is not easy. Dr. Pete is at retirement age, but he won't retire because he fears no one will take over from him. If that happens, his patients won't have access to a doctor."

I nodded. It was a shame that small communities didn't receive the types of services big cities did. Being able to see a doctor was a fundamental need.

Ann stopped walking. "And that's it. That's our town, except for the two pubs."

Because a town this size needed two pubs. And only one doctor, once a week.

"Can we have lunch at the pub, Peyton?"

"Yes. Which one?"

"We went to the Royal last time," Ann said. "It's the Doolan's turn this time."

"Will this be another gossip train experience?" I asked.

"No, Donna is nothing like Agnes."

"Good." I didn't want to experience that again anytime soon. It made me think about things I had no right to think about. Lachlan was the father of the children I cared for, and here I was thinking about whether I was the right woman for him. I didn't even know if I wanted another relationship. I didn't want to risk losing myself all over again.

We sat at a table, and when we were ready to order, Scarlet escorted us up to the counter.

"Hello, Scarlet," a smiling woman said. "That's a pretty dress you're wearing."

"It's Pop's favourite colour."

Donna leant over the counter. "Your Nan used to wear that colour. I think that's why it was his favourite."

Scarlet turned her eyes to Ann, who gave her a wistful smile.

Scarlet gave my hand a yank, pulling me forward. "This is Peyton. She's our new nanny."

"Nice to meet you, Peyton. Must be hard work keeping these rascals under control."

"They make it easy."

"That's not what the last four nannies said." She laughed. "What can I get you all today?"

We ordered and then made our way back to our table near the playground—a fenced-off outside area with a slide and swings. Donna came over with our drinks. She handed Ann and me a leaflet about a local singing competition.

"You should get Lachlan to enter," Donna said. "No one would have a chance against him."

"I didn't think he sang in public anymore," I said.

"No, but he should. Have you heard him sing?"

I shook my head.

"He could sing just one line, and half the room would fall in love with him."

"Wow." I probably didn't need to hear him sing, then. That sounded dangerous.

Ann studied the leaflet. "He could have made a career out of singing, but he never saw it that way. His heart was at the farm."

Donna nodded.

"He travelled through country towns and sang. He made a modest living from it, but it wasn't going to be his life's work," Ann said.

"He loved to get on stage," Donna said. "When he sang, everyone listened."

I looked between them. "Why doesn't he sing now?"

"You know Lachlan," Ann said. "He's devoted to the farm and his family. He doesn't feel like there's room for anything else."

"But it doesn't have to be one or the other. He doesn't have to sacrifice something he loves."

"You tell him that."

Why did she think I would have any influence over him?

CHAPTER TWENTY

Lachlan

THE HOUSE WAS quiet when I got home from work. I knew Peyton and the kids were back and was surprised they weren't outside. I walked through the kitchen. Someone had been baking. I could smell it in the air. Peyton, Scarlet and Thomas were on the couch watching TV.

Peyton was wearing a T-shirt. A *T-shirt*. It showed the extent of her burns. Not one piece of skin on her arm was untouched. It was worse than I'd imagined.

"How was your trip into town?" I asked.

They all turned to me. Scarlet giggled. Interesting.

"Donna called us rascals," Thomas said.

Oh no. What had they done? Better Donna than Agnes though. She was a busy body. By the end of the day, half the district would have known my kids were off the rails.

"But Peyton told her that we're easy to look after," Scarlet said.

"Did she just?" I turned my attention to Peyton.

She shrugged. "I wasn't lying."

They did seem to be on their best behaviour for her. Or maybe she brought out the best behaviour in them. In the time she'd been here, Thomas had had no full-blown tantrums. Even after the bath incident, he'd been quite calm, whereas normally he would have had a meltdown because he was upset with himself.

"Pop liked my dress," Scarlet said. She was still wearing it. I bet she had a full conversation with him too, just like Mum. "Donna said that it was his favourite colour because Nan wore it."

"That'd be right," I said.

I didn't know anyone who had a love like theirs. Right until the day he passed, Dad adored Mum. And she was the same. I couldn't even make it ten years in marriage. I'd had the perfect role models and still failed.

"And we met Agnes," Peyton said, her voice flat.

This wasn't going to be good.

"She felt compelled to tell me that you need a good woman in your life." She studied me.

I took a step back.

"Didn't you tell her we don't fraternise?" Her face was deadpan. There was that damn word again.

I took another step back. "N—"

She burst out laughing. The laughter stretched from her mouth to her eyes. They were full of glee. I stared at her. She had me good and proper.

"Shit head," I said.

"That's not a nice way to speak to your young nanny," she said, giving me a sly smile.

No, it probably wasn't appropriate to speak to the nanny like that. Why had I? What was it about Peyton that made me think that was OK? But friends call each other names. That's all I was doing—showing our friendship.

"According to Agnes, it's wonderful that we're so close in age," Peyton said in a teasing voice.

"Right." I couldn't be more blasé if I tried.

The age thing was good. Having a young nanny was turning out much better than the older battle axes I'd hired, but I wasn't going to say that. Because I, Lachlan Harris, was not going to admit anything like that out loud. Unless it was dragged out of me by Bruce.

"Go and have a shower. We have a surprise for you," she said.

The baking, no doubt.

"There's no arsenic in it, is there?"

"Oh no, that would never be rewarding enough." She gave me an evil grin.

"Mmm."

Her laughter followed me to my bathroom. That woman was dangerous in more ways than one. The shower eased my tired muscles. A day of fencing was hard work. I could stay in here all night, but the thoughts of Peyton wouldn't ease. They followed me everywhere. I walked back out to the kitchen, and the three of them were standing on the other side of the counter waiting.

"Sit down." Thomas paused.

He looked to Scarlet, who whispered, "Mr Harris."

"Mr Harris, we are going to—" He stopped again.

Scarlet stepped forward. "Present you with the first ever cake—"

"I've baked," Peyton finished. She placed a chocolate cake in front of me. It was risen on one side more than the other, making it lopsided.

"You've never baked a cake?"

A blush rose on Peyton's cheeks.

"No. In my house, we bought cakes." She smiled down

at Scarlet. "Never again though. Scarlet has taught me that cake batter is the best."

"The absolute best," Scarlet corrected.

"Well, let's see if your cake tastes the absolute best."

Peyton handed me a knife and some plates. Thomas and Scarlet came to sit beside me. I cut each of us a piece and handed them around. Everyone watched me as I took a bite. Fuck it was good. I took another bite.

"Good?" Scarlet asked.

"Bloody oath," I said.

Peyton tilted her head. Not something Americans would say by the looks of it.

"You bet," I translated for her.

Scarlet clapped. "I told you. The batter don't lie."

Peyton took a bite and nodded. "Not bad for my first cake."

"We can eat it every day," Scarlet said.

"Before dinner," Thomas added.

Peyton and I looked at each other. She was holding her laughter in.

"I don't think so," I said.

"I don't know what made you think your dad would agree to that," Peyton said, no longer holding in her laughter.

"You don't know if you don't try," Scarlet said.

She sounded just like Bruce. But trying opened you up to...everything. And I didn't think I could do that. I couldn't open myself up to another failure. My self-esteem couldn't take it. Anyway, Peyton never indicated that she was interested in me that way. We could be friends; I think we'd proved that.

"DADDY, you need to lift me higher," Scarlet said. "We need more tinsel at the top of the tree."

My arms were tiring. She was taking forever with the tinsel.

Peyton looked up from where she was sitting on the ground, untangling lights with Thomas. Her eyes widened. "That sure is a lot of tinsel."

She wasn't wrong. There was nearly as much tinsel as there was tree. I imagined her tree at home looked nothing like this. Hers would be so elegant it could be showcased in a sophisticated Christmas magazine.

Scarlet nodded with enthusiasm, making it even more difficult for me to keep her in position.

"Wait until we put all these lights up," Thomas said.

"I don't think we will need to use any lights in the house with all of these." Peyton pointed at the lights laid out in front of them.

Thomas giggled. "Uncle Bruce got them for us."

"Of course he did," Peyton said, smiling. "I bet he also said something like the more, the better."

"He said exactly that," I replied. She seemed to know him so well already.

"It's our new Christmas tradition," Scarlet said. She'd finally finished with the tinsel.

"What Christmas traditions do you have in Boston?" I asked.

"One of my favourites is the Faneuil Hall Tree Lighting. The tree is enormous, and the coloured lights are so pretty like the tree came from a fairy realm."

"What about family traditions?"

"Mom and Dad have breakfast together at a nice restaurant. And then we all get together for lunch."

"Will you miss not being with them this year?"

"I don't think so."

And that was it, the end of the home conversation. I knew her relationships in Boston weren't the best, but there must have been something good about home. Something she would want to share with us. But she never did.

Regardless, I didn't want her to feel lonely. No one should spend Christmas alone. It was wrong. Everyone should share in the love and joy. Mum would kill me if I didn't invite Peyton to spend Christmas with us.

"The children will have lunch with Jane and her family this year," I said. "And then will come over to Mum's for dinner." I shifted from foot to foot. "You're welcome to join us all."

She nodded. "That would be nice, thank you."

That's settled. She wouldn't be lonely, and I would live to celebrate another year.

CHAPTER TWENTY-ONE

Peyton

"Peyton," Scarlet called from her bedroom.

Lachlan was in there reading them a bedtime story. When he'd come home earlier, he'd noticed my short sleeves. His eyes had been drawn to my arm, but they hadn't lingered. He hadn't acted like it disgusted him. He wasn't treating me any differently. I put down my book and made my way there. Thomas and Scarlet were sitting together on her bed. Lachlan was sitting on her chair, holding a guitar.

"Daddy's going to sing us a song. Come and sit with us."

Lachlan shifted in his seat. Did he really want me there? I raised my eyebrows at him in question. He nodded. The two children scooted apart, and I sat between them.

"What song do you want?" he asked.

"I know," Thomas said. "Sing the one about the dog."

Lachlan played a couple of chords and then began singing. His voice sent shivers through me. The pureness mixed in with a huskiness. It wound its way through me, tightening around my heart, enveloping it. I filled my lungs with air as if breathing was now a voluntary action.

The song ended, and he started another one about two lovers staring at the moon. I watched his mouth form the words, so perfect. We made eye contact, and I lost myself in him and those words. The lovers' kiss warmed me. I could have melted; my only hope for salvation would be Lachlan holding me together with his strong hands.

He stopped singing, but I didn't stop staring until he smiled and his eyes averted to Scarlet. "One last song. What will it be?"

"The good night song."

I shook my head to escape his spell. Donna was right. Half the room would fall in love with him. In this room, we were equally affected. I listened to his last song, trying not to fall into the trap of his hot voice. It wasn't the only thing hot in that room. I almost needed to fan myself.

When he finished, I gave the kids a good night kiss and went to my room so he could finish putting the kids to sleep. I grabbed the leaflet out of my bag and then headed to the lounge room to wait for Lachlan. His footsteps sounded down the corridor. I held the leaflet tighter to stop my hands from shaking. I'd performed surgeries to save people's lives, yet somehow I was nervous about this.

He sat down next to me. "What are we watching tonight?"

"Nothing yet."

He was close. I could feel the heat radiating off him. I turned to face him, tucking one leg under me. "Donna gave this to your mum and me today." I handed him the leaflet. "I think you should enter."

He took it from me. Our fingers brushed, and tingles

spread through me. He read it and then raised his eyes to mine. "I don't sing in public anymore."

I'd prepared a whole host of arguments.

"You just sang for me."

"You're not the public."

"Well, I'm not family."

His mouth tightened. "You are. Sort of. You live here. And well, you know…"

He was rambling. Did he think of me as more than just the nanny?

"Why don't you sing in public anymore?" I kept my voice gentle so that he wouldn't be forced to defend himself.

"Because I'm busy with the farm and the children."

"I'm sure the children would love to watch you sing out there in the big wide world."

"And who will look after the farm?"

Lame excuse. I reached out my hand and rested it on his arm. "I just heard you sing. You're exceptional. It's not like you need to take a lot of time away from the farm to practice."

He raised his eyes to mine, totally exposed. "When I took over the farm, I didn't want singing to get in the way of what needed to be done. And then Scarlet came along. There was no time between getting married, having a baby, and looking after everything."

He gave up singing for his family. Was there anything else he'd given up?

"Maybe you're at a stage in your life where you can take it up again," I suggested.

I glanced down at my hand, still touching him deliberately. And it wasn't even my good hand. I chanced a look at his face. He was studying my hand. I blushed. I should take it away, but if I did, I might lose the power in my next comment. The killer blow.

"I think it would be good to show Scarlet and Thomas how important it is to do something that interests them."

Lachlan's hand took mine. His warm brown eyes searched my face. Every part of me was swirling, like cake batter in a blender, but his hand anchored me. No one had ever had this effect on me before. I wanted more of his touch, and that was disconcerting. I shouldn't feel like this about him, my boss, friend, housemate, whatever he was.

"I'll think about it."

"It would be a shame to deny all the ladies your talent."

And it would be a shame to deny me.

CHAPTER TWENTY-TWO

Lachlan

TALENT. There was one talent I'd really like to show Peyton. This was bullshit. I needed to stop thinking about her or what I'd like to do to her, with her. I thought about her at work, in the shower, and now, it seemed, while I was working out.

This was the time when I usually cleared my mind. But somehow, she kept pushing herself in. And my biggest problem was that this wasn't just physical. I was attracted to her in many ways. The way she opened up to me, became vulnerable. The way she was always happy. How much she worried about that fucking wombat. Nothing about her was selfish or self-centred. The way she trusted us with her burns tonight drew me closer to her too.

I worked on my triceps. They were dead tired. I wished other body parts would die along with them. Like my brain and my dick.

Knowing Peyton came in here to stretch and use the weights made me feel closer to her. The first time I'd seen her in here, she'd seemed shocked. She'd covered up but had taken the time to explain her burn recovery. Watching the video later, I thought about the many surgeries she'd had. But after tonight, after seeing her arm and the extent of her burns, I understood the magnitude of her recovery and why it had taken fourteen months. She must have felt so lonely during that time. Fuck, she was brave.

Nope. I couldn't stop thinking about her.

And now there was this bloody singing contest. I did miss performing and the adrenalin that came along with it. I wiped the sweat off my face. Could I do it? Would anything suffer if I did? Was I ready to put myself out there? With singing? With Peyton?

The lights in the shed died. I sighed. The power must be out. I put the barbell back on the rack and headed inside. Just as I did, Peyton came out of the bathroom wrapped in a towel.

"There's no water," she said.

"The power's out. The water pump doesn't work without power."

"Oh."

"The joys of country living."

I moved closer to her so she could see me better. That was a dangerous move because it also meant I could see her nearly naked body better. The torch from her phone illuminated her. My eyes followed water droplets as they made their way to the top of the towel. Other droplets emerged from under the towel and trickled down her shapely legs. My mouth was dry.

"What could have caused the power to go out?" she asked.

I lifted my eyes. Thank goodness for the distraction. "A

lightning strike or wind or a car crash. It could be anywhere between here and the substation."

"Do you think it will be out for long? I need to wash the conditioner out of my hair."

"It could be hours. We have some bottles of water in the cupboard. I can help you wash it out if you like."

"Yes, please."

"I'll grab a couple and meet you in the bathroom."

I was helping a friend. There was no need to think of her near-naked body. Or her breasts that caused the towel to jut out. Or her...anything. My only job was to pour water over her head. I entered the bathroom and swallowed hard. Just. Pour. Water. Over. Her. Head.

She gave me a tentative smile as I approached. The bath towel she had wrapped around her covered a decent amount of skin. It was both a blessing and a disappointment. She angled her body to the side and bent her head over the basin. I closed my eyes and drew a breath in before opening them and beginning to pour. She flinched, either at the suddenness or coolness, then massaged the conditioner out of her hair. Vanilla and coconut filled the bathroom. I watched the water and only the water.

"I think I got it all," she said. She grabbed another towel beside her and dried her hair before standing up. "Thank you."

"My pleasure," I said, my voice husky even to my own ears. I needed to get out of there before I became an awkward, stunned mute again. "I'll let you get dressed."

She looked down at her towel and blushed.

Fuck. I needed to rein my hormones in before they got me into trouble.

A FEW MINUTES after Bruce and I rocked up to the unit, Peyton joined us. The kids were in the sand pit digging out moats around their castle and lining them with plastic.

"Hi, Bruce," Peyton said, giving him a grin.

"Peyton."

He was playing tough guy, was he? Let's see how long he could keep this up for. I couldn't even keep it up for a week.

"I got a message from Kayley today," Peyton said.

"Uh-huh." He went into the bedroom and started removing the plaster. It had swelled with all the water and needed to be replaced.

Peyton followed him. "She said you gave her flowers. I'm so proud of you." She wasn't even being condescending.

He grinned. "You should have seen her face, Peyton."

Yep, the dam was broken. No more tough guy.

"I didn't know if she was going to smile or cry," Bruce said.

"It's the little things, Bruce."

"I never thought that a bunch of field flowers could make someone so happy."

Peyton smiled. "I told her I had nothing to do with it. That it was your idea."

He was beaming like a boy whose favourite teacher had just complimented him in front of the entire school.

He inclined his head to me. "You could take some lessons from me."

What did I need lessons for?

Peyton gave me a smile. "I think he's doing alright on his own."

That got my attention.

"Oh yeah?" Bruce asked.

"I heard him sing."

"Ooh, no one can compete with his panty-melting voice."

"I think it's more than just his voice." Her eyes widened as if her words surprised her.

"Like what?" Bruce asked.

Peyton blushed. Then she shrugged. She tried to make her way to the sliding door, but Bruce blocked her path.

"No way, you can't just leave after a statement like that."

You tell her, Bruce. I'd like to know too.

She poked him in the ribs, trying to move him out of the way. She didn't seem uncomfortable with him; her shoulders weren't tense, and her eyes weren't wide or apprehensive. Otherwise, I'd step in.

She stopped poking and nudged him with her elbow instead. "I have to get back to the kids."

He didn't budge. "Are you talking about his big muscles? Or those tattoos? Maybe his dreamy eyes."

The blush deepened.

"Don't think I haven't noticed you checking out his arse."

Peyton's mouth opened and then closed. She glanced at me and then back at him. Had she been checking out my arse?

"Lachlan is thinking of joining the singing competition in town," Peyton blurted out.

That was pure desperation. I was disappointed I didn't get to hear more about her checking out my arse.

Bruce grinned as he turned to me. "Is that true?"

I crossed my arms. "The operative word there was *thinking*."

"Oh, bro, you should do it. You'd win easy."

Peyton giggled. "How could the girls resist your panty-melting voice?"

Before either Bruce or I could say a word, she escaped through the sliding door.

And for good measure, I watched her arse the whole way.

CHAPTER TWENTY-THREE

Peyton

I couldn't walk away fast enough. My brazenness was next level. Was I flirting with Lachlan? My boss? Scarlet and Thomas's dad? I thought that checking out his butt was my own secret guilty pleasure. But it wasn't so secret after all. It was mortifying.

"Peyton, we're nearly done," Thomas called out.

I examined their creation. A huge castle surrounded by moats. "This looks fantastic. Do you think it will hold water?"

"For sure," Scarlet said. "We just need a few more decorations and we can test it out."

Thomas jumped up, ready and waiting, almost dancing on the spot. If he lost concentration, this could end in disaster. I moved to the other side of the sandpit, so I was in his line of sight.

"Thomas," I said.

He looked at me, still moving around like an excited puppy.

"Do you think now is the right time to be so boisterous? You don't want to accidentally damage the castle."

"Sit down, Thomas," Scarlett said, her voice high.

"No," he yelled.

"If you break it—"

"I won't break it. I'm not a baby." His feet didn't slow down. My stomach tightened. I had no control.

"You're acting like one." Scarlet stood up.

"I am not." He was getting loud.

"Are so."

Thomas' little hands were curled into fists.

"You're such a baby. Are you sure you're even ready for school?"

"Scarlet." My voice was firm.

"I'm not a baby." He kicked one of the castle towers.

"You broke it," Scarlet screamed. She launched herself at him, knocking half the castle over.

My heart raced.

He kicked her in the shin. "I hate you."

I climbed into the sandpit, right on top of the castle and pulled them apart, keeping hold of an arm each.

"That's enough."

They were taking swings at each other and kicking out, spitting out unintelligible words. I saw movement in my vision but couldn't pay attention to it.

A foot connected with my shin, and a punch got me square in the stomach. I tightened my grip and gave them a small shove. "I said *enough*."

I needed to separate them. I turned to Scarlet. "Go and stand next to the tree."

Her jaw was set as she stared down her brother. She didn't budge.

"Now." I let her arm go, pushing it in the direction of the tree.

"I—"

"I don't care. Go."

She swaggered to the tree. So much attitude for an eight-year-old.

"You." I glared at Thomas. "Sit on the bench."

He hung his head and walked away.

"I—" Scarlet called out.

I raised my hand up, telling her not to speak.

"I do not want to hear from either of you unless it's an apology."

Scarlet crossed her arms. Thomas pouted. I sat on the edge of the sand pit and rubbed my shin. I never knew bare feet were so hard. And that punch, I don't know who it came from, but it was good.

Movement in my peripheral vision. The bull was at the fence, his head swaying. I had enough to deal with without having to try to figure out his body language. Another movement, Lachlan, was coming toward us. I made eye contact with him and shook my head. This was for me to deal with. Without a word, he went back to Bruce who was watching from the verandah. Scarlet and Thomas gave each other death stares.

Which one should I deal with first? How would I deal with them? This was way beyond my level of expertise. Thomas first. He was younger, and the longer I left him, the more unlikely that he would listen to what I had to say.

I sat down on the bench beside him but didn't look at him. I didn't want him to become defensive.

"Do you think that worked out well?"

"She—"

"I'm not asking about Scarlet. Do *you* think that worked

out well?" I faced him this time. A little bit of pressure wouldn't hurt him.

"No."

"What could you have done differently?"

He swung his feet backwards and forwards. "Listened."

"And what would have happened if you listened?"

"The sandcastle wouldn't be broken."

"Right." I bumped his shoulder, a friendly gesture. "What Scarlet said about you being a baby wasn't nice."

"No. I'm not a baby."

"I guess it hurt your feelings."

"Yes."

I put my arm around his shoulders. "Do you think you acted like a big boy?"

He shifted in his seat. "No."

"That's right. You don't see Dad or Uncle Bruce acting like that."

"No."

"I know it's really hard not to act out when you're angry. But that's not the way we act in this family, is it?"

He shook his head, then leant in closer. "Dad and Uncle Bruce act like big kids sometimes."

We looked in their direction. I tried not to laugh. "I bet they do."

He nodded emphatically.

"I'm going to speak to Scarlet now. When I'm finished, I would like you to apologise to each other, and I'd like you to clean the sandpit."

"OK."

I walked over to Scarlet. She still had her arms crossed. But they were loose now, not tight in anger.

"Do you think that worked out well?"

She looked at the sandcastle. "No."

"What do you think went wrong?"

"I didn't stay calm."

She was quick to answer. I imagined this wasn't their first fist fight. And not the first time they'd been spoken to about staying calm.

"Yes, that would have helped."

"I shouldn't have called Thomas a baby."

"Do you think that was a nice thing to do?"

"No." She looked at her feet.

"I think that hurt his feelings. We try not to do that in this family."

"I know." Her voice was soft, full of remorse.

"I want you to apologise to each other. And I don't just want to hear the word sorry. I want to hear what you're sorry for."

She shuffled her feet. "OK."

"This is your chance to lead by example." I hoped that giving her this extra bit of responsibility would make her just that.

She unfolded her arms and went to the sandpit.

"Come and help me, Thomas," Scarlet said.

He came over slowly and glanced at me. I gave him a nod. They started work.

"I'm sorry, Thomas. I shouldn't have called you a baby."

Thomas started to pull up the plastic. "I'm sorry I broke the castle."

I watched them both, smiling, and then I glanced at Lachlan. His lips lifted at the corners. That was enough to tell me I'd done a good job. Why did his opinion matter so much to me? It's not like I had to prove myself to him anymore. I never felt like he wanted me to leave, not the farm or the house. Was there something more, could there be something more, between us? Did I want there to be?

CHAPTER TWENTY-FOUR

Lachlan

"Holy shit, she's a pro," Bruce said to me.

The children were cleaning the sand pit together. Peyton walked to the house, giving them one last look before she stepped inside. How? How did she do it? I was a parent, I'd been one for eight years, and I couldn't even manage what she'd just pulled off. If that were me, there'd likely be some yelling, some crying and everything in between.

"OK, I think we're finished here for the day," Bruce said. He closed the sliding door and walked down the steps. "You should check on her. She got a couple of heavy blows."

She had. And that was unacceptable. The kids needed to apologise.

I ambled over to them. Ben was no longer at the fence. When Peyton walked away, so did he. I couldn't figure that bull out. It was like he was attracted to her energy.

Scarlet and Thomas were gathering up the last of the plastic when I reached them.

Time to use the pro's example.

"Nearly finished?" I asked.

They nodded. As much as I wanted to rehash what had just happened, there was no point. There was nothing I could say to improve on what Peyton had already said.

"I think you need to apologise to Peyton. You hurt her in your little kerfuffle."

Thomas's eyebrows drew together. Scarlet openly stared.

"One of you kicked her, and the other punched her."

Thomas's eyes became wet. "We hurt Peyton?"

I nodded. "I know you didn't mean to."

"Why didn't she punish us?" Scarlet asked.

"She probably thought you felt bad enough already."

"I didn't mean to hurt her, Daddy," Thomas said. "I feel bad."

"That's something you need to think about before you decide to have a punch-up."

Scarlet stood up. She shoved the plastic into my hands. Thomas did the same. Then they ran to the house. I put the plastic in the bin and made my way inside.

Scarlet and Thomas were on the couch with Peyton giving her a hug.

"We're really sorry, Peyton. You're not going to leave, are you?" Scarlet said.

"I don't want you to leave," Thomas said, crying. "I love you."

Fuck, that kid was a goner. If she said she was going to leave, it would break his heart.

"I'm not going anywhere," she said, giving them both a hug.

"But we hurt you," Scarlet said.

"You didn't do it on purpose," Peyton said, rubbing Scarlet's back.

"No," Thomas sobbed.

"There are bad people in this world who wouldn't care if they hurt someone. I wouldn't want to stay with those people." Was she talking about that fuckwit of an ex she had? She had their full attention. "But you're not those people. What you did was an accident."

They gave her another hug.

"Why don't you go have a shower and get into your PJs? Maybe we can watch a movie after dinner."

"Can we, Daddy?" Scarlet asked.

"Sure. Call me when you're ready to turn the water on."

Scarlet headed off first. She called me soon after to help her turn the shower on. When I got back out, Peyton and Thomas were watching *Bluey* on TV. I grabbed an ice pack and wrapped it in a tea towel. She hadn't been kicked by a cow, but it still must have hurt.

"Here, put this on your leg," I said as I handed it to her. "It will help with the bruising and swelling." I can't believe I just told an actual doctor that an ice pack would help her.

Our fingers brushed. Heat rushed up my arm despite the coldness in my hand.

"Thank you."

"I'm ready, Daddy," Scarlet called.

"OK, buddy, your turn next," I said to Thomas.

He nodded, his eyes glued to the TV.

"It's nearly finished," Peyton told me.

I went to help Scarlet. She was old enough now to regulate the temperature, but I always liked to make sure. I let her turn the water on and off, but I checked she was doing it in the right order. Thomas was different altogether. I had to keep an eye on him. He got way too distracted. I got distracted in the shower too, usually by thoughts of Peyton.

I held Scarlet's towel out for her, and she stepped into it. I gave her a few rubs to help dry her.

"I like Peyton, Daddy," she said.

"I know you do."

She wasn't even attempting to dry herself, so I rubbed the outside of the towel.

"Do you like her?"

"Yes," I admitted. More than I should.

"She won't leave us like the other nannies, will she?"

"I don't think so." I hope not. "She likes it here."

"And she likes us, doesn't she?"

"Yes, she likes you and Thomas very much."

I gave her another rub. She still looked thoughtful.

"Does she like you too?"

"Yes." I hoped so.

She nodded. "Probably because you're not grumpy anymore."

I stood up straight. What was she talking about? I wasn't grumpy.

Thomas charged into the bathroom and started tearing off his clothes. I pointed at the basket. There was no way we were having two undomesticated Harris men. Bruce was enough. I helped Thomas shower, dry and get changed. By the time we got back to the living area, Peyton and Scarlet had served up dinner. This wasn't part of Peyton's job, but she willingly helped every night.

She was nothing like I'd imagined her to be.

Was I what she imagined I'd be?

CHAPTER TWENTY-FIVE

Peyton

"Peyton." Lachlan's voice aroused me from my sleep. I forced my eyes open. I was lying on the couch. Where were the kids? Lachlan reached out for the remote and turned the TV off. I must have fallen asleep during the movie.

"It's time for bed," he said.

I didn't want to move. My eyes were awake, but the rest of my body was in slumberland. My eyes wanted to follow.

"Do I need to carry you to bed like the kids?"

I let out a soft laugh. "I'm quite a lot heavier than a child."

"You don't think I could?"

"No."

Before I could swing my legs around to sit up, Lachlan had lifted me from the couch. I yelped. Then to help him with my weight, I wrapped my arms around his shoulders. I breathed in grass and man. Good man, not just aftershave and cleanliness. Earth and strength.

I melded into him, swaying with every step he took.

Being in his strong arms, I felt secure. I shouldn't feel like this. But I didn't try to jump out of his arms. What was I doing?

"Show off," I mumbled against his shoulder.

"Just proving you wrong."

He walked into my room and made his way to my bed.

"Is it wrong to like you?" I asked. My heart beat fast in my chest. Would he think I was stupid?

He lay me down on the bed. His face was shadowed. Was he going to answer?

"No, it's not wrong."

He bent down and kissed my temple softly.

Oh, the sweetness of it. I sighed. My eyes closed as my body floated in bliss.

"I like you too."

Was I dreaming?

I opened my eyes. He was gone.

WE WERE outside checking on the vegetable garden. Everything was growing well, and our preventative measures to keep Mr Harrison out had worked so far. No sighting of square poo in the garden.

Bruce stopped on his way to the unit. "Who's up for a bonfire tonight?" he asked, clapping his hands and rubbing them together beneath a wide grin.

"Me!" Scarlet's face was glowing.

"Mc!" Thomas jumped up and down.

Me? A fire? I don't know. I twisted my hands. The closest I'd gotten to a fire since the accident was a fragranced candle.

"It will be so much fun, Peyton," Scarlet said. "We can

toast marshmallows."

"And Daddy will sing," Thomas said.

I didn't want to disappoint them. If it was dangerous, Lachlan wouldn't let them go. I glanced at him; his jaw was set.

"OK," I said.

"Excellent. Kayley can't wait to meet you."

Bruce and Lachlan headed towards the unit.

"Don't you think that was a bit insensitive?" Lachlan asked.

"What?"

I listened harder as they got further away.

"Peyton has burns. From a fire. Couldn't you have told me first? Maybe I could have asked her without the kids."

My heart nearly exploded in my chest. Lachlan surprised me every day.

"Fuck," Bruce said. "I'm sorry."

"It's not me you need to say sorry to."

He nodded.

I needed to do something to keep my mind off what was coming.

"Do you want to go for a walk or ride to the dam?" I asked Scarlet and Thomas.

"Ride," they said in unison.

"OK. Go get the bikes ready. I'll meet you there."

They ran off at full speed. Afterwards the kids could help me with taking photos of Ben for my next assignment.

"Peyton," Bruce said as he approached me.

"Yes."

"I'm really sorry about the fire thing. I didn't think."

"That's alright."

"We can do a BBQ or something else if you like."

"It's OK. The kids are really looking forward to it."

He studied me, and I gave him what I hoped was a convincing smile.

He glanced back at the unit. "I think my brother has a thing for you."

My heart raced. I had a thing for him too.

"What makes you say that?" I asked.

"Just the way he stuck up for you. The way he looks at you. The way he talks about you."

He does those things? Tingles spread through me.

"Is it just my arse he checks out?" I joked.

Bruce laughed. "Sometimes, but he's not as obvious as you."

I blushed.

"I really am sorry," he said.

"If you can convince Lachlan to join the singing competition, I'll forgive you."

"Deal."

Was what Bruce said possible? Did Lachlan have a thing for me? I wanted it to be true, even if I shouldn't. Him, this family, the farm, were all ingredients in my happiness and security. I saw possibilities here that were never imaginable before. I saw a future where I could be me.

SCARLET BRUSHED hair from her face as she stood up with a weed in her hand. Dirt smudged across her cheek. Thomas was on the opposite side of the vegetable garden finishing his weeding.

"Can you help me take some photos with Ben, please?" I asked Scarlet and Thomas from the other side of the fence.

"What sort of photos?" Scarlet asked.

"The assignment is to take a photo of an animal from a

different perspective, so something you don't normally see. I thought maybe we could grab some flowers and rest them on his head."

Thomas giggled. "A bull with flowers."

"Not something you'd normally see," I said.

Scarlet grabbed Thomas's arm. "Let's go get some flowers."

Lachlan walked up the path from the carport as the kids ran past.

"Where are they off to?" he asked.

"They're going to get some flowers for a photo shoot with Ben."

"A photo shoot?"

"It's an assignment for photography."

"Right. Mind if I watch?"

"No."

Lachlan sat on the edge of the sandpit. My stomach fluttered. More than when I knew an experienced surgeon was watching me perform a surgery. The kids ran back with a bunch of flowers each. I went to the fence and climbed in. I wasn't afraid of Ben. I'd fed him scraps over the past couple of weeks, and he was always gentle with me. And he'd let me pat him through the fence, always reaching his head forward for more. The kids had even shown me how to brush him.

He came up close to me as I stood up.

"He likes a scratch between the ears," Lachlan said.

I glanced at Lachlan. He was watching my every move, just like the bull. I approached Ben and reached out my hand to give him a scratch. He closed his eyes as I did. Never in my wildest dreams did I think I would ever get this close to a bull. When I turned to the fence, Lachlan was standing there with the children, smiling.

"Are you ready for the flowers?" Thomas asked, holding his bunch out to me.

I took it from him and approached Ben. I held them out so he could smell them. I thought it would make him more comfortable to know what I was going to place on his head. He chomped them.

Lachlan chuckled as petals fell to the ground.

"Well, that wasn't part of the plan," I said and gave Ben a scratch.

I went back to the fence for Scarlet's bunch, took half, and handed the other half back to her. This time, I didn't let Ben smell them. I put them straight on top of his head. He lifted his head to see what was up there, and the flowers tumbled to the ground. This was not as easy as I thought it was going to be. I turned back to get the last bunch. Lachlan had them in his hand and was climbing through the fence.

"Let's tie these up first, so if he drops them again, they'll be easy to pick up," he said.

I nodded. Farmers were always practical. He grabbed a long stalk of grass and wrapped it around the stems before tucking it in on itself. I glanced at Scarlet and Thomas. They both stood as still as the fence post.

"How about you get your phone ready to take the photo, and then I'll put it on his head? If we're quick, you might get the shot you want."

"Good idea. Thanks."

Lachlan approached Ben and gave him a good rub. I crouched down, so I was on a better angle.

"Ready?" he asked.

I nodded. He placed the bunch on Ben's head and swiftly moved out of the way. I took some rapid shots in succession. Ben shook his head, and the flowers dropped.

"Did you get the shot?" Lachlan asked.

I scanned through the photos. There was a perfect one with the red bull and the bunch of yellow flowers. He looked sweet and almost as if he was smiling.

Lachlan stood beside me, and I showed him.

"Nice," he said.

I wrapped my arms around his waist and gave him a hug. That manly smell of his was intoxicating. I breathed it in. So good. Shit. What was I doing? I dropped my arms abruptly and looked into his eyes. The amber flecks were hypnotising. Those eyes were kind and sinful and oh-so-beautiful. My breath faltered.

"Can we see?" Scarlet asked, saving me from falling further.

"Thank you," I said to him before dragging my eyes away.

"You're welcome."

I went to the fence to show the children the photo. They clapped their hands in glee.

Lachlan climbed through the fence and gave them a little shove. "Go and have a rest. You don't want to be too tired for the bonfire."

I clambered through the fence and followed them to the house.

"Do we need to take anything to this bonfire?" I asked Lachlan as I sat next to him on the lounge.

"No. Kayley will have it all covered."

I nodded.

"If you feel uncomfortable at any point, just tell me, and we'll leave. Bruce can bring the kids home."

"Thank you." My shoulders relaxed. I stretched my neck, letting the stress escape.

"I don't know if I'm scared."

He took my hand. I loved the feel of mine in his. His

was big and strong but always gentle with me. "It's OK to be scared."

"I wasn't scared the night of the accident. The other driver, the mother, ran a stop sign and David crashed into her."

Once I started talking, I couldn't stop. I told him everything. Some people forget about traumatic events. I didn't. It was embedded into my brain. I told it to him like I was right there in the moment.

DAVID DIDN'T SEE the other car coming and only braked at the last second. Tires screeched seconds, maybe even milliseconds before the cars crashed, car against car, metal against metal. Glass shattered. The airbags exploded, the loud bang filling the car, smashing against my chest, vibrating through my bones. Smoke filled my nostrils. My brain worked in slow motion. Not fire smoke. Maybe a bit like gunpowder or smoke from a smoke machine.

I sat there, stunned. My ears were ringing. David was dazed, staring straight ahead.

"Are you OK?" I asked. The first few words were painful as I tried to get air back into my lungs.

"Yes." The word was lost to the ringing in my ears. But I saw his lips form the word. I knew what he'd said.

The other car. Were the people in the other car OK? I shoved the airbag down. Soft in my hands. Pliable. Weird.

I shoved my door open while fumbling with my seatbelt. I jumped out of the car. David followed suit.

The other car was maybe five feet away from ours. The distance didn't make sense to my foggy mind.

"Mom. Mom." The sound was muted.

My ears cleared just enough for me to realise there were

children screaming.

I rushed over to the driver. She was conscious. Very dazed.

"Are you OK?" I asked. I could barely hear my own words.

She didn't respond. I grabbed her shoulder firmly. "Are you OK?" I yelled.

She nodded. "I think so."

Doctor mode set in.

"Try not to move. You may have internal injuries." My yelling sounded harsh. My hearing was returning.

"My children." She whipped her head around. "Zoe. Megan."

"You need to stay still. I'll assess them."

I ran to the other side of the car and yanked on the bent back door. It screeched open. The girl had blood on her face. I examined her quickly. They were superficial wounds from broken glass. She was small. Maybe four years old. And in a harness and booster seat. Wearing pink pyjamas and pink fluffy slippers.

"My name is Peyton. What's yours?"

"Zoe."

"Zoe, are you sore anywhere?" I asked her.

She nodded.

"Where?"

"Tummy. Arm."

I could deal with that.

A piercing scream filled the air. Orange light caught my attention. Flames were coming out from under the hood. I needed to remove them from the danger. The girl in the front seat screamed again.

"Listen to me." Megan. She must be Megan. "Megan," I said loud and firm.

She didn't listen. I couldn't waste time trying to calm her down. The girl in the back started crying and gulping for air. I glanced at the mom. Her eyes were closed.

"Mom," Megan screamed.

I fumbled with the seat belt. I couldn't manage to get it undone. I needed to calm the hell down. Slow down. Think clearly. My fingers, hands, all of me needed to be purposeful. I leaned over the little girl again and undid the buckle. I gathered her in my arms and ran with her. I sat her down next to a tree.

"Wait here. I'm going to get Megan."

She nodded, tears streaming down her blood-stained face.

I ran back to the car. The flames were bigger and closer to the cabin. I looked at David and beckoned him for help, but he just stood there. A man came running up. I peered at him over the car.

"Help the mom. She's in and out of consciousness."

He opened the door, glancing furtively between me and the flames.

"We need to hurry. It might blow." He roused the mother. "We need to get you out."

"Zoe. Megan," she said.

"One is out," the man said. "Let's get you out so I can help your other daughter." He was calm. I didn't feel calm.

I pulled on the door. It wouldn't budge. Flames leapt out from under the car. Heat on my arm. Screams from inside. I grabbed hold of the door frame. Remnants of glass sliced through my fingers. I hardly noticed. The girl in the front seat screamed again.

"Look at me," I yelled.

She faced me but kept looking back at the flames. I braced my foot against the rear door and pulled. The door budged.

"You're on fire," the girl said, her eyes wide.

"Don't worry. We'll put it out."

The man struggled, pulling the mom out. He dragged her away.

I pulled on the door again. And again until it gave way. The heat on my arm, the burning, was distracting. I couldn't afford to be distracted. I shook my head.

My arm was in excruciating pain. But it didn't matter. I had a job to do.

"I can't move," Megan said. "My legs are stuck."

The dash was pushed forward. She needed space.

"It's OK. I'll get you out."

She nodded. At least she wasn't screaming. My arm was on fire. Piercing pain engulfed me as my skin burned, and I gritted my teeth to keep from screaming.

"I'm going to find the lever and push the seat back."

I bent my head and reached down, trying to get hold of the lever.

Flames licked at my fingers from under the dashboard. The fire had just started to penetrate the firewall. I grabbed the lever and shoved the seat back.

Please be enough space. Please. I grabbed hold of her and pulled. She was still stuck. Why was she stuck? Her seat belt. It was still buckled. I put myself between her and the flames.

I went to press down on the buckle. Nothing. Thin air. I looked at what I was doing. Why wasn't my hand working? Oh, the burns. The nerve endings must be shot. I couldn't feel what I was doing. Or not doing.

I needed to guide my hands with my eyes.

Sirens. Close. But not close enough.

The man came rushing back to the car. The buckle released. I grabbed hold of her again and pulled. She was free. Oh, thank God. The man helped us to the side of the *road. When I looked back at the car, half the front seat was engulfed in flames.*

The man took off his jacket and patted my hair. Then he wrapped the jacket around my arm, smothering the flames.

Sirens blaring. Close. The car was nothing but fire. People running.

"Over here," the man yelled. "She's burnt, bad."

Me. He meant me.

A blue uniform in my vision. He crouched down. A face. Serious.

"What's your name?"

"Peyton."

"OK, Peyton, let me have a look."

He unwrapped the jacket. We looked together. My shirt was almost gone. So was my skin. It just dropped off like it was melting away.

"Not much pain," I said. "Third degree."

I examined it closer. "Whole arm."

I couldn't see past my shoulder. "At least 9% body surface."

The paramedic's hands paused.

"Are you a nurse?"

"Doctor."

LACHLAN LET OUT A HARSH BREATH. I focused on him. His jaw was slack. He took my hands which were curled into fists and released my fingers. As they released, so did my other muscles. He kept his eyes on mine, holding me in the present, not letting me escape back to the past. I focused on the amber flecks in his eyes. He didn't say a word. He didn't force himself to fill the silence. And as profound as that silence was, it was the best comfort of all.

CHAPTER TWENTY-SIX

Lachlan

THE KIDS RAN AHEAD, each carrying their own chair. Thomas struggled. The chair was almost the size of him. He didn't give up. Just readjusted the chair bag on his shoulder every few steps.

Peyton and I followed. Bruce and I had worked on the fire set up during the day, and we'd made the fire smaller than usual. I didn't want Peyton to be intimidated by the size. A big fire might feel more out of control. I told him to arrive first and to make sure he set their chairs up further from the fire than we'd normally sit. It was summer anyway, so we didn't need the heat to keep warm.

Mum and Kayley sat a few metres away, chatting. Bruce was adding a small branch to the fire, which was burning slowly. Flames danced in slow motion, licking at the air above.

I took Peyton's hand and gave it a squeeze. "Are you OK?"

"Yes." Her voice was quiet, unsure. She glanced at the fire and then at me.

"We can leave anytime you like."

She gave me a small smile.

Hopefully, my family would keep her distracted so she'd have a good time. Kayley got out of her chair and came towards us. I rested my hand on the small of Peyton's back.

"You must be the infamous Peyton," she said with a warm smile.

"Just Peyton will do."

"Oh no, we have to celebrate the woman who has managed to domesticate that husband of mine."

Bruce appeared and put an arm around his wife. He gave her a sheepish smile. "It was always there. Just hidden deep."

"Too deep," Kayley said. "He might even be ready to be a father soon."

He poked her in the ribs. I smiled. Weeks ago, I would have said their marriage was stale. Kayley would be irritated by the smallest things. And Bruce was just his dumb arse self, with no idea how to fix it. The way they were looking at each other now, it was like their spark was back. Peyton had a hand in that. And a hand in my reinvigoration.

I set our seats up close to each other. Mum was watching us, amusement in her eyes.

"Hi, Mum." I bent down to give her a kiss.

She took hold of my arm to keep me close. "I saw you hold Peyton's hand. You know, that could be considered fraternising."

Bloody hell. "I was just offering her support. You know, with the fire and all."

"Whatever you say, Lachlan. Need I remind you that

I'm your mother? I know what you're thinking before you do."

I blushed. If Mum read half my thoughts about Peyton, I'd be in serious trouble. She patted my face.

"Hi, Ann," Peyton said.

"Come and sit next to me, love. Lachlan needs to learn to share."

This better not be the theme of the night.

I sat the small esky between Peyton's and my chair. The kids were off playing some made-up game.

"So, Peyton, how are you finding farm life?" Kayley asked.

"I love it. It's totally different to life back home."

I imagined it was. But she didn't talk much about it. It was like there were two different Peytons. One that lived in the big city with a prestige job and one who lived on the farm and was a nanny. Was there some reason she was keeping herself separate?

"Do you get bored when the kids aren't here?"

"The time goes so fast; they're back in no time. And I've joined an online photography challenge where they set assignments every week. It's a lot of fun."

"And she has Lachlan," Bruce said. "I swear the unit repairs are going slow on purpose."

"Good things take time," I shot back.

"Yeah, slow, deliberate time."

I took the top off a beer and threw it at him. "A bit like your domestication. Maybe you were just dawdling because you're scared of having kids."

I handed the beer to Peyton and got another for me.

Flickering flames caught my attention. I imagined Peyton looking down at her burnt arm and seeing the skin peel off. I shuddered.

Scarlet and Thomas sat next to Mum and chatted with her, telling her all about the things they'd been doing with Peyton. They hadn't been able to convince her to swim in the dam yet. Maybe she was too much of a city girl for that.

"Did you bring your guitar?" Bruce asked.

"It's in the car," I said.

Kayley's face lit up. "I haven't heard you sing for ages."

"He's going to enter the singing competition at the pub," Bruce said.

"Are you?" Mum asked.

I shrugged. "I'm thinking about it."

Scarlet jumped out of her chair and ran to me, launching herself into my lap. "That would be so cool. You're going to do it, aren't you, Daddy? Thomas and I will come and watch."

Mum glanced at Peyton and gave her a smile. Then she sat back in her chair, smiling like a bull who'd just got his rocks off. What was that all about?

"That panty-melting voice will win for sure," Bruce said.

Peyton and Kayley laughed, Mum shook her head, and Scarlet looked confused.

"Well, it's settled then. We can fill in the online entry tomorrow," Peyton said.

What the hell? I hadn't even agreed yet. The fire popped, and Peyton jumped.

I took hold of her hand. "It's just the gas build-up from moisture trapped in the wood."

She nodded and gave me a small smile. "It took me by surprise."

She took me by surprise every single day. And today, when she'd told me about the accident, was no different. She risked her life to save that family. Sure, she was trained as a surgeon, and surgeons perform lifesaving surgeries every day. But they don't put their life in harm's way doing so. And even when she was on fire, literally on fire, she didn't stop. She put the excruciating pain aside to save that little girl.

And what did her fiancé do? He just stood by while she did it. I would have been right there with her. If she was going to die, it would be with me by her side. And then later, he had the audacity to say she shouldn't have gone to the car to save those people. Like it was her fault she was burnt, her fault that she needed so many surgeries, her fault her career as a surgeon was destroyed.

Who the fuck does that?

"Go get the guitar, Lachy," Bruce said, drawing me back in.

"Will you be OK?" I asked Peyton. I still had hold of her hand, small in mine. But the size belied its strength. I ran my thumb across her knuckles, pausing in the dips. The rise and fall was like the melody in music, like the melody of a heartbeat.

She turned to face me. "I'm not as scared as I thought I was going to be."

I let go of her hand and went to retrieve the guitar. When I got back, Bruce was helping Scarlet and Thomas toast marshmallows. The three ladies were sitting together talking. Kayley looked my way and then started talking faster. They all looked at me. Mum smiled.

"What are you three up to?"

"Oh, nothing," Kayley said.

Meaning *something*.

"We're just discussing which song you should sing," Mum said.

I didn't believe that was all they were talking about.

"You only get to sing one song in the first round," Peyton explained. "With each round, the number of songs increase, and in the final round, you sing one of your own as well."

I nodded. A song of my own. I could sing one I'd already written or a new one. I needed to start preparing in case I got through.

"So, we were thinking," Kayley said, "you should play us five of your faves tonight, and we would vote on which one you sing."

Scarlet presented a marshmallow to Peyton from the end of her stick. Peyton pulled it off and stuck it in her mouth. She licked her lips.

"Mmm, good."

If I kissed her now, I could share that sweet taste on her tongue. I huffed and shook my head. Because that's not something I wanted to do in public. No, our first kiss did not need an audience. First kiss? What the fuck?

"Start playing, Daddy," Scarlet said. "We need to vote."

Thank goodness for music. It might be the only thing to keep my mind off Peyton. But what about when it stopped?

CHAPTER TWENTY-SEVEN

Peyton

WE CARRIED the children into the house. I waited with Thomas in my arms while Lachlan put Scarlet to bed. As he was about to stand up, she flung her arms around his neck and said, "I love you, Daddy."

He kissed her cheek. "I love you too."

My insides turned to goo.

In all of my childhood, I don't remember ever sharing such a tender moment with my father. We must have said the words though. I didn't have a loveless childhood.

"Thank you for your support tonight," I said as Lachlan joined me in the hall.

"You're welcome."

We walked to Thomas's room together, and I set him down on his bed. Lachlan pulled Thomas's flip-flops off, and I pulled the covers over him.

"I'm glad you're entering the competition," I said. "You're setting a very good example for Thomas and Scarlet."

We walked out of Thomas's room and down the hallway together. I stopped outside my bedroom door and gazed up at him. He was watching me. My stomach pounded, rising into my chest. Did he want to kiss me as much as I wanted him to?

His hand reached out to cup the back of my head. His thumb grazed my cheek bone. I was trapped in his gaze. And his touch. Heat swept through me.

Lachlan's head bent, and his lips touched mine, soft and slow. Such control when all I wanted to do was ravish his mouth.

"Peyton," he whispered.

I laid my hands on his muscular chest. His heart hammered against my palm. Light breath brushed my lips as his other hand pulled me in closer. Chest to chest. Body to body. I pressed my lips against his. He teased mine open. Still slow, our mouths moved in unison. He held me tighter. Beer and sweetness danced across my taste buds. So perfectly Lachlan. I sighed. My whole body sighed.

Our lips stopped. But we didn't pull apart. We shared our harsh breathing. I needed more, wanted more.

Lachlan pulled away from me. I opened my eyes. His were already open, watching me.

"Goodnight, Peyton," he said.

I watched him, with his great arse, walk to his room.

I lay in bed, but my eyes wouldn't close. I relived the night. Lachlan's presence alone had reassured me. But his words meant so much more. He was considerate and didn't admonish me for my feelings. Finishing it off with a kiss was perfect.

What was I doing? Falling in love with Lachlan was crazy. But why was it crazy? The fact that he was virtually my boss didn't matter. Not when it felt so right. Not when he gave me what I'd been missing—respect.

LACHLAN and I were watching the kids in the sandpit from the shade of the tree. They were digging a hole and building the sides up around it, trying to replicate a dam. Scarlet was wetting down the sand with the garden hose. Lachlan turned his head as Jane's car pulled into the driveway.

"Mummy," Thomas yelled as he ran to her.

Jane picked him up and swung him around.

"Daddy is going to sing in a competition."

She looked at Lachlan and raised her eyebrows. "That's exciting."

"It's tomorrow night," Scarlet said as she turned off the hose at the tap. "Can we go?"

"Of course, we can go. We'll be his groupies."

"His what?" Scarlet asked.

"His biggest fans. Always there to cheer him on."

"Yes." Scarlet gave a decisive nod. "His groupies."

"Go and get your bags so I can talk to Daddy about it."

That was my cue to leave. I went to follow them inside, but Lachlan touched my arm, stopping me. My heart lurched as I stood beside him.

Lachlan gave me a half smile. "It was Peyton's—"

"You're singing again?" Jane interrupted.

"I've always sung, just not in public."

"It's about time. You loved singing in pubs before."

He shrugged. "I didn't have the time. There's always so much to do here."

She shook her head. I think we all felt the same.

Lachlan deserved to have as much as he wanted—his family, the farm, singing, whatever. He should have something just for himself.

"So which pub? And what time?"

Lachlan turned to me.

"At Donna's. 6 pm," I said.

"We'll be there. Dan will love to see you in action."

Dan. I hadn't met him yet. He was Jane's new partner. From all accounts, he was nice. He treated the kids as his own and always made time for them. He never begrudged the relationship Jane and Lachlan still had. I think that was very mature and showed an immense amount of respect.

Scarlet and Thomas emerged from the house. They gave Lachlan a kiss. Then it was my turn.

Scarlet looked at me, her face serious. "When we used to leave to go home with Mum, I was always a bit sad because Daddy would be alone. But he has you now."

Yes, he had me.

But did I have him?

CHAPTER TWENTY-EIGHT

Lachlan

We walked into the pub. Usually sleepy mid-week, it was lively tonight. People were standing around chatting, drowning out the background music. Most of the tables were taken up. A table was reserved for us. The sign said *Lachlan and his Groupies*. I smiled. I looked around at my groupies. They were all the people I loved most in the world. If I didn't progress to the next round, it was enough to know they were all here for me.

Peyton sat next to me. "Are you nervous?"

"Yes." It had been a long time since I'd sung in a pub, nine years. And I'd never been in a singing competition. What if I didn't cut it?

The pub was filling up. Excitement buzzed through the air.

"We're all here for you," she said.

I nodded, wiping my sweaty palms on my jeans.

She glanced around the room and smiled. Leaning in close, she whispered, "Lots of panties here to melt."

I laughed. I would never have thought this big city girl would have fitted in so well.

Before she pulled away, I replied, "I'm only interested in melting yours."

She blushed. "Well, best you sing your heart out then."

Before I could reply, Donna hopped up on stage. "Welcome to the first round of our inaugural singing contest. We have some very talented singers here tonight."

A cheer went up through the crowd.

"First up on stage, we have Stacy Lightfoot."

We all clapped loudly as the teen from a neighbouring town went up on stage. She was good. Her voice was soulful, and she had beautiful harmonies. The crowd gave her a well-deserved round of applause. As the singers went through their turn, I realised there was some tough competition. Some didn't quite make their mark either because of nerves or from talent that had yet to be honed.

"Last up, we have Lachlan Harris with a song chosen by his family."

Mum must have been speaking to her. First, the groupies sign, and now she knew my family had chosen the song.

Loud whooping erupted from the crowd. Or maybe it was just my family. It didn't matter.

I walked up to the stage and looked out at the crowd. The guitar slung across my shoulder was my trusted friend. I swung it around, my hand caressing the neck. Faces stared back at me. Some I knew, some I didn't. I took a deep breath, adrenalin running through my veins. My fingers tingled, ready to get playing. My whole body was ready to get playing. I knew this feeling. I'd owned it nine years ago; I could own it again.

The crowd wanted something from me, and I was ready to deliver.

"What a fantastic night. Thank you for being an amazing audience."

Cheers and whistles. The sound and vibrations reverberated through my body.

"Let's see if we can lift the roof off."

I played a few chords of an upbeat Keith Urban song. The music coming from my fingers flowed through my body. Then my voice took over. It was in every cell of my body. It was a part of the people in the room. I glanced at my family, all smiling up at me. Peyton. She couldn't take her eyes off me. My heart slowed as I watched her watch me. I wanted to stay lost in this moment with her. But I couldn't. I had a crowd to entertain. She gave me the hand signal for hot. Mission accomplished. I sang one more line to her and turned my attention back to the crowd as I sang the last chorus. I sang that to them.

Cheers and clapping exploded through the room. I missed this. I missed making people feel. To have them lost in me.

My heart was pumping as fast as the song I'd just finished.

Donna joined me on stage. "Well, if that wasn't the best way to finish the night, I don't know what is."

"Thank you, everyone." I kissed Donna's cheek before leaving the stage.

"Daddy. Daddy," Scarlet and Thomas called out, running to me before embracing me in a hug.

"You were so good," Scarlet said.

"Yeah," Thomas agreed.

"Even better than at home?" I asked.

Scarlet stopped to think. "Maybe a little better."

I laughed.

"Bro, you were fantastic," Bruce said, giving me a one-armed hug.

Kayley nodded.

Mum smiled with tears in her eyes. "I'm so proud of you."

Anyone would think I'd just won the final.

"You haven't lost your touch, Lachy," Jane said. She was beaming, as was Dan standing next to her. He shook my hand and clapped my back.

Peyton was standing back, quiet, watching. Before I could make my way to her, Stacy, the young singer who'd sung first, blocked my path.

"Wow. Where have you been hiding?"

"Been busy on the farm."

She took hold of my arm. "What a waste."

"Not really."

She squeezed my biceps. "You should wear a tighter shirt next time."

Was this girl flirting with me? She couldn't even be twenty yet. But these days, it was hard to tell. I tried to step away, but she held on.

"Maybe we can get together...and talk singing."

No hope in hell.

I looked for Peyton. She was right where she'd been before, with a bemused look on her face.

"Peyton, come over here and meet Stacy."

She ambled over. Could she walk any slower?

"Stacy, this is my girlfriend, Peyton."

OK. That might have been stretching the truth a bit. Or a lot. I needed help.

"Nice to meet you, Stacy. I loved your song."

"Thank you." Stacy looked Peyton up and down.

I don't know what this ambitious girl saw, but I could tell her they weren't even close to being equals. There was no point in even comparing the two. Peyton outclassed every woman in this room.

Someone called out to Stacy. She started to walk off but then turned back. "Think about what I said."

Yeah, for maybe two seconds. And all two of them would be spent in distaste.

I turned my attention to Peyton. She had her hands on her hips. My stomach dropped.

"Do you think this girlfriend-boyfriend thing is something we should have discussed?" Peyton asked.

"I was desperate."

"Desperate? You only want me to be your girlfriend because you're desperate?"

I struggled to breathe...like you would if a cow had kicked you in the chest.

CHAPTER TWENTY-NINE

LACHLAN RUBBED HIS JAW. "No."

"You're not desperate?"

He shifted his weight. "I needed to say something. She was coming on to me."

Bruce was shaking his head and chuckling as he tugged on Kayley's arm. She turned, and he nodded toward us.

I liked watching Lachlan squirm. "So you don't want me to be your girlfriend?"

He widened his stance. "No."

"Fine then." I started to walk back to his family. Jane turned around to see what Kayley and Bruce were gawking at. Lachlan was making this way too easy. I glanced back as he ran his hand through his hair and shook his head.

"No, I didn't mean no," he called out in frustration at my retreating back.

I chuckled and kept walking.

"Peyton." His voice was commanding.

I turned back to him as unhurried as I could. "Yes, Lachlan."

He closed the distance between us. "I want you to be my girlfriend."

"And do I get a choice in this?" I wasn't going to let him off lightly.

"Only if you choose correctly."

"Correct for me or correct for you?"

"Correct for us."

My lips quirked.

The speakers crackled. "OK, ladies and gentlemen, the judges have made their choices," Donna announced.

I moved to Lachlan's side and held his hand. I had no doubt he would get through. He was the best one up there. But until his name was called, my convictions would count for naught.

"Stacy Lightfoot."

The crowd cheered.

"Walter Green."

Clapping.

I stood still, my hand gripping his tighter with every name that was called.

"Lachlan Harris." At last.

"You did it." I turned to him and gave him a kiss on the cheek.

He held me firm. When we made eye contact, the whole room disappeared.

"Will you be my girlfriend, Peyton Carter?" He gave me a choice. My whole insides felt like jelly.

"Yes, Lachlan, I believe I will."

He smiled, and then he bent his head down to mine. "Good."

"About time," Bruce mumbled.

I snuck a look at his satisfied smile.

"I guess the fraternising rule is null and void now," Jane said.

"Who actually asks someone to be their girlfriend?" Bruce said. "It's like he's from another century."

Jane and Kayley laughed as Lachlan gave his brother the finger.

Lachlan touched my chin and brought my attention back to him. I was swept up in his gaze. His lips found mine and he kissed me—intimate, chaste, full of promise. He pulled away and smiled. "Did I make your panties melt?"

I didn't get a chance to answer as his family swarmed him to offer congratulations. Bruce gave my shoulders a squeeze on the way past. If I'd had the chance to answer, I would have said yes, both the song and the kiss had the same effect on my panties.

"You'll have to up your game for the next round," I said as Lachlan and I drove back to the farm. "You need three songs."

He nodded. His features were lit up by the lights on the dashboard. He was composed, thoughtful. "My biggest competition is probably Stacy. We need to be strategic about which songs we pick."

"So, not just panty-melting songs?" I teased.

"It did melt your panties, then?" He smiled.

"And Stacy's." I laughed.

He took my hand. "Yours are the only ones I'm interested in."

I blushed. He knew how to make a girl feel special. And it wasn't just his words or his thoughtfulness. It was the way he never had any qualms about holding my scarred hand.

"Back to the song choices," I said. "What are you thinking?"

"Maybe some sort of ballad. I can't match Stacy's soulful voice, but I can do one justice."

"Good idea." The crowd would be swept away by his voice.

"A love song. And maybe a good old rock song."

"Sounds like a good range."

We turned into the driveway, and the car thumped over the cattle grid. It no longer sounded strange to my ears.

"Kayley is eager for another vote," he said. "Probably after Christmas dinner."

Christmas. It was only three days away. I hadn't thought much about it beyond buying Scarlet and Thomas a present. I'd gotten one for Lachlan as well. Just something small. I didn't know if giving gifts was an important thing in his family.

"Do you have a big get-together?" I asked.

"Everyone will be here, including my sister Lydia. The kids will come over once lunch with Jane's parents is finished."

"Well, you have three days to get your list together."

"I can think of better things to do over the next three days." He grinned over at me, and tingles spread through me.

"Such as?"

"Spend time with you. Watch movies, read... some more kissing would be nice." He raised my hand to his mouth and kissed it.

I breathed a sigh of relief. He wasn't being presumptuous after all. Kissing was good. Sex? I didn't think I was ready for that. That would involve too much nakedness.

"Thank you for supporting me," Lachlan said as we pulled into the carport.

"You're welcome."

No one had thanked me for my support before. It was just expected. This was all so new to me. Being appreciated for being me was more than I expected.

We got out of the car and headed toward the house. Lachlan stopped me before we went inside. He looked up at the sky.

"Full moon tonight."

I gazed up. It was amazing how much light the moon gave off out here in the country. It lit up whole fields with its brightness. This, us, staring at the moon, reminded me of the song Lachlan had played for us the first time I'd heard him sing. It was the first time I'd realised I was falling in love with Lachlan Harris.

He pulled me close and wrapped his arms around my waist. I lifted my face to his, eager for his lips. And when they met, little explosions went off through my body. I wrapped my arms around his neck, and his biceps pressed tighter to my sides. His tongue searched out mine—soft, insistent, so very good.

He kissed me more. Not just with his lips but with the power of his body. The muscles in his legs as they rested against mine. The muscles in his chest were hard but somehow contoured to my body. And the muscle between his legs that pressed against me, revealing his desire. I couldn't have pulled myself closer to him if I tried.

His hands made their way to my waist and then higher, resting under my bra. They lifted higher and cupped the outside of my breasts. I flinched ever so slightly at the weird sensation.

Lachlan pulled his hands away and stopped kissing me. "I'm sorry."

Was it always going to feel this awkward? Would I ever

get used to someone touching my scarred tissue? It felt weird sometimes—dead, alive, tingly. I needed to explain.

"Scars give a different sensation to touch."

"Scars?"

"Yes. The side of my breast was burnt. Not as bad as my arm, but there is still scarring."

"Oh."

And that was it. The moment anything sexual stopped. The moment I no longer felt like a normal person. Tears filled my eyes, and I stepped away from him. I hated myself. I hated my body. I hated this fake belief that I could be loved for being me, scars and all.

"Can I see?" Lachlan asked, his voice soft.

"What?"

"Can I see your scars?"

I took another step backwards. "Why? Can't we just pretend you like me as I am?"

I crossed my arms over my chest. I couldn't do this. Every one seeing my arm was one thing, but this? Exposing my whole self to someone who wasn't on my medical team?

"I do like you as you are," Lachlan said.

"You don't see all of me, Lachlan." I was crying. "You won't like what you see."

Lachlan moved forward. "Why don't you let me decide what I like?"

I shook my head. "I can't."

"It's OK, Peyton." And then, as if his words weren't enough for me to trust, he wrapped me in his arms. As he stroked my back, he told me it was OK. I wanted to believe him. I wanted to believe in the safety of his arms.

He released me, and we retreated to our separate rooms. I lay in bed, unable to sleep. What I'd done was wrong. I should have trusted Lachlan. Shutting him out because of my fear was wrong. I was allowed to be scared. I was allowed to feel negative feelings. But I shouldn't project those feelings onto him.

How could any relationship be successful if you couldn't expose your greatest fears to the other and trust that they'll be there for you?

Tears wet my pillow. I couldn't stay here while Lachlan lay in his bed, wondering if what we had was real.

I swung my legs out of bed. The carpet below my feet was cushiony. I crossed to the door and then over the hardwood of the corridor. I couldn't stop now. Lachlan's door was open. I'd been in there before when I'd put his washing on his bed. But I'd never been in there with him.

"Lachlan," I called softly from the doorway. I could see his form illuminated by the moon light coming in through the window. He opened his eyes instantly. He hadn't been asleep. I stepped over the threshold. "I'm sorry."

He sat up. "It's OK, Peyton. You don't need to apologise."

"I'm ready to show you."

"You don't need to show me. It's OK."

I'd ruined it. My fear had ruined everything. I started to cry. So much for being strong and independent. One rejection and I was falling to pieces. I needed to leave before I looked even more stupid.

Before I could retreat, Lachlan was standing in front of me. "Come to bed."

"Not before you see me."

"Do you think after I see you, I won't want you to come to bed?"

I nodded.

He pursed his lips and released a breath from his nose. I grabbed the hem of my sleep shirt and pulled it over my head. My muscles were tense. My toes dug into the carpet. Lachlan's eyes raked over the top half of my body. The length of my arm, my shoulder, the side of my chest and my breast. The air may have been warm from the summer's night, but my skin still prickled. He walked around and looked at my back. Only a small portion of that had been burnt. He took my arm and lifted it so he could see my chest better.

"You can touch it."

He raised his eyes to mine. I nodded.

He laid his hand against my side. His touch was firm. I was grateful for that. He pressed the side of my breast; his fingers examined the scarring there. I held my breath. What was he thinking? Not once did his face show displeasure. He didn't hesitate to touch me. When he was finished, he took the shirt from my hand and held it over my head for me to put on. I stretched my arms up, and he slid it on.

"Are you ready to come to bed now?" he asked.

He still wanted me? I nodded and went around to the other side. We lay facing each other.

"Thank you," he said.

I nodded again. Saying anything was too risky.

"To be clear, I see you no differently now than I did before."

How could that be?

"Your scars are a part of you, just like some mothers have stretch marks."

They didn't really compare. He must have seen the doubt on my face.

"I will not love you any less because of your scars. In fact, I will love you more because I know what you did to get them."

My heart raced.

Did he mean he loves me now? Or in the future, he will love me?

It didn't matter. The affirmation in his voice was all I needed. In a few weeks, Lachlan had shown me more about love than I'd seen in twenty-six years. He never made me feel he was more important than me or that I was only there to address his needs.

He put his arm around me. I closed my eyes and sank into his secure embrace.

CHAPTER THIRTY

Lachlan

Softness in my arms. Vanilla and coconut. Quiet breathing. These were the things I would always remember about Peyton. With those things came her fear, bravery and determination. But it was the fear that ran the deepest. The fear of being seen and the fear of being unseen.

I wasn't unhappy with my life before Peyton came into it. I fulfilled my duty every day, and I was happy about that. I never thought anything was missing. I didn't think I needed anything else. And I didn't until Peyton had come along. Now I need it all. I need extra in my life. I need her.

She stirred against me. Her back nestled against my chest, and my arm was draped over her. I kissed the back of her head. She snuggled closer, right into my hard-on. She tensed. She must have felt it.

"Good morning, beautiful." I kissed her neck and was rewarded with a shiver.

She rolled around to face me and smiled. It was different to all her other smiles. It felt shy, yet unguarded.

I stroked her short silky hair. "I thought I had everything I wanted before I met you. But that was because I hadn't met you yet."

She brushed her lips against mine.

"Do you think it's safe to want someone so badly?" she asked, her hand resting on my arm.

"Fuck no. You could come to your senses at any moment and realise that this, what I can offer you, isn't enough."

She withdrew a fraction. "Why would you think that?"

"If it wasn't enough for Jane, how could it possibly be enough for you?"

"What do you mean?"

Peyton had opened up to me on more than one occasion. She trusted me with her fears. I needed to trust her too.

"I failed at marriage, Peyton. I had the perfect parents, the perfect role models. But not even following their example was enough. I couldn't make Jane happy. Even though I tried to be the best father, a great provider, she still left."

She slid her hand down my arm and entwined her fingers in mine. Our eyes met, and she held them firm. My heart thumped as fast as cows running in a paddock.

"Lachlan, you give me things no other person ever has. I'm brave with you, brave to speak. But it's not just that you let me speak; it's that you listen."

I wanted to listen to her scream my name. But not yet. She needed to be ready. And until then, I would kiss the fuck out of her. I let go of her hand and pulled her close to me until our faces were millimetres apart. I rested my hand on her back and captured her smile with my lips.

Mine moved slow at first as I tested the suppleness of

hers, their willingness. And fuck were they willing. I pulled her closer and moved my hand to her arse, grabbing it. I squeezed, feeling the softness. I was rock-hard in my underwear. There was no way she couldn't feel it. But just in case, I drew her closer.

My lips left hers, and I kissed along her jawline to the spot below her ear. She moaned. Her head tilted back. I suckled down her neck to the top of her sleep shirt. This wouldn't do. I needed more of her skin exposed. I rolled her onto her back and pushed her top up. Lowering myself, my mouth followed the trail of my hand. She quivered. When my hand cupped her breast, she moaned and pushed herself into my palm.

My dick throbbed. I pulled her top higher so her breasts were exposed and higher again until she helped me take it off. My hand went back to her warm breast. Her nipple hardened under my fingers. I needed it in my mouth. Another illicit moan as I sucked on it. And again, as she arched her back. I moved my mouth to the other and got the same response. I rolled on top of her and nestled between her legs, rubbing my hardness against her.

I kissed her hard and fast. Our tongues met stroke for stroke. Need spread through me until every muscle was as taught as a guitar string. Fuck. Kissing her wasn't enough. I wrenched my lips away, breathing hard.

"I'm ready," she said.

I couldn't be any more ready. I pulled her sleep shorts down. She pulled one leg out and then the other. She was naked before me. Holy shit.

Fuck. "I don't have a condom."

She smiled. What was there to smile about? My dick was aching.

"I thought farmers were always prepared."

"I wasn't prepared for you."

I started to roll off. Peyton grabbed my shoulder, stopping me.

"I'm on the pill."

Yeah, but still. It was a lot to ask of her, even if I was certain I was clean, and she was likely the same. She placed her hands on either side of my face and pulled me towards her.

"I'm ready."

I studied her. I wanted to be sure.

"You could always drive into town to buy condoms if you want." Her voice was teasing.

That would be at least a forty-five-minute trip.

"But then everyone will know what we're doing. Tamworth would be the better option." She shrugged. She knew that would take at least two hours.

"Yeah, that's not going to work for me."

"I didn't think so."

I pulled my underwear down and kicked it off. She pulled me closer and kissed me deep. Her hips came up, encouraging me. I let my fingers find their way first. She was wet. I guided my dick to her entrance and pushed myself in.

I stopped kissing her as she gasped. I slowed.

"Are you OK?"

"It's been a while."

"For me too."

She moved beneath me, adjusting her position. "Don't stop."

I pushed in further. Her hands held tight to my shoulders. I slowed again.

"It's OK. You're big. Keep going."

I moved in and out slowly, allowing her time. She was so fucking tight. But each movement in and out became easier until I was gliding all the way in. When she moaned, and her hips met mine, I knew she was fine. Her head tipped back, and I kissed the taught muscles in her neck.

Tightness built in my groin and my balls. Peyton clutched at my shoulders, her fingers digging in. She lifted her hips, and I thrust in deeper. She opened her legs wider. I thrust deeper, harder. My balls squeezed.

Peyton cried out my name. A guttural growl escaped as I thrust again, emptying myself inside her. Were they her tremors or mine? I couldn't tell. All I knew was that I wasn't ready to move yet. Her fingers loosened on my shoulders. I looked down at her. She was breathing hard.

She smiled up at me. "That was good."

"It sure was."

I rolled off her and held her hand. She turned her face to me with a wide grin. "Is that classed as fraternising?"

Peyton

My parents smiled at me through the computer screen. I was in my room. I'm sure they studied my surroundings and compared them to home. The walls here were not adorned with artwork. The furniture was simple and functional.

"Merry Christmas, Mom, Dad."

"Merry Christmas, Peyton."

"What do you have planned for tomorrow?"

I knew that they'd have a busy day, and Christmas Eve was a better choice for a call. I didn't want to interrupt their plans.

"Dad has arranged a breakfast on a boat sailing on the harbour." She looked at him. "He reassures me they have a set up where even a naked Eskimo would feel warm."

Dad smiled at Mom.

"Sophia, Michael, James and Ingrid are coming for lunch," Mom said.

"That sounds wonderful."

Lachlan was moving around the kitchen. Drawers opened and closed. Then the fridge.

"Next year, it will be good to have the family together again," Dad said.

I didn't reply. He was always dropping comments about my coming home, like my being here was some sort of short-term sabbatical. I didn't want it to be. I'd found something here that I didn't have back there—acceptance and independence. Not just from Lachlan but the whole family too. He helped me feel comfortable in my own body, that my scars didn't need to stay hidden.

"We saw David last week," Mom said. "His superiors are full of praise for him."

"That's good."

What else was I supposed to say? I was happy for him. But that is as far as my thoughts and feelings extended.

"We've emailed you some information about specialist avenues you could consider. Have you been able to review them?" Dad asked.

I nodded. "Yes. They all look interesting, but it's not something I want to pursue."

"You can't stay hidden in Australia forever."

It was always the same thing.

"I like it here."

I didn't want to tell them the farm felt like home. They'd never understand. I wasn't hiding here. I was doing something for myself.

"What are you doing for Christmas?" Mom asked, changing the subject. She was in denial like Dad. My opinion didn't matter to them.

"Lachlan and I are going on a picnic; then tonight, we're going to have dinner with the family."

"Lachlan, the farmer?" Mom asked, her voice flat.

"Yes." I refrained from rolling my eyes.

She knew exactly who Lachlan was. But not what he was to me. I kept the information about my life here sparse. It was better that way. Less opportunity for them to judge or interfere.

"Anyway, I've got to go. We're heading off soon."

"Look at the email again. They're all sensible options," Dad said.

I nodded, not wanting to commit or make waves. The more I pushed back, the more determined they would become. "Wish everyone a Merry Christmas for me."

I disconnected before they could say anything more, but I continued to stare at the screen even after their faces disappeared. It was always the same. I tried to think of it as them trying to do the best for me. But was it really about me or them?

I was happy here, but they would never understand. To them, happiness came from high achievement. Enough about them. I closed the screen and went out to the kitchen.

"How are your parents?" Lachlan asked.

"They're good. They'll be spending Christmas with my sister and her family."

"Is it hard not being with them for Christmas?"

"No." It was an honest answer.

He studied me for a moment but didn't say anything. Why was he looking at me like that? I didn't want to explain to him and risk putting a dampener on the day ahead. I wanted to enjoy our time alone without my parents invading it.

"Have you got everything we need?" I asked.

"Sure do. Even got some towels for our swim."

"Swim?"

"In the dam." He grinned.

I placed my hands on my hips. "I never agreed to a swim."

He shrugged. "Didn't ask you on purpose. Figured in this case, it was just best to tell you."

Smart move. It didn't mean I was going to go along with it though.

"Mmm."

"Before we go, I have a present to give you," he said.

My stomach lifted. Although I'd gotten him a gift, I hadn't expected one from him. He handed me a box wrapped in bright shiny green paper. I opened the lid. There was something rectangular on top, about the size of a book wrapped in tissue paper. I unwrapped it, revealing a frame inside with the photo of Ben with the flowers. The one that had received the most votes for our weekly photo submission. Tears brimmed in my eyes. I opened the next package. Another frame but this time a photo I'd taken of tall grass with the sun setting. And the third was of the children playing under the sprinkler. All from my photography assignments.

I raised my eyes to his. He shifted his weight. The lump in my throat made it hard to speak. I swallowed it. "Thank you."

"I thought we could start a gallery in the hallway if you wanted to."

I nodded and wrapped my arms around him. He believed my photos were good enough to display. My chest constricted, making breathing hard. I held on tight. This was where I wanted to be.

As I pulled away, I said, "I have something for you too."

I went to my room and grabbed his present off the bed. When I handed it to him, my hands shook. He unwrapped it. My heart beat fast as he studied the leather-bound notebook and the emerald and silver pen. He smiled up at me.

"For your songwriting," I said.

He nodded as if he knew exactly what they were for. Leaning down, he brushed my lips with his. "Thank you."

I hugged him again.

We placed our gifts on the counter, and I followed him out the door. The back of the 4WD was packed with blankets and pillows. He added the picnic basket and cooler.

When we got to the dam, he parked close to some shady trees. I helped him get everything out. He laid the blankets down and then the pillows.

"This is quite luxurious," I remarked.

"Eating should be done in comfort."

I sat on the blanket and eyed the dam. My uneasiness was unrealistic. The kids swam here all the time under supervision. Lachlan wouldn't let them if it wasn't safe. And he'd once told me that the plants around the edges added filtration, so the water, although brown, was quite clean.

Lachlan brought out the food. Cold meats, salad and rolls. Perfect for a summer's day in Australia.

"I didn't know what you'd like to drink. There's beer, water and wine."

"Beer, thanks."

That's another thing I liked about Lachlan. He never assumed to know what I liked. He would always ask. Whenever I went to dinner with my parents or David, they would always order for me.

I filled a plate with food and leant back into the pillows that were stacked high.

"When the kids are here for Christmas, we all have

lunch at Mum's and then come for a swim. It's a nice way to cool off on these hot summer days."

"Do you miss them more at Christmas?"

"Sometimes. But I know I'll get to see them for dinner. I like waking up with them all excited about Santa coming."

I forked some salad into my mouth. I could only imagine their little faces with wide eyes and exuberant laughter.

"Jane and I work hard to make it fair for both of us."

"It seems like it works well. The kids are well adjusted."

"I worry about Thomas starting school. His kindergarten teacher didn't think he was ready."

"It will be hard for him at first. I think with the right teacher he'll be fine."

Lachlan nodded. "I sometimes wonder if he is so boisterous and absent-minded because we separated when he was so young."

Lachlan worried about a lot of things. He didn't share those concerns out loud often. He should. Sometimes talking to others would reassure him. In a family like his, burdens didn't need to be suffered alone. Knowing he was willing to share with me gave me confidence in our relationship.

"I think you'll find a lot of boys his age have a lack of control."

"Yeah. I guess I can only compare him to Scarlet who was completely different at his age."

"You know, it's a scientific fact that girls mature earlier than boys." I sipped my beer.

"Did you learn that at medical school?"

"I learned a lot of things at medical school. Some not so useful."

"Such as?"

I watched Lachlan eat while I thought.

"Seventy-five per cent of women don't orgasm from sex."

Lachlan's eyebrows furrowed. "And you learnt that because?"

"I think it was to make the male students feel better."

Lachlan laughed. "Lucky you're in that other twenty-five per cent."

I blushed. "Only with you."

"What do you mean?"

"I never orgasmed during sex before you. I was good at faking it though. It helped get it over and done with quicker."

Lachlan shook his head. "We have so much to make up for."

I crossed my legs. Just thinking about it made me hot and bothered. Maybe I needed that swim after all.

CHAPTER THIRTY-TWO

Lachlan

I PUT the leftovers and rubbish back into the basket. One way to make a guy feel good is to tell him he's good at sex. It was next level to tell him he was the only person to make you orgasm. I was feeling pretty happy with myself. I mean, sex isn't everything, but it matters.

"Ready for a swim?" I asked.

"As ready as I'll ever be."

I couldn't hide my smile. "What have you got against the dam?"

She looked at the dam. "I don't know. Maybe it's because the water is brown, and I can't see the bottom."

That was reasonable. "The middle of the dam is deep. You won't be able to touch the bottom there. As you walk in, your feet will sink. But they shouldn't get stuck."

"Shouldn't?" She eyed the water again.

"I mean, it could happen, but it's unlikely."

"And if it does happen?"

"I'll save you."

She laughed. "My hero."

I stripped off my clothes. As I pulled down my underwear, her eyes widened.

"We're going in naked?"

"I didn't bring bathers, did you?"

She shook her head. "There are no animals in the dam, are there?"

"Nothing will touch your privates except for me." I gave her a wink.

"But what if someone comes?"

"No one will come. Everyone is busy with Christmas."

She looked around. Nothing but quiet farmland surrounded us.

She took off her clothes, eying our surroundings, and then followed me. I liked how all the good parts of her wobbled. Sections of the ground were rough, and she winced as she stepped on them.

"City girl feet," I remarked.

She laughed.

We reached the edge of the dam.

"Ready?" I asked.

She looked back at our clothes and the water. "Yes."

I stepped in. The mud clay beneath my feet was quite firm. But the next step had me sinking. Peyton followed me gingerly. When I was hip-deep, I pushed forward and then turned around to watch her. It was the opposite of those movies where a goddess would glide out into the water. Her face scrunched up with every step, and I stifled laughter. There was no grace in that look. Once she was deep enough, she swam to me, and I pulled her towards the centre of the dam.

"The water is cooler here," she said as we treaded water. "If we moved to the middle more, would it be cooler again?"

"Yes."

"I can see why the kids like swimming here so much. It's refreshing."

"Well, have a listen to you, anyone would think you're turning into a country girl."

"That wouldn't be so bad."

No, it wouldn't. But a few weeks in the country didn't compare to twenty-six years in the city. Even though she didn't speak about it, there must have been things she missed. There were no five-star restaurants or shopping here. No convenience. Even buying condoms would be a feat.

I rolled onto my back and floated. Peyton did the same.

"It's weird to be heated so quickly by the sun on top while this coolness lay beneath you," she said.

I'd never really thought about it. But now that I concentrated on it, I was ultra-aware.

"Lachy," a female voice called out. I rolled over and looked in the direction of the voice. Lydia and Matt had parked their car beside mine and were walking towards the dam.

And we were butt naked.

"Bet you're grateful for the brown water now," I said to Peyton.

She held her head above water. Her face was so red it could have been a beacon for a bull.

"Hi, Lyd, Matt. This is Peyton."

Peyton managed a small wave.

"We saw your car from the road. How's the water?"

"Nice. You should try it sometime."

Peyton positioned herself slightly behind me. Lydia and Matt stayed at the water's edge.

"Are you going to come out to introduce Peyton properly?" Lydia asked.

A little gasp escaped Peyton's mouth.

"Ah, now's probably not a good time," I said.

"Why not?"

I glanced towards our picnic spot. Lydia did the same.

She smirked. "Oh, right. OK, see you at dinner then."

She pulled on Matt's arm and led him to the car. They laughed, and he put his arm around her shoulders. Peyton and I watched as they drove away. As soon as their car disappeared, Peyton turned to me. How bad would she rip into me?

CHAPTER THIRTY-THREE

Peyton

I SIGHED IN RELIEF. "That's the last time I listen to you, and your *no one will come*."

Lachlan chuckled. He turned around and pulled me towards him before cupping my butt.

"Now that we're alone."

"What's that saying you use for no chance? Buckley's?"

He nodded.

"Yeah, well, you've got Buckley's." I pushed him away.

He grinned. "Your loss."

He swam towards the bank and walked out. That view was just as good as him in jeans or shorts. I couldn't take my eyes off him even as he picked up his towel and turned to face me. Lordy, what a body. The grin topped it off. If I had panties on, they would have melted off by merely looking.

I swam to where I could touch the ground and scanned the paddocks and roadway. I couldn't see another human. And I didn't want to. Lachlan seeing me in the flesh was one thing, but others? No, thank you.

Lachlan held his towel in his hand and watched me. I scanned the area again just to make sure. Lachlan picked up the other towel and came towards the dam.

"No one's here," he said.

"That's what you said last time."

But there was no one there, so I walked out of the water, and as soon as I was close enough, he wrapped me in the towel.

"Thank you."

"Do I get rewarded for my hero move?"

I raised my eyebrows. "You're the reason we're in this mess in the first place."

"I wouldn't call it a mess. Just unfortunate timing." He grinned.

I rolled my eyes.

"Maybe I can make it up to you in the shower," he said.

"And how would you possibly do that?"

"We can test that twenty-five per cent theory again," he said, giving me a smirk.

I TURNED the water on nice and warm and dropped my towel. My stomach did that weird swirling batter thing again. I stepped in and turned back to face Lachlan. He stood watching me, licking his lips. Then he followed. His mouth found mine, and he kissed me in that longing way of his that turned me on. My core clenched. As his mouth moved to my neck, his hand took hold of my breast, and he squeezed it slow and firm.

"Let me wash the mud off you," he said, his voice husky.

He grabbed the soap and lathered his hand. With deliberate strokes, he washed my neck. He massaged my shoulders and then my arms. He never hesitated on my scars, just treated them like the rest of my body. His hands caressed me like his voice when he sang. When his mouth followed his hands to my breasts, I trembled.

"So fucking beautiful."

No one had ever worshipped my body like this, even before the accident. Heat erupted between my legs. And the legs were where he went next. Long, languid strokes from my ankles up to my thighs. I reached a hand out to the cold wall to steady myself. I opened my thighs before his hands even reached there. As soon as he touched me, I moaned. My body was tight and loose at the same time. When he slid his fingers between my folds to find my clit, small explosions erupted over my body.

"Lachlan," I half moaned. It felt so good. His fingers inside of me, the way he stroked, sent me closer. So close.

I looked down to see him staring up at me. He licked the water from his lips, inciting another moan from me.

He stood up and turned me around. "I want you so bad."

My core clenched again at the need in his voice. Bracing my wrists, he planted my palms against the wall. He let go and took hold of my waist to position me. I tilted my hips, and he pushed himself inside me.

"Fuck Peyton, you feel so good."

He slid in and out, hitting the right spot every time. I adjusted myself again, giving him better access. He went deeper, holding me close with one hand on my waist. His other hand slid around the front, touching me, playing with me. His breathing became ragged behind me.

His fingers matched his thrusts. I pushed against the wall, against him. Every thrust brought me closer. My legs trembled. How was I still standing?

I clenched around his dick. Tremors spread through me, increasing like his voice when it reached a crescendo. I tried to hold on a little longer, tried to ride it out. His movements were no longer measured, no longer controlled. I cried out as I went over the edge with him. His ragged groan. His fingers. His dick. And my pulsating. That's all that existed.

He collapsed against me and placed his hands next to mine. His harsh breaths heated my shoulder. I couldn't move. I was stuck in place, waiting for the tremors to disappear. He pulled himself out, and I sighed.

"That was amazing," I said.

"Still in the top twenty-five per cent."

I turned my face to him, and he kissed my cheek.

"It doesn't count. You used your fingers."

"You're a hard taskmaster." He claimed my lips with his.

Technicalities didn't matter. Sex with Lachlan was the best sex I'd ever had. Lachlan was the best man I'd ever had.

There was nothing that could top this feeling.

CHAPTER THIRTY-FOUR

Lachlan

WE WALKED around the back to Mum's patio. I put my guitar down as Mum got up to greet us.

"Merry Christmas, Lachy." She gave me a kiss and then turned to hug Peyton. "Merry Christmas, Peyton."

Lydia smirked at us. "Lachy and Peyton had a lovely picnic by the dam today."

Mum patted my cheek. "I knew I raised you right."

Lydia failed at stifling her laughter. Matt nudged her just as Mum sent a querying look her way.

Bruce pulled into the driveway. We could hear him coming before we saw him. He was singing some song about skinny dipping. Kayley walked behind him, shaking her head.

"You're just jealous," I said.

"I've seen enough of your naked body to last a lifetime."

Mum looked between us all. I saw the moment it clicked. She opened her mouth, closed it, sat and grabbed her glass of wine. I glanced at Peyton, who was blushing.

"Aw, come on, Mum," Bruce said, leaning down to kiss her cheek. "Don't pretend that you and Dad never went skinny dipping."

"That's none of your business."

Bruce laughed. "Looks like you're really fitting in, Doctor Peyton."

Peyton blushed. "What nice thing did you do for Kayley today?"

She was an expert in diverting conversations.

"Breakfast in bed," he announced, puffing his chest out.

"And the dishes afterwards," Kayley said.

Lydia shook her head. "I don't know how Peyton did it. I wish she'd been here twenty years ago when Lachy and I always got stuck with your chores."

Bruce laughed. "You always did them though."

Lydia and I rolled our eyes.

"Yeah, or else we didn't get to go out to play," I said.

Bruce shrugged.

Matt looked over at Peyton as he brushed his blond hair out of his eyes. "Would it be snowing where you're from?"

"Yes. We'd have a pleasant fire going inside."

"What do you prefer?"

"I think something in between the dry heat here and the freezing cold there."

"Yeah, the two extremes."

"We have a boy who comes and shovels our path for us every morning. Otherwise, we might never leave the house."

She truly lived in a different world. If we wanted our paths cleared, we'd do it ourselves. If we wanted *anything* done, we'd do it ourselves. I bet they had a housekeeper and even a cook. That's why she'd never baked a cake before.

"Daddy," Thomas yelled as he ran across the grass. He

launched himself into my arms and covered my face in wet kisses. "Merry Christmas."

I held him tight. "Merry Christmas, kiddo. Have you had a good day?"

"Oh yeah. I got a new bike from Santa. It's blue and has a loud bell and goes really fast."

I glanced at Jane and smiled. We'd chosen well.

He wriggled out of my arms and went to Peyton. "Merry Christmas, Peyton."

She gave him a hug. It seemed it wasn't tight enough for him because he squeezed her with all his might.

"Where's Scarlet?" I asked.

"She'll be here in a minute. She had a meltdown in the car," Jane said.

I glanced in the car's direction. "A meltdown?"

Jane threw her hands up.

Everyone sat around, chatting, eating crackers, dips and cheese. Five minutes passed, and still no Scarlet.

Peyton leant over and said quietly, "Do you want me to go get Scarlet? She might feel embarrassed knowing everyone will be watching her."

I nodded. As we continued talking, I watched out for Scarlet and Peyton. They were taking longer than I thought they would. Should I check on them? Before I had the chance, they came across the lawn holding hands. Scarlet was in a cornflour blue dress. Peyton let her sit beside me and chose the spare seat next to Mum.

"Merry Christmas, Daddy," she said. She wasn't as excited as her brother.

I kissed the top of her head. "What did Santa bring you?"

Her face lit up. "A really cool science kit. It has loads of experiments."

"Awesome. Which one are we going to try first?"

Scarlet jumped up and sat in my lap. She started chatting about what we should try. Her mood had changed completely. I glanced at Peyton. She was watching us. She gave me a small smile before I turned my attention back to Scarlet.

"You should have seen him, Lyd. It was like he'd never left the stage," Jane said, pulling me back to the conversation at the table.

"So, we have Peyton to thank for this as well?" Lydia said.

Peyton laughed. "No, it was a group effort."

"But she was the most convincing of all of us," Bruce said.

Mum was smiling as she looked around. Thomas was in her lap, nearly asleep. They would have been up at the crack of dawn, and he was probably too excited to nap in the car.

"We will need to come up for the final," Matt said. "I need to see Lachlan in action."

"Do you want to get my guitar?" I asked Scarlet.

She jumped off my lap to grab it.

"You're getting ahead of yourself. There are two more rounds yet," I said to Matt.

"Don't be ridiculous," Kayley said. "All the girls want you, and the guys want to be you."

Bruce started laughing and couldn't stop. He slapped his leg and then took a sip of his beer. "He had to beat a nineteen-year-old off by using Peyton as a shield."

Cue time for me to start. I strummed the strings to get their attention. No way I needed them to share groupie stories in front of Peyton. "I thought I could start with a ballad. Suggestions?"

Mum brought out the cold roast chicken and salads she'd prepared for dinner. As everyone ate and opened their presents, I sang. They voted, and I had my playlist ready for next week. Bruce was very strategic, always thinking about the audience and judges.

"OK. Bring on next week," I said, packing my guitar in its case.

Jane stood up. It was late, and they still had the hour's drive home. Scarlet was dozing off in the chair next to me. Thomas hadn't even made it through the first three songs.

"We'll walk you out," I said.

Jane took Thomas from Mum. He wrapped his arms around her neck. Scarlet looked up at me. Peyton stepped forward and took my guitar.

"Hop on my back," I said to Scarlet. She stood on her chair and jumped on. We all made our way to Jane's car. Peyton stood back, waiting for me, and I put Scarlet down so she could get in the car. Instead, she ran to Peyton to give her a hug.

"Thank you," Peyton said softly. "Give Thomas a kiss for me."

We watched as they drove away and then went to our car. Peyton was quiet as we made our way home.

"Are you OK?"

"Yes. Thanks." Short and sweet, but her tone was off. Maybe she was tired. It had been a big day. Perhaps being with the family made her miss her family. But she'd been quiet since going to get Scarlet earlier.

"What was wrong with Scarlet?"

"She was feeling a bit left out." Peyton took a breath. "Something about how excited you were to spend Christmas with me."

Fuck.

"I explained you were just as excited about spending tonight with her and Thomas."

I nodded.

"I think we should have discussed how we were going to talk to the children about our relationship," she said.

I sighed. "That would have been a good idea."

Mind you, *we* hadn't even talked about our relationship or how it affected her job.

I should have learnt from what Jane and Dan had gone through. I'd gotten so caught up in Peyton that I'd forgotten about how my children would feel. No, that wasn't true.

"I thought they'd be happy. Scarlet said almost as much when she left."

"I know. I think her feelings confused her."

I never wanted my kids to be confused about how much I loved them.

"She's not confused anymore. We had a good talk. And you wanting to do science experiments with her proved that."

I smiled. "She was so fucking excited."

"She was. I told her you would want to."

Peyton to the rescue again.

"We need to talk with them when they come back," I said. "I don't want them thinking that I don't love them anymore." I glanced at Peyton. "What do you think?"

CHAPTER THIRTY-FIVE

Peyton

HE WAS ASKING MY OPINION? And on something this important? I already knew the answer. I'd given it a lot of thought over the past two hours.

"I agree. I think we need to be open with them but move at a pace they're comfortable with."

Lachlan reached over and took my hand. "That's a good plan."

"Maybe you can speak to Jane too. She's already been through this."

"Yeah. I will."

We pulled into the carport and went inside. I hesitated at his bedroom door. Would Lachlan want me to join him in bed? Maybe he wanted some alone time. We'd spent nearly every minute together since the children had left. The unit was finished, but we'd never mentioned my moving back there.

"Goodnight," I said before heading off down the hall.

Lachlan followed me to the bathroom. I got my toothbrush out of my toiletry bag. I still hadn't unpacked. I was in limbo, not knowing if I'd be staying in the house or going back to the unit.

"Are you coming to bed after you've done your teeth?" He was always giving me choices.

"If you'd like me to."

"Yes."

I nodded and started brushing my teeth. It was strange. I made decisions for myself now, and when the children were in my care, I made decisions for them too. And no one ever questioned me, so I never doubted myself. It was liberating.

Lachlan was already in bed when I got there. I hopped in beside him. He rolled over and kissed me.

"I much prefer to say good night like this," he said as his lips drew away.

"Me too."

"Don't ever think I don't want you in my bed."

My stomach squeezed. I'd never felt so wanted.

"OK. But not when the kids are here," I said.

"Not yet. But we'll build up to it." He rolled onto his back.

Were we moving too quickly? We'd known each other for such a short time—four weeks. I knew what type of man he was from the way his family loved him and the dedication he had to the farm and his children. But what if there was another side I didn't know? Anyone could fall into the trap of enjoying something new.

"What are you thinking?" he asked.

What do I tell him? It had to be the truth. I could pretend I was thinking of something else, but I wasn't here to hide my feelings.

"Do you think we're moving too fast?" I asked.

"We have moved from zero to one hundred very quickly."

He felt it too.

"But it feels right to me," he said. "You fit."

"I fit into my old life too."

"But from what you've told me, you were forced to fit. It wasn't a choice."

"Do you think you were ever forced to fit?" I asked.

"I think Dad's death forced me to fit quicker than I wanted. But it was always going to be this way."

"And you never begrudged that?"

"In a way, I was disappointed that I didn't get to see my plans through. But I couldn't change that." He was silent for a while. "I think the most difficult thing was not being able to grieve the loss of Dad."

"How do you mean?"

"As soon as I got back, I had to take over. I threw myself into the farm and helped my family. Bruce was only sixteen, and Lydia was fourteen. They needed me."

"That's a lot of responsibility for a nineteen-year-old."

"I didn't have a choice."

The freedom of young adulthood had been taken away from him. Just like the freedom of my teenage years—and my young adult years—had been taken away from me. There had been no parties, no experimenting; those things hadn't fit into my parents' plans. And then, when their plans had been coming to fruition, my career was ripped away. I hadn't had a chance to grieve that. Maybe that's another reason why I'd come here. But being all consumed by this family hadn't allowed me to grieve. Losing a career was nothing like losing a parent though. And saying it out loud would be selfish.

I rolled onto my side. Lachlan followed and put his arm

around me. I lay still, waiting for his breathing to even out. It didn't take long. Then I let my thoughts go to a dark place they hadn't been to before. My recovery hadn't allowed them to stray there.

Years of my life had been wasted. The career I'd worked so hard for was torn away from me. What was left for me? People changed careers all the time. But I'd never even practised as a surgeon. Not a fully-fledged one.

What purpose did I have? My life would never be the same. I didn't want it to be the same. I wasn't truly happy before, but I knew where I was heading. I wasn't lost. Not like now. My throat ached from the tears I was holding in. Lachlan was asleep. I didn't need to hide them. I let them flow.

Sometimes, while I had been lying in that hospital bed, I'd thought about how it would have been different if I hadn't gotten out of the car that day. I would have been safe. But that family wouldn't have. And that is not something I could have lived with. I would never have forgiven myself.

My career or their life? Life as I knew it or their future? My arm, my scars or them? There was no choice. It would always be them.

I cried for my pain. I cried for my career. I cried for my family.

The tears wouldn't stop.

All the while, I felt the comfort of Lachlan's arm around me.

CHAPTER THIRTY-SIX

Lachlan

PEYTON SHIFTED BESIDE ME. Last night I held her while she cried. I didn't let her know that I was awake while she silently broke beside me. It wasn't my place to intrude. If she had wanted to share it with me, she would have done so while I was awake.

I'd played the conversation over in my mind. The last thing I'd said was that I didn't have a choice in my duty to my family and the farm. Was she crying because she didn't have a choice? A choice about what? She'd told me she hadn't had choices growing up. Her destiny was pre-determined for her. I know that made her sad. But sad enough to break down?

She rolled over and smiled at me. "Good morning."

She was happy. Her normal self. Was it all a facade? This happiness she projected?

"Morning."

"What's on the agenda for today?" she asked. She rolled into me and stretched before laying her hand on my chest. I looked into her eyes. Her gaze didn't dart away, and my shoulders relaxed.

"I need to do the rounds and check on the cattle."

That was not the answer I wanted to give. The answer should have been that I wanted to talk about last night. But she needed to be ready to talk. I needed to give her time. She'd been open with me in the past. I just needed to wait, even if it was eating me up inside.

"And then?" Her hand drifted down my chest to my bulge.

"And then we have the whole day to"—I pulled her on top of me—"do whatever we desire."

I gripped her arse and pulled her higher. She straddled me. I could feel the heat between her legs as she pushed herself down onto my dick. Her chest pressed against mine as she kissed me.

"I'm not sure I can wait that long," she said, her breath brushing my lips.

Fuck, neither did I. The cattle could wait.

She moved her lips across my jaw. "This is our last day alone." She kissed my neck. "I think we should make the most of it." Her mouth moved lower, down my chest, my stomach. "Maybe we could just..." She pulled my underwear down. My dick, no longer contained, showed her exactly how ready I was. She straddled me again, pressing down on me. Holy fuck. There was too much material between us. She grabbed at the hem of her top and pulled it over her head. Her breasts were like magnets. My hands were drawn to them. She sighed and rubbed against my dick. Still too much material.

"You better get naked before I rip those shorts off you."

She smiled. It was small and too fucking sexy. "So bossy."

She manoeuvred her shorts and underwear off. Now it wasn't just the heat I could feel but her wetness too. She took hold of my throbbing dick and guided it inside her. She moaned as she lowered herself down. She took her time. She was tight and hot. My dick throbbed. She reached the hilt and rose again. Down and up.

I needed more. I grabbed her hips and thrust, guiding her up and down. She lost balance and rested her hands on my chest. Her moves matched mine, sliding down as I thrust up. Her breathing became heavier, faster. Moans mixed with cries of pleasure.

My groin tightened. I clenched my jaw. She needed to come with me. She wasn't there yet. My balls tightened. I slammed into her pulling her down hard. And again. Her hands pushed into my chest. Her legs shook. My whole body shook. I exploded inside her.

"Lachlan," she cried out.

She pulsated around me. Tremors spread through me. I held her there until we were both still. Then she collapsed onto my chest.

"Thank you for bringing me to the top twenty-five per cent," she said.

I chuckled and kissed the top of her head. She rolled off me and cuddled into my side. She was a woman of contrasts. At times she was unsure. But she still managed to have steely resolve. Reserved out in the open, almost shy at times. But sex brought out a different side. Open, willing to share things. But closed, keeping secrets behind a steel door.

I'd told her I loved her when she'd first showed me her scars. But those words were never returned. Why? Was she afraid to say them? Maybe she wasn't ready. It made sense. She'd only broken up with her fiancé a couple of months ago. But she admitted it was practically over the night of the accident. If I were her, being disappointed and rejected by the one she loved, I'd be hesitant to say those words too.

I WENT OUTSIDE to meet Jane and the kids.

"Daddy, I brought the science kit," Scarlet said, hauling a plastic container out of the boot.

"Excellent. I can't wait to do an experiment with you."

"We could do one tonight," she said, beaming up at me.

"I think we could make time for that." I ruffled her hair.

"And then can we go for a bike ride," Thomas said. "I can show you how fast my new bike is."

"How fast is it?"

"Super-fast."

I laughed. Jane pulled the bike out of the boot. I grabbed his helmet and bag.

"Take your things inside," I said. "I'll be in soon."

Thomas grabbed his bag and took off.

"Where's Peyton?" Jane asked.

"She's gone for a walk. She said I should spend some time alone with the kids."

"That was thoughtful."

I nodded.

"How are things going with you two?"

"Good."

"Is that all you've got for me?"

"The last week has been great. I've had time off work, and we've spent all that time together." I ran my hand through my hair.

Jane narrowed her eyes. "But?"

I shrugged. Why did she know me so well? How much do I tell her?

"Spit it out."

"Nothing. We're back in the real world now. It will be different with the kids here."

"Well, yes. But you'll figure it out."

"How do you and Dan manage?"

"It was different for us. We weren't living together like you are. It was a slow introduction."

"And now?"

"We share the parenting. Our lives revolve around each other and the kids."

I guess we already did that in a way. Peyton looked after them during the day, and then we shared responsibility for them at night. It didn't need to be different now that we were a couple.

"Do you think the kids miss having you to themselves?" I asked.

Jane shook her head. "Not really. I usually do the bedtime routine alone with them."

"You know that's what Scarlet's meltdown was about at Christmas?"

"I put two and two together when Peyton sat away from you."

"I don't want them to think I'm choosing her over them." My heart ached at the thought.

"Lachy, you're a good dad. The best. You'll figure this out." She hugged me. "And Peyton will support you."

"True."

"I'll see you tomorrow. I hope you're ready to wipe the floor with those other competitors."

CHAPTER THIRTY-SEVEN

Peyton

WE WALKED INTO THE PUB. Thomas gripped my hand, and Scarlet held Lachlan's. People greeted him from every direction, telling him how great he was and how good it was to see him singing again.

"You're famous, Daddy," Scarlet said.

Lachlan chuckled.

Kayley was talking to Jane. "I've ordered the shirts. They'll be here before the next round."

"What shirts?" Lachlan asked, looking between them.

"Our groupie shirts. Every star should have them."

We'd all agreed on his favourite colour—emerald green. I didn't know what slogan they'd chosen, though.

He groaned. "I shouldn't have asked."

Before we could sit down, Stacy appeared. The fact that Lachlan was with me didn't deter her one bit.

"Hi, Lachlan," she said, flipping her long hair over her shoulders. She had legs for days and showed them off in tight jeans.

Lachlan's shoulders tightened. "Hi, Stacy, ready for your performance?"

"So ready." She smiled, flashing her straight teeth. "I can't wait to hear you sing again."

"Likewise."

She looked over at me with her judgy eyes. "Do you sing?"

Scarlet giggled. "Peyton *tries* to sing."

"Peyton's talents lie elsewhere," Lachlan said.

"Oh yeah, where?" Stacy asked as if I couldn't possibly have any talents. And she was right.

Scarlet turned to me. "She makes us happy."

That girl was my hero.

"That's right. You're the nanny." Could she have used a more condescending tone? Blood rushed to my face, and I stared down at my feet. I had no comeback.

"She's my girlfriend," Lachlan said.

Stacy gave me another once over and walked away.

"That young lady could learn some manners," Ann said.

"I'll say." Jane sat at the table, studying Stacy's retreating figure.

I gave a small smile, sat down, and tried to engage in the conversation around me. I didn't want Lachlan to see how much the comment upset me. I didn't want him to be distracted from his performance.

I was the nanny who fell for the single dad. A walking cliche. No longer a surgeon. Someone without purpose. I'd thought I'd found my place in the world, but did Lachlan just like me because I was convenient?

Lachlan stepped away to talk to Donna.

Bruce took his seat. "Don't let that little upstart upset you."

"I won't."

"But you have."

I shrugged. What had happened to speaks-her-mind Peyton? One comment from someone I shouldn't even care about had sent her packing.

"I don't know why it bothered me so much," I admitted. "Sometimes I feel a little lost."

"If someone told me I couldn't be a farmer anymore, I'd feel lost too."

I nodded.

"You'll figure it out. There's no rush."

I nodded again and remembered the unanswered message on my phone from my mother. I couldn't keep avoiding her. According to my parents, there was no taking it slow when it came to deciding my future. And no matter what I decided, if it wasn't what they wanted, they'd never approve. Like my coming here and choosing a different direction, I was happy, but that wasn't enough for them.

Bruce sat up straight as Donna climbed onto the stage. "All right, let's get this round started. We have six singers tonight. Each will sing three songs. To start off, welcome Walter Green to the stage."

We all clapped as a middle-aged man made his way to the mic. Bruce squeezed my shoulder before returning to his seat, and Lachlan sat beside me. I reached out for his hand. Tonight wasn't about me.

Stacy was third up. She sang a couple of pop-country songs and a folk song. I hated to admit it, but she was good. She looked good. Her voice was good. Everything about her performance was good.

Lachlan performed next. He started with an upbeat love song that had the crowd smiling and clapping to the beat. When he finished the first song, he stood still and closed his eyes. The crowd waited. He strummed the first few chords of Amazing Grace. That wasn't the song we'd all chosen.

And then he sang. His voice was pure and in perfect melody. Just him, his guitar and no pretence. Every word spread through me and opened my heart. The crowd was transfixed. When Lachlan locked eyes with mine, my breath stuck in my throat.

Lachlan was my grace.

When he stopped singing, the room was silent. Tears rolled down my cheeks. The beauty of the song, the truth of it, was all-encompassing.

Lachlan gave the crowd a smile. "That is one of my favourite songs. Thank you for letting me share it with you."

He started the next song. It seemed like a crowd favourite, with half of them singing along. When he finished, he said, "Thanks, everyone. You've been a great audience." He waved as he stepped off stage.

Bruce clapped him on the shoulder when he got to the table. "Well, if that doesn't get you to the next round, I don't know what will."

Lachlan picked up Thomas, who planted kisses all over his face. I loved how that kid was so affectionate. Scarlet gave him a high five as she told him he was the best singer in the whole world. I glanced at Stacy, who was watching Lachlan's every move.

He sat down next to me. "Did your panties melt?"

"No. But my heart did."

He gave me a lopsided smile.

Lachlan Harris had the power to crush that heart.

I CHANGED and hopped into bed before calling my mother. After five rings, my hopes lifted. Maybe she wasn't going to answer.

"Hello, Peyton."

No such luck.

"Hi, Mom."

"You're up late, seeing you have the children to look after tomorrow."

"Yeah, been busy."

Yeah? I was actually starting to sound the opposite of someone from upper-class America. I nearly laughed.

"We're busy too. We have the annual hospital fundraiser this weekend."

What a relief I wasn't there. Dressing up and talking to people I hardly knew was not something I enjoyed. That was one good thing about the accident—I wasn't forced to go.

"Remember how much you loved attending with us?"

Time for honest Peyton to make herself heard. "I didn't enjoy them."

"Oh hush, of course you did. You always looked so beautiful."

I sighed. She never listened to me. If my opinion was different, it didn't exist.

Time to change the subject. "How's Dad?"

"Marvellous. He played a round of golf with the head of paediatrics on Sunday."

"A good round?"

"Oh yes. They spoke about you."

I tensed. "Why would they do that?"

"You're working with children in Australia. We thought it would be the perfect career path to follow when you return home."

I clenched my fist. "Please stop talking to people about my future. I can make my own decisions. And my decision is to be here."

"It's been nearly sixteen months since the accident."

I took a deep breath, stood up and started pacing. "Need I remind you that for fourteen of those months I was recovering?"

"We are fully aware of how long it took you to recover."

What the fuck?

"Are you implying that I took too long?"

"No, no."

She was.

I took some slow breaths, trying to steady myself. I couldn't believe what I was hearing. I'd put every effort into my recovery. I'd worked as hard as my body allowed me to. I'd done everything my specialists advised.

"Peyton—"

"Mom, if the only reason you're going to call me is to tell me about some decision you've made for my future, please don't."

She sucked in a breath.

"I'm happy. The least you could do is be happy for me too."

I hung up before she could say another word.

Yes, Mom, I'm just a nanny. But that's my choice. And if I want to love a farmer, that's my choice too. But were they smart choices? The right choices?

Lachlan and his family loved me for me. Or at least I thought they did.

Maybe I was delusional. Maybe they just loved me because of how well I looked after the children.

If my parents couldn't love me for me, perhaps no one could.

CHAPTER THIRTY-EIGHT

Lachlan

I stood in the hallway outside Peyton's door. Her phone call to her mum hadn't gone well. I could hear her from my room. Not the actual words but the hurt and betrayal in her voice.

I wanted to make sure she was OK. But would she feel like I was intruding, that I'd been eavesdropping? It didn't matter. She was what was important here.

I knocked on her door and counted the seconds until the door handle turned and opened. Peyton stood there and looked at me. She didn't smile. Part of me expected she would. That she'd put on that bright persona of hers.

"Are you OK?"

She shook her head. I crossed over the threshold and wrapped my arms around her. She let out a long breath before her arms circled my waist.

"Do you want to talk about it?" I rubbed her back.

"I'm so tired, Lachlan."

Tired of what? She wasn't tired of us, was she?

I didn't ask. I was too scared of the answer. I just waited for her to tell me more.

"It always feels like I'm in a battle with my parents. My decision to be here, to be a nanny, isn't good enough for them. "

I held her tighter. I couldn't imagine what it would be like to have every decision I made questioned.

"Being a nanny is an important job. You care for my children and are helping to mould them. It may not be saving lives, but it's changing lives."

She spoke into my chest. "I don't even know if I'm doing the right thing anymore. I feel happy. But they make me doubt if that's even true."

My chest squeezed, and I held her tighter.

I thought she was happy. Did I only believe that because I was happy?

"You make us happy, Peyton. Every day, in so many ways."

She sighed. "My mother insinuated tonight that I took too long to recover."

My jaw tightened. Who would say that to someone, let alone their own child?

"I worked hard, Lachlan. I did everything my specialists told me to."

I stroked her back. "I know you did."

And I did know. She'd told me all about the surgeries and physical therapy. How when she felt despondent and wanted to give up, she wouldn't allow those thoughts to take over.

She pushed herself away. "We need to go to bed. You have to get up early for work."

"Come to bed with me."

She shook her head. "Not until we talk to the children. I don't want them to come in and get a shock."

I wanted her with me. I wanted to comfort her. But she was right. My hands were tied, and I hated it. I lowered my head and walked back to my room.

***

IT WAS a late start to the morning. I didn't sleep well knowing that Peyton was hurting and I could do nothing to help her. Was she destined for greater things, and I was holding her back?

"Celebrate too hard last night, did you?" Bruce asked as I walked into the shed.

"No."

Bruce eyed me, his brow creasing. He continued putting the spray equipment in the ute.

My shoulders sagged. "Do you think I'm doing the right thing with Peyton?"

"Uh, yeah." He sounded like he thought I was an idiot.

"Scarlet had a meltdown at Christmas because she thought I didn't love her as much anymore."

"That's normal. I'm sure she's over it now."

That wasn't the point.

"I never want my kids to feel that way."

Bruce finished what he was doing and gave me a hard stare. "Stop this shit. You always think that it has to be the farm and your children and nothing else."

I ran a hand over my face. "The farm is all we have."

"Yeah, we. Not just you. We're all responsible for it. "

I shook my head. "It's my duty to look after it all."

"Really? Just yours?"

I shrugged.

"Don't use us as an excuse because you're scared."

Scared? I guess I was. Bruce knew what I was like when Jane left. I never wanted to be like that again, where there was no joy left in my heart, and everything just seemed too hard, even getting up in the morning.

"Don't risk your happiness because of some perceived duty or because you're scared."

"Yeah, I suppose."

I grabbed the PPE and put it in the tray of the ute.

"Do you think Peyton is happy?" I asked.

"Yes."

I screwed my mouth up. How was he so certain?

"Have you seen the way she looks at you? It's like you're the best thing that's ever happened to her."

"What are you talking about?"

"She fucking cried last night listening to you sing."

I didn't get it. Bruce strode to me and stuck his finger in my chest. "She sees you here." He poked me again. He kept eye contact with me. "Not even Jane ever truly saw you."

I shook my head. Was this my brother? "What has she done to you?"

"Opened my eyes."

And opened my heart.

"Got everything?" I asked.

Bruce nodded, and we hopped in the car.

"She spoke to her mother last night," I said. "They're trying to get her to continue a medical career. Do you think being here is holding her back?"

"I don't know. Some highly esteemed career isn't for everyone."

I sighed. That wasn't an answer.

Maybe that was why she never spoke about her life in Boston. Maybe if she didn't speak about it, she could pretend it didn't exist. She could pretend that it wasn't calling her back. That Boston wasn't where she was supposed to be. So, if she kept that steel door closed, she could stay here and not make the decision to return to the life she should have.

CHAPTER THIRTY-NINE

Peyton

Donna studied Lachlan as we placed our orders. "Eating here is not going to sway the judges."

"Would you rather I take my date to the other pub?" Lachlan asked her.

Donna gave me a wink. "Oh no, the fact that Lachlan Harris is actually on a date will bring people in here on this quiet night."

I leant in close to her. "Hopefully not Stacy."

She laughed. "This one's a keeper. Pretty, with a sense of humour."

I blushed. Lachlan put his arm around my shoulders. "Let them come, so I can show her off."

I glanced around the dining room. People were already watching us. I didn't need to be scrutinised by these strangers. I was happy to live in our insulated world. But we couldn't just hide away. The real world was here, and every now and then, we had to venture out into it. The kids had gone back to Jane's a day early, and this was the prime opportunity to get out.

We ordered, and then Lachlan led us to a table by the window. It was six o'clock, and the sun was still making its way to the horizon. The dining room was warm, but I kept my light cardigan on. I didn't need everyone looking and staring any more than they already were.

"Peyton."

I turned my attention to Lachlan. "Yes."

"What's wrong?"

"Nothing. Sorry. I was distracted." I gave him a smile.

"By what?"

"By everyone looking at us."

"That's small-town life for you."

"Do you ever get accustomed to everyone knowing everything?"

Lachlan grinned and waggled his eyebrows. "*Every-thing* would really get them excited."

Everything got me excited. A giggle tumbled out. Lachlan reached out to take my hand and raised it to his lips. He kept hold of it.

"Where would you go for dinner at home?" he asked.

"Surgical rotations didn't leave much time for dinner."

"What about girls' lunches?"

I gave him a small smile. "My Mom, sister and I would go to lunch once a month. Usually to my Mom's favourite restaurant, famous for its French and Italian cuisine."

"That sounds nice."

I nodded. "The food was good."

"Not as good as our pub grub," Donna said as she placed plates in front of us. Golden chicken schnitzel covered half the plate with vibrant vegetables and mashed potato on the other half.

"Never this good," I replied.

She glanced behind me. "Incoming."

Before I could turn around, I heard Stacy's voice. "Lachlan, it's so good to see you."

She didn't even acknowledge my presence.

"Hi, Stacy."

I studied her while she paid no attention to me. Tight jeans again and a satiny musk camisole top that showed off her flawless tanned skin.

"You should join us for drinks later," she said.

"We're on a date," he said pointedly.

She forced herself to look at me.

"Bye, Stacy," Lachlan said.

She strolled away, and Lachlan rolled his eyes and dug into his food. I couldn't agree more with that eye roll. I tell you, that girl outdid my mother in making me feel inferior. It was like I was nothing. And in the scheme of things, I was. I picked up my fork and pushed some vegetables around my plate, not really hungry anymore.

I was just the nanny. Lachlan said I did a lot for the family, the kids, and that may be true, but any good nanny could do that.

I scanned the room. Lachlan could have any one of these women. Why would he want to be with someone broken like me?

"Thomas is excited about school tomorrow," Lachlan said, drawing my attention.

"I can't wait to see him in his school uniform. He'll be so cute."

Lachlan nodded. "He has matured so much this summer. I think that will help him settle in."

I took a bite of my schnitzel. It was melt-in-your-mouth delicious. The food in Australia was fresh and natural. There was a limitation to the preservatives and chemicals they were allowed to put into their foods. And from what I'd seen on Lachlan's farm, the animals lived a good life and were well cared for.

"Do chickens in Australia live the same good life as your cattle?" I asked.

"Chickens live in barns, and some have outdoor access. Nearly twenty per cent are free range now. They're fed a special formula with lots of energy in it, so they grow quickly. No hormones or steroids."

I imagined happy chickens like Lachlan's, which got to warm themselves in the sun and have dust baths. Animals were happier here. So were humans. Well, I was, at least. Life was lived at a different pace, and I didn't feel like I had to prove myself all the time. And I didn't have to constantly worry that I was going to disappoint someone.

I hoped Thomas felt the same. We would love him no matter how long it took him to settle into school. But I was sure he'd be fine.

DAN and I watched as Jane and Lachlan walked the children into school. Thomas had been excited all morning. Taking his photo had been an effort.

"What are you going to do now the kids are at school?" Dan asked.

"I'll do the school run every day. Lachlan doesn't think Thomas is ready for the school bus."

Dan laughed. "I don't think it would be fair on the bus driver."

That would be four hours of my day taken up. The remaining five, when the children were at school, still needed to be filled in.

"I might see if I can volunteer at the school or some-where else in town some days."

He nodded. "The kids would love that. Jane and I don't get to spend much time at the school with work and all."

He always treated the kids as his own. He made time for them and included them in his plans. It was like Lachlan and me in a way. I never felt excluded.

"Do you ever think of becoming a doctor here?" he asked.

"I haven't really thought of being a doctor anywhere."

"Why's that?"

"I don't know. When I was told I couldn't be a surgeon anymore, I ceased thinking about medicine being a part of my life."

It was like I'd slammed the door shut. My parents' insis-tence that I choose another specialist field didn't help. They pushed me further away from medicine. But was that distance good? I didn't need to follow the path they wanted me to. Could I practice medicine on my own terms?

CHAPTER FORTY

Lachlan

JANE and I stood beside her car in my driveway. It was our child swap day.

"It's only been two days," she said. "They can't expect him to behave like he's been at school for a month."

"Did the teacher say anything about the other children in her class?"

Peyton approached us.

"Just that they'd started to settle in already."

Peyton looked behind her. "Maybe you can speak to the teacher about me assisting in class in the morning. It might help settle him."

Just the idea helped relax me.

Jane nodded. "That might help."

"Let's see how the rest of the week goes. If she's still concerned, I think we should try that," I said.

By the end of the week, Thomas still hadn't settled. The teacher had a video conference with Jane and me on Friday afternoon to tell us that Thomas had gotten into a fight.

"Is there something in the home environment that could be affecting him?" the teacher asked.

"No. There have been no changes," Jane said. There was this tiny tenseness in her voice. Was she thinking about Peyton and me? She wouldn't have appreciated the accusation even though that's probably not how the teacher intended it.

"OK then. We can just put it down to settling pains. Some children take longer to settle in. We expect that. But we do need to put a stop to any aggression."

I didn't understand it. Thomas was a happy-go-lucky kid at home. Sure, he got into fights with Scarlet, but Scarlet picked fights just as often with him.

"Do you think having someone familiar in the room at the start of the day might help?" Jane asked.

"If one of you want to come in and sort readers or do some other things for a short while, it could help."

"It wouldn't be Lachlan or myself, but Lachlan's partner has offered."

She looked between us. "That's generous of her to offer her time."

"Yes," Jane said. "She's very close to the children. She looked after them all summer."

"Let's try that," the teacher said before she disconnected.

"Here's hoping," Jane said to me.

"I'll talk to Peyton." I disconnected.

Was Thomas behaving like this because of Peyton and me? No, even his kindergarten teacher had concerns, and that was before Peyton had arrived. But still, maybe I wasn't giving him enough attention. Was I failing him and Scarlet? They were my first priority. They always would be.

Peyton was getting dinner ready, so I heated the frying

pan for our steak. Scarlet and Thomas were vegging out on the couch.

"Thomas got into a fight today," I said to Peyton.

She stopped chopping the vegetables. "Do you know why?"

Good question. I was more concerned with the fact that he wasn't settling in and was called aggressive instead of asking why.

"The teacher didn't say."

"I think you should talk to him about it later to understand what's going on."

"She also said he's still not settling."

"Have you and Jane spoken about me helping in class? I'm happy to."

I didn't even need to ask her. I leant over and gave her a hug. "That would be great."

"I'll go in for as long as he needs me."

We worked in companionable silence until dinner was ready. And then we all sat at the table together to eat.

Scarlet glanced at Thomas. "Thomas got into a fight today."

Thomas said nothing. Just continued eating.

"What was the fight about?" I asked.

Scarlet looked at Thomas. He stopped chewing and swallowed. "Some grade two kid stole a little girl's book and wouldn't give it back."

The teacher neglected to mention it was a grade two child Thomas had a fight with. It seemed like she'd forgotten to mention a few other things as well.

"That kid is nothing but trouble," Scarlet said matter of fact.

I had to stop myself from laughing. I turned my attention back to Thomas. "What happened after he took the book?"

"The girl was crying. She asked for it back, and he wouldn't give it to her. So I took it back. "

I couldn't see the problem yet. "How did the fight start?"

"I gave the book back to the girl; then he hit me. So I hit him back."

Sounded reasonable to me. Perhaps he could have handled it a different way. Although, in Thomas's defence, I always encouraged my children to be problem solvers, and he'd done exactly that.

"I think you should tell a teacher what's happening next time," I suggested.

Scarlet sat up straighter. "Why? They never do anything. That boy is a bully, but he never gets into trouble."

Interesting. There seemed to be some issues at that school. And those issues had nothing to do with Peyton and me.

"Thomas should tell the teacher so he doesn't get in trouble," I said.

"I think that's a good idea," Peyton said.

Scarlet shrugged.

Thomas said nothing. He continued eating.

Scarlet looked between us. "Dan says we're lucky to have two families."

I nodded. "That's true. Some kids don't have that." That was my cue to talk to them about Peyton and me. I glanced at Peyton before I said, "You have Mum and Dan and Peyton and me. How do you feel about that?"

"I think it's excellent," Thomas said. "I love Peyton."

Scarlet nodded.

Peyton beamed. "I love you too."

I wanted to hold them all close in this moment forever. I don't know what I was so worried about.

"Peyton is going to start sharing my bedroom. Don't be shocked if you come in and she's in the bed."

Thomas chewed his food and nodded. "That's good. Your bed is bigger than Peyton's. There's more room for us."

Scarlet gave her brother a high five.

And that was it. A conversation I'd thought would be hard wasn't at all.

"I KNEW there must have been more to that fight," Peyton said from beside me in bed.

"Yes, I should have asked more questions."

"I hope they haven't labelled Thomas as a troublemaker just because he is taking a little longer to settle than the others," Peyton said.

I hadn't thought of that. "I'm glad you're going in on Monday. I think it will help Thomas and the teacher."

"I think it would be good to see what the teacher's concerns are."

"Thank you for offering." I rolled over to kiss her.

"Maybe you should thank me properly," she said.

I smiled. "What do you have in mind?"

"Use your imagination."

"My imagination can be wild." I looked at the door. "You'll have to be quiet."

I straddled her legs and pulled her up into a sitting position. I lifted her top over her head and then captured her mouth with mine. The warmth of her mouth, her eager tongue and her soft moans made me hard. Pushing her back down, my lips left hers, and I sucked on the soft skin of her neck. Her hands wrapped around my forearms. My mouth made its way lower to her breasts. I paid attention to them equally. She squeezed my forearms, her breaths coming out in small sighs. What would she be like when I reached that warm spot between her legs?

I moved lower, pulling my arms from her grip. Tugging her shorts and underwear off, the smell of her desire filled my nostrils. My dick grew harder.

I pushed her legs open and licked the crease at the top of her thigh. Her smell was intoxicating. I closed my eyes, breathing in deeply. My tongue found her wet folds.

"You taste so fucking good," I said between licks.

She opened her legs wider. I explored with my tongue and fingers. So wet. I concentrated on her hard clit—flattening my tongue against it, swirling around it, sucking it. Peyton's legs tensed. And shook. I thrust two fingers inside her. Her hands clutched at the sheets. She pulsated around my fingers and let out a muffled cry.

I didn't stop until she did. I wanted to wring every last bit of ecstasy out of her. When she fell backward on the bed, I moved on top of her.

"Was that a proper thank you?" I asked.

"Indeed, it was."

"Do you think you could handle two thank yous?" I nudged my dick closer to her entrance.

"I think I could manage."

She raised herself up to kiss me nice and slow. I pushed myself in. Her kiss halted for a moment and then continued its languid pace. My thrusts equalled it.

A noise sounded in the house. We stopped in unison. Our bodies still, we listened. It was the fridge making its weird sound. Peyton giggled as I released my held breath.

"I hope that doesn't happen every time you're thanking me," she said.

"Or when you're thanking me." I started moving again and met her lips.

Every time we had sex, it was a thank you to the sex gods. I felt like one every time she orgasmed. Knowing I was taking her to a level she'd never been to before was powerful.

Peyton pulled her lips away. Her breaths were heavy in my ear. The harmony of our lips was now shared in our breaths.

The conversation we'd had at the dinner table had been perfect. Peyton was perfect.

I pumped faster. My balls tightened. I groaned through my release. Peyton tightened around me. Her muted cry against my shoulder was perfect.

CHAPTER FORTY-ONE

Peyton

THOMAS and I walked into his classroom on Monday morning. His teacher was placing handouts on the desk. She was probably in her fifties and had a stern look about her—her eyes were piercing, and her face appeared like it was set in a permanent frown.

"She reminds me of the last nanny," Thomas whispered. I'd heard all about her and her fun police ways.

"Good morning, Mrs Smythe. I'm Peyton. I believe Lachlan and Jane, Thomas's parents talked to you on Friday about me helping in class."

She stopped what she was doing and studied Thomas and I. Sweat pooled under my arms. Is this how Thomas felt?

"Yes, right. So Thomas and his sister have two stepparents, do they?"

I don't know whether I'd classify myself as that, but I didn't like the tone in her voice, so I said, "Yes."

"Mmm."

Mmm, what? This was the most functional family I knew. There were parents who remained together that weren't as happy as Jane and Lachlan. Or who placed their children and their needs so highly.

"Where would you like me to help?" I asked.

"The children will all bring their readers and folders in." She pointed to a corner with books. "Take their readers out, check them for damage and place them on the shelf. They will choose new ones this afternoon."

"OK."

"I'll show you," Thomas said, pulling me towards the books.

"I'm not finished yet, Thomas," Mrs Smythe said, her voice like ice.

Jeez, no wonder Thomas was struggling. He wasn't accustomed to being spoken to like this. I would come in every day if I needed to, just to make him comfortable.

"After you've done the readers, you can clean all the scissors and sort the supplies the children brought in last week."

"Got it. Where are the scissors and supplies?"

"The scissors are at the back of the room, and the supplies are in the office storeroom area."

"OK. Thanks."

Thomas led me to the reading area. He put his folder in a plastic tub. "You take the folders from here, take the books out and put the empty folders here." He put the folder in another tub.

"Don't forget to check them for damage," Mrs Smythe said.

"If I find damage, what do I do?"

"Put a sticky note on the front with the child's name and put it in my office."

"We lose points for damaged books," Thomas whispered.

I nodded. "Show me your desk."

He showed me to a desk with two seats. "Who sits next to you?"

"No one."

"He's too disruptive."

Disruptive, my ass. I took in a deep breath. I was here to help Thomas not to get upset by everything the teacher said.

The other children started coming into the classroom. They put their bag on a hook. Mrs Smythe reminded them in her firm tone to put their readers and folders in the tub. Thomas stuck close to me as I waited for the tub to fill. When the first bell went, we gave each other a kiss, and he went to his desk.

As I did my reader duty, I watched Thomas. He sat still mostly and was attentive. He got in trouble when he turned around to speak to someone behind him. My jaw tensed. Every other child had someone to talk to, some even sat in groups of four, and there was Thomas on his own. Whenever he looked my way, I gave him a smile or a thumbs-up. I wanted him to know he was doing good.

I stayed until recess, completing the jobs Mrs Smythe asked me to do. I wasn't going to say anything to Lachlan and Jane yet about Mrs Smythe. I couldn't just base my opinion on one day. I needed to know more.

***

"HI, HONEY," Mom said, smiling at me through the screen. What was she up to? I swear if she started talking careers again, I'd hang up on her.

"Hi, Mom."

"How have you been?"

I didn't want to tell her anything but the bare minimum. "Fine. How about you and Dad?"

"We're good. Dad's been very busy. There's a new specialist hospital opening in Chicago. He's been doing some consulting work."

"That's great."

"You received a letter from the mayor's office today."

I'd received a few since the accident. I hadn't replied to any. I hadn't told my parents about them either.

"It says that they've been trying to contact you about the local hero award."

I tensed. "Yes, I know. Please throw it away."

"Peyton, this is a prestigious award."

I sighed. "How about you show me some decency and don't open my mail?"

"Peyton, you're being praised for what you did."

I bet the only thing she was concerned about was how good this would look.

"You should receive accolades," she said.

"Mom, drop it."

She glanced to her side. I'd won this battle, for now. But she wouldn't give up.

I didn't deserve that award. What I'd done was instinct.

"How is Lachlan?" she asked.

"He's good."

"And Scarlet and Thomas?"

What was she up to? She never asked about them so directly.

"They're good. They started school last week."

"Does that mean your nanny job is over?"

"No. It's just different from what it was before."

"I thought the completion of your nanny contract would mean you're returning home."

That's what she was up to.

"My contract wasn't just for the summer. It's ongoing."

"Is there another reason you're staying?"

"Yes. I'm happy here."

She scrutinised me. What was she seeing?

"Speak soon, Mom." I hung up before she could reply.

I was not going to let her ruin my happiness or poison my mind. I loved what I had here. This was nothing like what I'd had with them. I wasn't putting myself last anymore.

CHAPTER FORTY-TWO

Lachlan

My phone rang. The number on my screen said the call came from the United States. That was weird. I didn't have any contacts over there.

I pressed the answer button. "Lachlan Harris speaking."

"Hello, Lachlan, this is Cecily Carter, Peyton's mother."

Peyton's mum. Why was she calling me?

"Hi. Did you need to speak to Peyton? She's not with me at the moment."

"No, Lachlan. It's you I wanted to speak to." She was very formal and pronounced her words crisply.

I walked away from Bruce and the water trough we were cleaning.

"How can I help you, Cecily?"

"I would like to speak to you about Peyton's return home."

I stopped dead in my tracks, my stomach in my mouth. "She hasn't told me she's leaving."

"I don't believe she would have. But I believe it's in her best interests."

"What do you mean?" I was surprised I could even find words.

"A farm in Australia is no place for a lady like Peyton. She is accustomed to the finer things in life."

"She likes her life here just fine."

"She deserves much better, Lachlan. She deserves a better career than a nanny."

I planted my feet firmly. "That's for Peyton to decide."

"Perhaps. But she is not making any sensible decisions while she's there with you."

"She'll decide when she's ready."

"Becoming a doctor is no easy feat. She went through eight years of college before starting her internship. She has dedicated more time to her career than the time your children have been alive. She shouldn't throw that away."

What was I supposed to say about that?

"While we are on the subject of *decisions* and *you*, I don't believe staying with you is wise."

I clutched the phone. "Excuse me. You know nothing about me."

"I know you are a farmer, and she was engaged to a surgeon."

"A person you chose for her. A person she was not happy with. A person who did not support her through her recovery."

"And you believe she is happy with you?"

"Yes. And I'm happy with her."

There was a pause, too long of a pause. I stood rigid.

"The relationship is new," Cecily finally said. "Do you think you and your children will be enough for someone like Peyton in the long run?"

Who the fuck did this woman think she was?

"Lachlan, let me explain the life Peyton led before she started working for you. She never wanted for anything. She never suffered any economic hardships."

I kicked at a tuft of grass.

"She led a lifestyle where she could buy whatever she liked and go wherever she liked. How does that compare to living on a farm?"

My heart pounded. How many more things were on her list?

"She can't keep hiding. She needs to come home."

"Thank you for your call, Cecily. I will leave the decisions about our lives to Peyton and me."

I hung up and stared at the phone. What the fuck was that? I strode back to Bruce.

"Are you OK to finish on your own?" I asked.

His eyebrows drew together. "Why? Where are you going?"

"I'm going to walk back."

"From here? Why? What's wrong?"

"I need to think."

I left before he could ask anything else. I walked across the paddock, not paying attention to anything around me. I'd never been spoken to by anyone so rude in my whole life. Cecily knew nothing about Peyton, me, or our relationship. We were happy. Peyton got us. She fit in perfectly. I didn't need to compromise my children or the farm for her. Was that why our relationship was good? Because I didn't have to compromise anything for her? Would I compromise my duty for her? Yes, no, I don't fucking know. Was that fair? No, it wasn't fucking fair. She deserved someone who would burn the world down for her.

I was so fucking stupid to believe this could work, that I

would be enough for Peyton. She deserved so much more. She had so much more before she came here.

Jane knew what farm life could be like, she'd been born into it, and she never wanted to live it again. And here was Peyton, someone who lived at the top of American society, living it every day. But she hadn't seen the hardships yet—the drought, the starving cattle, the mouse plagues. The honeymoon period would be over then.

And what about the kids? They'd get closer to her, and she'd leave them. How much closer could they get? Thomas had already declared that he loved her, and Scarlet told Stacy that Peyton made her happy. They'd be destroyed.

Fuck.

I kept walking.

The crux of it was that she wouldn't stay. Like Jane before her, she would leave. And it wouldn't just be because of the farm. It would be because I couldn't give her what she needed. I can't give her riches or status or whatever else someone from her standing should have. Me, myself—I'm not enough. I could never be enough.

I balled my hands into fists. I would never be enough.

Bruce caught up to me once I got to the road. He stopped the car next to me. "Getting in?"

I wanted to keep walking, but there was no point. I'd thought about all there was to think about. I got in the car.

"Do you want to talk about it?" he asked as we drove off.

"No."

"Who was on the phone?" He wasn't going to give up.

"Peyton's mother."

Bruce looked at me from the corner of his eye. "What did she want?"

She wanted lots of things. But I didn't want to share

them all with Bruce. I didn't need him to reason with me. Everything Peyton's mother said was true.

"Just to remind me how different Peyton and I are."

Bruce grunted. "Are you though?"

"Yes."

We drove in silence. When we got back to the shed, I got out of the car.

"Don't do anything stupid," Bruce said.

Doing the right thing wasn't stupid. I knew where we were heading; I might as well get there sooner. I'd been fooling myself this whole time, living in some dreamland where Peyton was happy with us, with me. I'd never thought of forever, but now that I did, forever was impossible. I couldn't keep someone like Peyton happy.

There were so many thoughts running through my head that I didn't know which one I was going to start with when I got home. It didn't matter. None of them were good.

My heart was tearing. It would hurt less if it was ripped out of my chest. Each word from the phone call stabbed me harder and deeper—a farm is no life for Peyton, she deserves better, you are not enough for her, it's time for her to come home. Peyton was hiding here, and I was hiding from the truth. Those words were the truth.

I walked in the back door. Peyton was on the lounge watching TV.

She looked at me and smiled. "You're home early."

"The kids get home, OK?" Dumb question. I had to start with something.

"I dropped their things off at Jane's after I helped in class."

I nodded, then headed to the bathroom to shower. Peyton followed me. Normally that would excite me, but now it made my stomach churn.

I turned to her. I took a deep breath in. I needed to stay calm.

"Your mother called me today."

Her arms crossed over her chest. "My mother?"

"Yes. She told me that you're hiding here."

Peyton frowned. "I'm not hiding. I'm living."

That was bullshit. I clenched my fists.

"Until what? You realise there's something better out there?"

"Better than what? You? The kids? Love?"

I grunted. "Love? You don't love me."

My breaths were coming fast and shallow. We needed to stop fucking pretending. It was time we both saw this for what it was—an illusion.

I needed to stop the pain before it consumed me and ruined me.

And she needed to go back to her real life.

CHAPTER FORTY-THREE

Peyton

MY STOMACH CLENCHED as if it had just been punched. I stumbled back. "Excuse me?"

"You don't love me. You've never even bothered saying the fucking words."

"I do love you."

A mirthless laugh seeped from his lips. "Oh, come on, Peyton. You're hiding here from your real life. One where you have everything, including a boy to shovel snow from your front path."

"What are you even talking about?"

He ran his hand through his hair. "Your home is not here. As soon as you get bored with us, you'll go back. Save us all that heartbreak, and go back now."

I sucked in a breath and backed farther away from him.

Lachlan nodded as if something just dawned on him. "It all makes sense now. You never speak about home. It's like if you opened that door, you'd be tempted to walk straight back in."

I shook my head.

Lachlan huffed and gave me a hard stare. "Farming is fucking hard. There are no five-star holidays here. You're not made for this."

Tears sprung to my eyes. How could he speak to me like this? I'd expect this from my mother, not him. She'd gotten into his head. And he'd let her. He didn't believe in me. I was stupid to think that anyone ever would.

"What do you want from us?" he said.

Want from them?

"What do you want from us?" he asked again.

What did he think? I loved them. Obviously, my love wasn't enough. I wasn't enough.

"I want nothing from you," I said. "You're just like them."

He stepped back, blinking.

"I'll pack my things and move back into the unit."

"Good."

"I'll wait for you to employ a new nanny unless you want me to leave straight away?"

I didn't want to leave yet. I still needed to help Thomas. Thomas. Scarlet. I loved them both so much, and now I had to leave them. And Lachlan. My heart plummeted. His love for me may not have been real, but theirs was.

"I'll speak to Jane," he said.

"You do that. Make all the decisions for me that you want."

I stormed off. When I got to the bedroom door, I turned around. "Don't forget to call my mother as well, seeing that you're best buds."

I slammed the door behind me. I grabbed my suitcase out from under my bed and started shoving my things inside. Crap. Half my things were in Lachlan's room. I wasn't going in there while he was at home. I'd get them tomorrow when he was at work.

As soon as I heard the water turn on for the shower, I made my way out. What if he decided to bring the rest of my things over? Forget that. I didn't want to see him unless it was absolutely necessary. I wrote him a note to tell him I'd pick them up while he was at work.

I walked to my unit. Bruce was sitting on the step, waiting for me. I stopped in front of him, gripping the suitcase handle to stop my hands from shaking.

"Are you OK?" he asked, standing up.

"Fine."

"What did he do?"

"Told me I was leaving. He just needs to decide when."

He shook his head. "Dick head."

I shrugged. "I shouldn't have believed someone could love me for who I am. That someone could believe in me."

My mother must have painted a very good picture of me. The me she wanted me to be. Not the me I was. And he believed every single word. He'd seen me, listened to me, knew who I was. At least, I thought he did. But it was all a fallacy.

Bruce strode towards me and pried my hands from the handle. He held them tight. "I love you for who you are, Peyton. He does too."

His strong hands were comforting. Not like Lachlan's. But Lachlan's comfort was nothing but a lie.

I gave him a weak smile. "It doesn't matter. He's decided. And I need to respect that. And I need to respect myself."

Bruce hugged me. "I'll see you tomorrow."

I went inside my unit. I'd loved this space when I first

got here. It had been my own private oasis. Now it was a prison where I awaited my sentence.

I WATCHED the class while I sorted through the readers. Thomas still sat on his own. I clenched my teeth. Enough was enough. I didn't know how much longer I had here, and I needed to speak my mind while I had the chance.

At recess, Thomas came up to me and gave me a hug. Mrs Smythe was watching.

"I love you, Peyton," he said.

I hugged him tighter and gave him a kiss. My throat clogged. "I love you too, Thomas." I separated from him. "Go out and play. I'll see you tomorrow."

He gave me a kiss and then ran outside.

I turned to Mrs Smythe. "Do you have a minute? I'd like to discuss something with you, please."

"Recess is short."

"That's OK. I can come back after school if you prefer."

She sighed. "No. No. Now is fine."

I looked at the door to make sure Thomas had left.

"I would like to understand why Thomas is still sitting on his own."

"He's disruptive."

"Is he? I haven't seen any evidence of that."

"You wouldn't, would you? Loved ones are often biased and can't see faults in the students."

"He talks to the other students in class because that is the type of person he is. He is kind and friendly."

"Friendly children don't get into fights."

I took a deep breath. "Do you know why he had a fight?"

Mrs Smythe stared at me.

"The bully in grade 2, who teachers seem to know about but can't control, or won't—I'm not sure which—stole Susie's book. He wouldn't give it back. Susie was crying. Thomas took it off him and gave it back to her. Then that bully punched a five-year-old."

Mrs Smythe raised her eyebrows.

"I take it from your reaction you didn't know that. Why didn't you ask him?"

"I—"

"Is it because you had a preconceived idea about his home life?" I didn't hide the anger in my voice.

"I must admit I was confused about how he explained his family."

"Right. Let me tell you about his family. They are the most functional family I know. Everyone in Thomas and Scarlet's life loves them." I couldn't stop now that I'd started. "Their parents remain friends, even though they're divorced. They attend school functions together. They share milestones together. They're better than a lot of traditional families."

We stared at each other. I wanted to give it to her, all my anger and frustration. But I was here to help Thomas. Not make it worse for him.

"I don't think it's fair that no one asked Thomas what happened that day," I said in a measured tone.

"I'm sorry."

"It's not me you should say that to. It's Thomas."

She nodded.

"Please put Thomas at a table with someone. Maybe Susie. Because his friendliness will help with her shyness."

She released a shaky breath. "That's a good idea."

I wiped my hands on my jeans. "Thank you for taking

the time to listen to me."

She smiled. Actually smiled. "I don't think I had much choice."

I returned her smile. "Probably not. I got a bit passionate there."

"Will you be back tomorrow?"

"If that's OK with you."

"Yes, I appreciate your help."

"Thank you."

She didn't know how much that meant to me. And I hung onto it as I drove home. It wasn't really my home. It was a place that held my heart, that had helped me learn who I was. I thought I knew who I was until yesterday. I thought I was loved until yesterday.

I walked into the silent house. I had an hour before Lachlan came home for lunch. I went into my old room to make sure I had everything. I sat on the bed and scanned the room. This bed was where Lachlan placed me that night when I told him for the first time that I liked him. Why was I so brave then and not now?

I went into his room next. Only yesterday, I referred to it as our room. I stood in the doorway, the one I'd stood in when I'd invited Lachlan to look at me. And he had, without an ounce of disgust. The bed was the place he'd first told me he loved me. I took a shaky breath, then rushed in and grabbed my things. The tears made it hard to see, but I knew my way around. I didn't need clear eyes. I shoved things into my bag with trembling hands.

I needed to get out of there before Lachlan returned. I went into the ensuite. I pushed the memory of our first shower sex out of my mind. That was Christmas Day. Christmas Day would never be the same again. Best I ignored its existence for the rest of eternity.

CHAPTER FORTY-FOUR

Lachlan

BRUCE DUMPED a box of cattle lick blocks onto the quad. He strode back to the shelf to grab another one. He swung around to face me.

"You're a fucking idiot," Bruce said, shaking his head.

"I don't want to hear it."

"I don't care. What were you thinking?"

I huffed. "I was thinking about the children. The longer Peyton stays, the more attached they'll be."

Bruce gave me a sarcastic smile. "The more attached you'll be, you mean. "

"No, they'll be heartbroken when she leaves. My duty is their wellbeing."

Bruce stared at me. "Stop hiding behind your fucking duty." He walked to the quad. "Do you have any idea how much you hurt her?"

I didn't mean to hurt Peyton. But this was best for all of us. "She needs to go home. She doesn't belong here."

"Argh. You don't get to decide where she does or doesn't belong."

"She wasn't going to decide."

"Uh, I reckon she already decided. But you're too fucking dumb to see it."

I rubbed my hand down my face. He wasn't listening. There was no point to this conversation. She was leaving, and that's all there was to it. Better to do it now than months down the track when she decided she belonged in her comfortable high-society life and we weren't enough.

My phone vibrated.

Jane - *Mrs Smythe would like to talk to us. Is 10 am OK?*

Oh no, was Thomas in trouble again?

Me - *yes, I'll make the time.*

Jane - *good, speak to you then. She'll send a meeting link.*

After the call would be a good time to talk to Jane about Peyton.

Me - *we need to talk about something else after the call. Do you have time?*

Jane - *sure.*

I turned to Bruce. "I'll check the southern paddocks. I need to be back by ten. We have a meeting with Thomas's teacher."

Bruce stopped scowling. "Is everything OK?"

"Jane didn't say."

He hopped onto the quad. "I'll go north. I'll see you when I get back."

I headed out. Was Thomas in trouble again? We'd never had to speak to Scarlet's teacher twice in a month. Peyton hadn't said anything to us. Why wouldn't she tell us about something as important as this?

10:00 a.m. took forever to come around. I set myself up in the workshop, but it was stifling. I moved outside instead and clicked on the link. Jane was already waiting. She gave me a concerned smile. Mrs Smythe came on the screen seconds later.

"Thank you for taking the time to speak to me."

"Is Thomas alright?" I asked.

Mrs Smythe smiled. "Thomas is fine. Peyton has made sure of that."

What did Peyton have to do with this apart from helping in class?

"Thomas and I have had a good talk about the fight and how he's settling in."

Jane and I made eye contact.

"Thomas is a very kind boy. Too talkative sometimes, but I'm sure we can work with that."

I released a relieved breath.

Jane let out a small laugh. "Sometimes he can't help himself."

Mrs Smythe nodded. "Peyton has given me some tips."

Peyton again.

"That's it, really. I'm sorry that I didn't take the time initially to understand Thomas. I'm sure everything will be great going forward."

"Thank you for letting us know," Jane said.

"I cannot tell you how highly Peyton speaks of you and your family."

Jane smiled. "We feel the same about her."

I nodded. Jane was going to kill me.

"I'll keep you updated on Thomas. Thanks again for making the time. I know you're both busy. Goodbye."

"Bye," Jane and I said in unison.

We hung up, and Jane called me straight back.

"What did you want to talk about?" she asked.

"We need a new nanny."

"What?"

"Peyton's leaving."

"Leaving? What are you talking about? Why would she leave?"

I didn't answer.

"What did you do?"

My jaw stiffened. "Why do you assume that I did something?"

"Because Peyton wouldn't leave otherwise. She loves you and the children."

Why did everyone say that? Peyton didn't love me. The children, maybe, but not me.

"Peyton doesn't belong here, Jane. She has a better life to go to."

"Peyton is not me, Lachlan. If she wasn't happy or didn't want to stay, she would have told you."

I sighed. Why couldn't they see what I saw?

"I love you, Lachlan, but you have to be one of the stupidest people I know."

"Can we just get back to the nanny replacement?"

"I'm not doing anything until I speak to Peyton."

For fuck's sake, what was the point?

CHAPTER FORTY-FIVE

Peyton

My phone rang. It was Jane. I took a deep breath and answered. No point avoiding the inevitable.

"Hi, Jane," I said as her face appeared on my screen.

"Hi, Peyton. Are you OK?"

What was I going to say? I closed my eyes. I hadn't hidden from my feelings since I'd been here. I needed to stay true to myself. I opened my eyes.

"Not really. I wasn't expecting this." I did well keeping my tears at bay.

"I'm so sorry. I don't know what has gotten into Lachlan."

I shrugged. "I guess it's better that it happened now."

"It would be better if it didn't happen at all." She pursed her lips. "You two are perfect for each other."

"I thought so. But Lachlan doesn't."

"What happened exactly?"

"He told me I didn't belong here and asked me to leave."

There was no point rehashing it. He'd made his decision.

"Bruce said your mother called him."

"Yes."

"And?"

"He chose to listen to her and not me."

"Listen to her about what?"

I shrugged. I had no idea what they'd actually spoken about. I didn't care. His reaction was what mattered. He'd torn my heart in two.

She shook her head.

"I have to leave," I said. "I can't stay here."

"I don't want you to leave."

The whole purpose of my job was to help Lachlan with the children. Being close to him was no longer an option. Therefore, I couldn't do my job.

"I can't stay where I'm not wanted."

She sighed. "I'll advertise tomorrow. Let me know if you change your mind."

I was grateful that she didn't try to convince me to stay. At least someone respected my decisions.

"I'll stay until you find someone."

I'd probably regret that decision. But more time with Scarlet and Thomas would outweigh seeing Lachlan every day.

"Thank you. And thank you for all you've done for Thomas at school."

I smiled. That kid was the best. "It was my pleasure."

"I don't know how you're going to break it to Mrs Smythe. She thinks you're the best thing since sliced bread."

The tear in my heart got its very first stitch.

"Talk soon," Jane said.

"Bye."

I put my phone down and stared at the blank TV screen. Breaking it to Mrs Smythe was going to be easier than breaking it to Scarlet and Thomas. But that wasn't my job. That's what they had parents for. So much for being a part of their family.

But I couldn't stay. I couldn't stay with someone who took my choices away. I couldn't stay in a place where my decisions weren't respected. Or where I wasn't loved.

My chest squeezed.

He didn't believe I loved him. He said I'd never said the words. That day he said the word love, he said he would love me more because of my scars. I hadn't known exactly what he meant. Had I told him that I loved him? I searched my memory, but nothing came to mind. Had I really never said the words? I felt them. I felt them in my whole being.

I sighed. I needed a plan for what I was going to do next and where I was going to go. Boston wasn't an option. I didn't want to find myself back in the same situation I'd been in before, where I had no control over my life.

I could stay in Australia and find another job. That would allow me to keep my independence. As a nanny? Maybe not. In the medical field? Maybe. It would mean my eight years at college weren't for naught. As my parents pointed out, there were lots of options. I didn't necessarily need to be a surgeon or specialist. If I did choose that avenue, it would be on my own terms, my own choice, what I wanted.

Heavy footsteps sounded on the stairs. My heart raced, and I turned toward the sound. Bruce waved at me through the door, and I got up to let him in.

"How are you?" he asked as he stepped inside.

"Shit."

He nodded. "I bet. Do you need anything?"

"No thanks."

He sat on the couch. "Do you want to talk about it?"

I gave him a nudge as I sat beside him. "Listen to you, all ready to talk about feelings."

"I learnt from the best."

"Maybe you can teach your brother a thing or two."

"I doubt it. He's as stubborn as a bull."

Even Ben wasn't that stubborn.

"I thought that I'd found my home." I started to cry even though I didn't want to. "Now I need to find somewhere else to go."

"You won't go back to your parents?"

The tears wouldn't stop. "Not after what my mother has done."

He put his arm around me. "You can stay with Kaley and me."

"And interrupt your baby-making activities? I don't think so."

He gave my shoulders a squeeze. "Are you coming to the semi-final tonight?"

I shook my head.

I wanted to hear Lachlan sing. But I couldn't. I couldn't sit there and let his voice capture my heart. Not when it was the same voice that tore it apart.

CHAPTER FORTY-SIX

Lachlan

THE EXCITEMENT in the pub was almost palpable. I didn't take much notice. Without Peyton by my side, everything felt pointless. The only reason I was here, singing, was because of her. Everyone at the table was more sedate than usual. Thomas and Scarlet had asked for Peyton. Jane gave some lame excuse.

Stacy came over and gave us all a quick scan. "Where's your girlfriend?"

"She was sick of seeing your face," Kayley said.

With wide eyes, we all turned to her. Kayley never said a bad word about anyone.

Stacy grabbed my attention by touching my arm. "Do you want to catch up for a drink later?"

I pulled my arm away. "Stacy, you're an excellent singer, but you lack eloquence. I'm not interested in you, nor will I ever be interested in you."

She pouted. "So why do you talk to me then?"

"Because that's what polite people do."

"Your girlfriend doesn't talk to me. That's not very polite."

I took a deep breath. "Is there something you need, Stacy? I'd like to get back to my family."

She glanced around the table. "No."

"OK. Good luck tonight."

I turned away and took a seat at the table. Stacy stood still for a moment as if considering something and then walked off. Donna pulled her aside and started talking to her. Donna's stance was stiff, and her set jaw showed she wasn't happy. What was that about?

"That girl doesn't know how to take no for an answer," Mum said.

"Yeah."

"I'd take Peyton over her any day," Bruce said.

Me too. But there was no point thinking about it. She'd be gone soon.

"Have you spoken to her?" Mum asked.

I looked pointedly at the children. Now was not the time to talk about Peyton. Mum shook her head at me and frowned, disappointment written all over her face.

"What songs are you singing tonight?" Jane asked.

I was still undecided. This was something I would have spoken to Peyton about. She would have helped me.

"I don't know."

"Well, you better decide quickly. What have you narrowed it down to?"

I told them the songs.

Bruce shook his head. "No one wants to hear depressing shit."

Kayley elbowed him. "I think one of those songs would be good."

Mum nodded. "Yes, one is good. Then something upbeat."

"Yeah, and maybe bang out a rock song," Jane said.

We discussed the songs until my set came up. I needed to put my feelings aside and put my best effort in. As I sang and looked out into the crowd, I searched for Peyton's face at our table. She was always mesmerised when she looked back at me. My heart dropped every time I couldn't find her. But what did I expect?

I concentrated on the rest of the crowd and gave them a good show.

BRUCE STOOD in the doorway of the gym like he had all that time ago when he came to give me shit about Peyton.

"What do you want?" I asked as I finished a set of shoulder presses.

"Nothing."

"Bull shit."

Bruce shrugged. "Just wanted to see how you are."

"I'm fine. "

Bruce laughed. There was no humour in it. "Right. You've been in a bad mood for days."

"What? Because I expect you to pull your weight?" I wiped the sweat off my face and faced him.

"Because I don't?"

"You never do."

Bruce stood up straight. "Don't start a fight with me because you fucked up."

"I'm not in the mood, Bruce."

"To hear the truth?"

I turned away.

"Peyton was the best thing that ever happened to you."

"My kids are the best thing that's ever happened to me."

"They're two different things."

I wanted to say one mattered more than the other, but saying that was disrespectful. Why the hell did I care about respect now? I'd shown none to Peyton. I hadn't even given her a chance to talk for herself. I'd just run over the top of her like a stampede of cows. She was right; I was no better than her parents.

"Is there anything you actually want?" I asked him, exhausted.

"Like I said, to see how you are."

I spun around, the towel clenched in my fist. "I'm shit. OK? Is that what you want to hear?"

"The truth at last."

"I just need to live with it. She's leaving. I did that."

He went to say something but stopped himself.

I walked Bruce out and watched him drive away. I stood outside the house and gazed at the moon. Peyton and I had kissed under that moon only months ago. The night that she was brave enough to let me see her. She showed me parts of her no one had ever seen. She'd trusted me with all of her, and I had doubted her. What was wrong with me?

Love wasn't just about words. It was about trust. She told me things and shared her feelings and her fears. You don't do that unless you trust someone, unless you love someone. The truth slammed into my chest, and I couldn't breathe.

I tore my gaze away from the moon and looked at the unit. Peyton was in there now, only hundreds of feet away. What was she doing? Thinking? I had no right to ask.

I walked inside my house. It was empty now without Peyton. How could one person make a house feel alive?

Make me feel alive? Even when it was announced last night that I'd gotten through to the final round, I was numb. It wasn't the same without Peyton.

I sighed. I'd never disappointed someone so much in my life. I knew her fears. I knew how she'd been treated. And yet I'd done the same to her.

The house was empty, and my bed was empty. I'd had a chance at happiness, and I'd thrown it away. Bruce was right. She was the best thing that'd ever happened to me, apart from the children.

I could have had the farm, my family, love and singing too. Peyton had shown me it was all possible. I was through to the grand finale. I needed to write a song. All I could think of was heartbreak. And Peyton.

CHAPTER FORTY-SEVEN

Peyton

Mr Harrison was making his way out for his nightly walk. How funny that I had been scared of him that first night. Now, I looked forward to hearing him. He was my tie to the real world when I was alone at night. And alone I was.

I should have stood my ground with Lachlan instead of retreating into my old self. I should have respected myself enough to tell him he was wrong and that he had no right to treat me like that. I should have told him I wanted to stay. I should have told him that I didn't speak about Boston and my life there because I didn't need it. My happiness was here. He was angry, and he wasn't listening, but I still should have told him. If for no other reason, I should have done it for myself.

But not only that, Lachlan may have said the words, but I believed them. In that moment, I believed I couldn't be loved for who I was. But the more I thought about it, he did love me for who I was. Until that last day, he listened to me.

Not just my words but the intent behind them. He asked for my opinion. He made me feel loved. I'd never felt like that before.

Lachlan made me feel loved.

I stared up at the ceiling. Would I ever feel like that again? He loved all of me, including my scars. It was about time I did the same. I shouldn't be ashamed of them or embarrassed by them. They were a testament to me saving a life. Lachlan saw that.

Lachlan's treatment of me was wrong, but so was my reaction. As soon as he'd mentioned my mother, my defences had gone up. I couldn't reason with myself, let alone him. I knew the power she had and how she could zero in on your weaknesses, your doubts. But for her to zero in, they must have existed in the first place, even if they were minuscule. She'd grab onto them and twist them so much they were on the outside, completely exposed.

Because of her, him, and me, I'd lost my chance of happiness. His touch at night. The way he looked at me with adoration. The children joining us in bed in the morning. My feeling of being enough. Lost. All lost.

I could go to him now and speak to him. But he had the same opportunity. He could come to me and start the conversation that could begin to repair our relationship. But he chose not to. Bruce said Lachlan loved me, but maybe he didn't love me enough.

I WAITED at the school gate for Thomas and Scarlet. When they saw me, their faces lit up, and they ran to me. I hugged them both and soaked up their love. Coming home day was the best day for me.

"How was your day?" I asked as I bundled their stuff into the car.

"I did art today," Scarlet said. "We had to draw a picture of our family."

"That sounds like fun."

"I was going to draw everyone, but there wasn't enough room. So I drew you and Dad, Thomas and me, and Mum and Dan."

My chest constricted. If only I was her family. I was still part of her life now. But soon, I wouldn't be. They would get a new nanny, and I would fade from their memories.

"That sounds great."

We drove out of the car park.

"I'm going to put it on the fridge. I bet it makes Dad happy when we're not there."

"I'm sure it will." Except for the picture of me. "What reader did you bring home, Thomas?"

He was getting good at reading now. Mrs Smythe had given me a new job in class. I listened to the children read. A few every day. It was fun seeing which books they chose.

"The tractor one."

I laughed. I think he'd taken that home five times already. "Again?"

"It's my favourite."

"Mrs Smythe might have to find you some new farm ones."

His eyes lit up.

I listened as they told me about their friends and their playground antics. The hour drive didn't feel like an hour with them in the car. When we parked in the carport, they jumped out of the car and started toward the house.

"Hey," I called out. They both turned.

"Have you forgotten something?" I headed to the trunk to get their bags out.

"Sorry," Scarlet said as she retrieved her school bag. Thomas did the same. I carried the remainder and followed them to the house.

I hadn't been inside since I'd collected the last of my things. The place I'd considered home was no such thing anymore. I went through the kitchen door. Unwashed dishes were in the sink. Bread was left on the kitchen counter instead of being put back in the fridge. The washing was in a basket sitting on one of the dining room chairs.

I'd never seen it like this before.

I put the kids' bags down. "Can you take these to your room, please?"

They collected the bags, and I made a start on cleaning the kitchen.

"What's for afternoon tea?" Thomas asked.

"I made some frittata with our homegrown zucchini. I'll have to go get it from the unit."

"Why's it in the unit?" Scarlet asked. Lachlan hadn't told them I'd moved out of the house? How had he kept that a secret?

"I've moved back there. Uncle Bruce and your dad finished it."

Scarlet cocked her head. "It's been finished for weeks. I thought you lived here now."

"No, your dad and I thought it was best I move back there."

"Why?" Thomas asked.

Damn Lachlan. Why hadn't he told the kids?

"Did you have a fight?" Scarlet asked.

I put the bread away. My mind raced. How was I going to answer them?

"When are you coming back?" Thomas asked.

I couldn't answer. I didn't want to. I did something I'd never done with them before; I avoided their question. "I'm going to get the frittata. I won't be long."

I strode out of the house and across the lawn. I shouldn't have avoided the question. I'd always been honest with them before. Ben walked along the fence line, following me. That bull was my most loyal friend.

When I got back, they were sitting on the lounge watching *Bluey*. I cut up some frittata for them and took it to the table.

"Here you go."

They came to the table, and I went to the kitchen to wash the dishes. Lachlan's car pulled into the carport. That was my cue to leave.

"Your dad's home now. I'll see you both in the morning."

"Aren't you staying?" Scarlet asked.

"No. This is time for you and your dad."

Thomas chewed his food quickly. "I don't want you to go."

Tears sprung into my eyes. I needed to get out before I was trapped in here with Lachlan. I could hear his boots along the path. My palms became clammy.

"I'll see you in the morning," I said, heading toward the door. It opened before I had a chance to open it myself. I jumped.

Lachlan stood on the threshold. He had stubble on his jaw like he hadn't shaved for a couple of days and dark circles under his eyes. I stepped forward, closing the distance between us. Still, he stood and stared. I stepped forward again, forcing him out of the way.

"The kids have had afternoon tea," I said to his chest. I couldn't make eye contact with him. I couldn't fall into the trap of his warm brown eyes. Or dark and angry. Angry was the last thing I'd seen. The coldness of that anger in his once warm eyes was imprinted on my brain.

"Thank you," he said.

"I'll come over after you leave for work."

I didn't wait for his answer. I walked so fast that it was almost a jog. My chest constricted to the point that breathing was hard.

Jane needed to find a nanny soon. The pain in my chest was just too much.

Why hadn't Lachlan told the kids?

Surely they'd asked for me when they called at night. He'd have to face the music now.

CHAPTER FORTY-EIGH T

Lachlan

As soon as I stepped into the kitchen, Scarlet asked, "Why is Peyton living in the unit?"

"We decided it was best."

"That's what she said," Thomas replied.

"What did you fight about?" Scarlet asked.

I didn't want to answer their questions or admit my stupidity. But that was the coward's way out. I needed to be strong like Peyton. She was always honest, even when the answers were hard.

"I listened to someone I shouldn't have and said some bad things."

"Then why don't you just say sorry?"

"Yeah," Thomas said.

"Sometimes sorry isn't enough."

"When I was mean to Thomas, Peyton made sure we said sorry to each other. It made us friends again."

"I don't think it will work. Sometimes it's different for adults."

"So you're just going to give up?"

I studied my eight-year-old daughter. I would never tell one of them to give up on something they wanted. So why was I?

"No. I'm not going to give up."

"Good."

Scarlet and Thomas watched me. Then they began talking quietly together, glancing at me every now and then.

I needed to speak to Peyton. I needed to start with sorry. Even if she couldn't find it in her heart to forgive me, she deserved an apology. But she wouldn't even look me in the face and was avoiding me like the plague. We lived on the same property, but I hadn't seen her in days. I could have seen her if I had had enough balls to go to the unit. Why hadn't I? What the fuck was I even doing? She'd been honest and open with me from the beginning. She even had the strength to tell me I made her feel uncomfortable. And I hadn't afforded her the same respect. I should have said something the moment I began thinking even the smallest negative thought.

I'd hurt her so bad I couldn't see a way back from this.

I might need to enlist some help.

"You can write her a love song," Scarlet said.

That kid was a genius. I had five days before the final.

I LEFT the house and walked towards my car. Peyton had been waiting for me to leave. Before I'd even made it to the carport, her door opened. I listened hard, wanting to hear her footsteps, but they were too soft against the grass.

This is what it had been like since the kids had come home. I was always desperate to hear or see her. But she was too careful, always timing her arrival or departure for when I wasn't around. I was lucky to see her retreating back.

It wasn't enough for me. I needed more. I needed her.

And knowing she was scurrying to get away from me tore me apart. I'd hurt her so bad she couldn't even be near me. I picked Bruce up from the shed, and we drove along the fence line. We needed to spray the grass before it got out of hand.

"I fucked up," I said.

"That's already been established."

I took a deep breath. "I can't live without her, Bruce. My life is so empty."

He was quiet for once.

"I need your help," I said.

"With what?"

"Scarlet said I should write Peyton a love song."

Bruce nodded. "Smart kid. You want me to help you write it?"

I swallowed my laughter. "No. I want you to convince Peyton to come to the final."

He whistled. "You're going to sing it to her there?"

"I can't think of a better place."

He nodded. "You do have a lot to make up for."

"I know. I don't know if it'll be enough, but I have to try."

"Have you written the song?"

"Mostly. I think it's OK."

"OK, isn't going to cut it. OK, won't win you the competition."

"I'm only interested in winning Peyton's heart."

Bruce grunted. "About bloody time."

"So, will you help me?"

"Fucking oath, I will."
This might just work.

CHAPTER FORTY-NINE

Peyton

BRUCE KNOCKED ON MY DOOR.

"Hi," I said as I opened it. I moved aside to let him in. Before I closed it behind him, I glanced toward the house. Lachlan was nowhere to be seen.

"How are you?" he asked.

I shrugged. "Not great."

"You should come with us to the pub tomorrow. It's the final round in the singing contest."

I'd planned to go. I wanted to watch Lachlan one last time. I'd thought about hiding up the back unnoticed. But hiding was not what I was about anymore. He needed to see me. Even if he didn't love me, I loved him, and I needed to show him.

"OK."

"That was easier than I thought it would be," Bruce said, cocking his head.

"I was going to go anyway. I want to support him."

"And don't try to sit by yourself. Sit with us," he said. "You wouldn't want to get stuck alone with Stacy."

"Ugh, that girl."

The words she said to me, the way she'd judged me, wouldn't have affected me so much if I'd just believed in myself. The way Lachlan believed in me.

"Lachlan told her straight out that he wasn't interested."

"I bet that went well."

"It went better than Kaley saying that you're sick of seeing her face."

My mouth dropped open.

"Your face looked like ours." He laughed.

"I wish I'd seen Stacy's face."

"It looked a bit like this." He pouted. I couldn't help but laugh. "We'll pick you up around six. OK?"

"Yes."

I let him out and sat on the lounge staring at the blank TV. I think this was a good plan. Being with Lachlan's family would help ease my nerves. I didn't want to let Lachlan go. Being there to support him on his big night would show him I was still there for him.

I deserve love, and I wanted Lachlan's. Bruce wouldn't have asked me to join them if Lachlan didn't want the same. But having Lachlan back wasn't all I needed. I needed to stand up to my family. My mom ought to know what she'd done was unacceptable. And I had to do it before tomorrow. I didn't want it hanging over my head or over Lachlan's head.

I picked up my phone and called my mother.

"Hello, Peyton." Her voice was light.

"Hello, Mom."

"Are you coming home soon?"

I gritted my teeth. She didn't even ask how I was. She set out to ruin my life here and didn't even care.

"No, Mom. I'm not coming home. I'm staying here."

"Oh."

"Your little act of sabotage didn't work." Well, it had, but I wasn't going to tell her that. Even if things didn't work out tomorrow night, I wouldn't tell her.

"Until you can respect me and my decisions, I don't want to speak to you."

"Peyton—"

"I don't want to hear it. I am doing what I want to do, what I need to do, to be happy."

"I want you to be happy."

"You don't get to choose what my happy is. I do. And I'm happy here with Lachlan and his family."

Gosh, I was really stretching the truth now. What if Lachlan didn't want me?

"I don't need to hide who I am with Lachlan. You and Dad are always pressuring me to do what you want, to be who you want. Here, I can be who *I* want."

"We only want what's best."

I sighed. "You're not listening to me. It's been like this my whole life. Anything I said was dismissed. No one dismisses me or my thoughts here. They want what's best for me too, but they let me decide what that is."

That is until she'd called and interfered.

"Please don't call Lachlan or me again. Not until you can respect us and our relationship."

I didn't give her a chance to respond. I hung up.

CHAPTER FIFTY

Lachlan

Bruce and Kaley hadn't arrived yet. Were they able to convince Peyton to come?

Donna came to our table. "Are you ready, Lachy?"

I looked toward the door. Still nothing. "Yes, do you need me to come up now?"

"Yes. Stacy is ready and waiting."

"OK."

I stood up to follow her.

"Good luck, Daddy," Scarlet said, giving me a hug.

Thomas joined her. I gave everyone a smile and headed to the stage. Stacy was checking her guitar.

"Hi, Stacy. Ready for the big night?"

She gave me a quick glance. "Sure am."

Donna approached. "OK. Stacy will go first. She will do one song and then hand over to you. After your first song, you will stay on stage for your second one and continue like that. You have three songs each. One of which needs to be an original."

"Too easy," I said.

Stacy nodded.

Never had a night meant so much. I wanted to win, but I wanted Peyton more. Was she here yet?

I looked back at the table. She was there. My heart raced. I watched her as her eyes searched the crowd. Her sandy brown hair was longer now and just touched her shoulders. My fingers itched to run through its silkiness. She was in a summer dress with short sleeves. My favourite colour—emerald green. It showed off her curves, and her breasts poked out the top with just the barest of skin revealed. Damn, she was beautiful. I bet she was self-conscious wearing those short sleeves. My heart swelled in my chest.

Her eyes met mine, and I nearly jumped out of my skin. She gave me a smile and a small wave. Fuck. I just wanted to run over there to kiss her.

"Hey lover boy, you keeping your mind on the job?" Donna asked.

Stacy looked up and stared at Peyton. Then she gave her a genuine smile. "She looks pretty."

What the hell? Was she trying to throw me off my game?

"She does."

"I'm sorry for being such a brat."

I swung around to face her.

She shrugged and gave Donna a sidelong glance. "Donna put me in my place in her own special way."

I laughed. "So basically, she told you that you were being a brat."

"Yeah."

We laughed together. Donna rolled her eyes.

"What do you think about doing our last song together?" Stacy asked.

I considered her.

"Sort of like a make-up song," she said.

"We haven't practised anything."

"Yeah, bad idea."

It was the first time I'd ever heard her doubt herself. I guess we would go down and burn together if it was bad.

"What would we sing?" I asked.

"I don't know. Maybe *Somewhere Over the Rainbow*. Do you know it?"

"Yes. I think we can pull it off." I had no idea why I'd agreed. Maybe because she was making an effort or maybe because I didn't want to see her lose her confidence.

Stacy turned to Donna. "Can we have an extra fifteen minutes to practice?"

"I'll give you thirty," Donna said, smiling at us.

Stacy clapped her hands. "Let's check out a couple of videos. If we can't get it right, we can just go back to our original plans."

I couldn't believe I was doing this.

CHAPTER FIFTY-ONE

Peyton

I KEPT WATCHING THE STAGE, wondering where Lachlan and Stacy had gone. She'd given me a smile when she saw me. Then she and Lachlan started talking animatedly and even laughed together.

Donna came over to our table.

"Stacy and Lachlan have a surprise for you tonight."

"What sort of surprise?" Bruce asked.

Donna rolled her eyes. "It's a surprise."

Then she turned to me. "You look stunning, Peyton."

I blushed. "Thank you."

"Stacy had trouble dragging Lachlan away. He couldn't take his eyes off you."

"Why is Stacy dragging Lachlan anywhere?" Kaley asked.

I wanted to know the same thing.

"It's a surprise," Donna said.

I clenched my jaw.

Donna rested her hand on my shoulder and laughed.

"Jealousy looks good on you. Seriously, you have no need to worry. Stacy's seen the error of her ways."

That was not comforting enough. Stacy had been downright awful for weeks. How was I supposed to believe she'd changed? And now she was off somewhere with Lachlan. The man I loved. And trusted. He wouldn't be tempted by her.

Donna's eyes paused on the green T-shirts the others were wearing. There was a picture of a guitar on the back with the saying *Lached and Loaded*. "Nice shirts."

Kayley grinned. "Do you want one?"

"I can't be seen favouring anyone," Donna said with a smile.

Lydia looked around. "You've got a big crowd here, Donna."

"You should see the beer garden. It's chockers. We've got speakers set up out there and a screen."

Dan nodded, impressed. "Is Lachlan nervous?"

Donna grinned and looked at me. "He has a lot to be nervous about, something about laying it all on the line."

What was she talking about?

"Where's Daddy?" Thomas asked.

"He's getting ready," Jane said.

"Maybe he's practising his special song," Scarlet said.

"Yeah. It's going to be so good." Thomas clapped his hands. Then he and Scarlet hugged each other. Jane gave them a look only a mother could master. They sat still in their seats. I looked around at the family but couldn't figure out what was going on.

"OK. I've got to go. I told them they only had thirty minutes to sort themselves out."

Donna went out the back. I shifted in my seat, sitting up tall, trying to see what was happening back there. Lachlan appeared. He looked amazing in jeans and a muted green, long-sleeve button-down shirt. Butterflies fluttered in my stomach. When he caught my gaze, my body froze while my insides turned to molten chocolate. He gave me a crooked grin. And that's all it took for me to know I'd done the right thing.

And for my panties to melt.

I gave him a wink.

CHAPTER FIFTY-TWO

Lachlan

HOLY SHIT. I was spellbound by the person I loved.

I couldn't tear my eyes away from Peyton. I was scared if I did, she would disappear. My heart pounded in my chest. I didn't know if I could speak, let alone sing.

She'd winked at me. It reminded me of when we teamed up and teased the kids. Was she ready to team up again?

"Lachlan," Stacy said.

"Huh?"

"Lachlan." More urgency this time. "Oh, my God. Wait until you get home."

I faced her. "What?"

"Rather than fu—having sex with your eyes, wait until you get home and do the real thing."

"I wasn't doing that."

"What were you doing then?"

"Falling in love all over again."

Stacy sighed. "Now is not the time. You need to focus."

I narrowed my eyes at her.

She put her fists on her hips. "I do not want to win because you can't concentrate."

I chuckled. "Who says you're going to win?"

"I have no choice but to win. This is my chance, and I'm going to take it."

"Chance to what?"

"Chance to prove that I can do this. My chance to prove that I can make something of myself."

"You don't need to win a competition to do that."

She gave me a small smile.

"No matter what happens tonight, Stacy, you're a talented singer. You can go places."

"Stop being so perfect," she said.

"I'm far from it. You see that woman out there." I looked towards Peyton. "She's the best thing that's ever happened to me, apart from my two kids. My fear pushed her away." I faced Stacy again. "Tonight, I'm going to win her back."

"Well, you better put on a good show then."

I would, for Peyton.

"Stacy, you're up," Donna said.

I turned to her. "Remember, the singing is not just about you. To take it to the next level, connect with the audience."

Stacy nodded, then walked on stage and waved. "Thank you for coming tonight."

Make it about them, Stacy.

"Lachlan and I are here to entertain you."

And I was going to throw fear out the door and win back the only woman for me.

CHAPTER FIFTY-THREE

Peyton

"Wow," Bruce said. as the crowd applauded for Lachlan. "They've got to be neck and neck."

He was right. They'd both sung an amazing first song. My stomach tumbled. Gosh, if I was this nervous, imagine how Lachlan was feeling.

He walked out on stage for his second song looking strong and poised. I wiped my sweaty palms on my dress. He looked straight at me, took a deep breath, and then looked around the crowd.

"Three months ago, a special person walked into my life. She is the best thing to ever happen to me."

People in the audience looked towards our table. I shifted in my seat.

Lachlan spoke directly to me. "Peyton, because of you, I believe in a forever love."

Goosebumps spread across my skin. An audible sigh spread through the room.

"This song is for you." He started strumming at a slow, steady pace with a mixture of low chords.

He sang directly to me, not even glancing at the crowd.

> "The moment I saw you, I was a goner.
> You moved my world like no one can.
> Because of you, I now believe in a forever love,
> And I want to be your forever man."

The pace picked up.

> "You took the bull by the horns.
> That bull was me.
> You could have set your sights on the world.
> Instead, you set your sights on me."

A smile appeared on my face without any command. That stubborn bull was more than I'd expected to encounter.

> "You showed me all of you,
> And you saw all of me.
> No one has ever done that before.
> You are more than my best dreams.
>
> You took the bull by the horns.
> That bull was me.
> You could have set your sights on the world.
> Instead, you set your sights on me.
>
> The light of the full moon is not as bright as
> your love.

It's more than I could ever deserve.
I will give you everything, my heart, my
    love.

The pace slowed, and his low, husky voice wrapped me in tenderness.

    Because of you, I believe in a forever love,
    And I want to be your forever man."

WITH EVERY WORD, my heart expanded until it felt like there was no room left for it in my chest. The end of the song didn't deflate it.

The people around us would have no comprehension of what the words meant to us. Tears rolled down my cheeks. He was declaring to me that I was as important as everything else in his life. The room was silent.

"I love you, Peyton."

Everyone in the room turned towards me. The silence crashed down. Their expectant faces sucked the breath out of me. But I didn't care about them. At that moment, only Lachlan mattered.

"I love you, Lachlan Harris. I want you to be my forever man."

Cheers and wolf whistles drowned out the sound of my thumping heart. Lachlan grinned and walked off stage. His arse never looked better.

"Stop staring at his arse," Bruce said.

I wiped the tears off my cheeks. Scarlet and Thomas gave each other a high five.

Stacy came out on stage and gave me a huge smile. "Phew, I don't know how I'm going to beat that."

The crowd clapped.

"That was a proposal, right?" she asked.

Cheers erupted.

"Yeah, I thought so." She looked back at Lachlan. "Did Lachlan propose or was it Peyton?"

The crowd called out our names. I blushed. Who would have thought a song about a bull could have such an effect?

"Yeah, I say Peyton too." She turned to me. "All the power to you."

The crowd quietened down.

"OK. My turn, I guess."

She sang a beautiful ballad about farmers and life on the land. We were all captivated. I bet every farmer in that room felt that song was for them, about them. When she finished, Bruce stood up and clapped. One by one, everyone did the same. Stacy smiled, waved, and left the stage.

They had one song left.

CHAPTER FIFTY-FOUR

Lachlan

"Ready?" I asked Stacy.

"Yes."

I grabbed her hand, and we walked out onto stage together. I kept hold of it as I addressed the crowd.

"Stacy and I are going to sing this last song together. I would like to thank Stacy for being a great competitor. Every round, she has inspired me to be better."

Stacy smiled at me. "Lachlan has not only made me a better singer but a better entertainer. And tonight, he has taught us all about love."

Applause from the crowd.

"This one is for all of you," I said. I let go of Stacy's hand and swung my guitar around to begin playing.

Stacy and I sang our hearts out, blending our melodies and voices. When we finished, the crowd was on their feet.

We took a bow.

"Thank you, everyone," I said.

"Thank you," Stacy said.

We walked off stage together as Donna walked on.

"What a perfect ending to such a great night," Donna said. "Let's give Stacy and Lachlan another round of applause."

Stacy gave me a hug. Once I would have cringed, but now I accepted it. All I wanted to do was go to Peyton and my family. But I couldn't just yet.

"Looks like you won the prize you wanted," Stacy said.

"I sure did."

I looked at Peyton. Thomas was sitting on her lap. Their heads were together as they talked. My heart expanded. She'd opened my stubborn heart, and it would never close again. Not as long as she was in my life, which would be forever.

"OK," Donna called out, getting everyone's attention. "The judges have made a decision."

Stacy and I walked on stage. Donna stood between us, smiling at both of us.

"The winner of our first ever singing competition is"—she looked around at the audience—"Stacy Lightfoot."

Stacy stood there, her mouth hanging open. Donna hugged her.

I picked her up and twirled her around. "Congratulations."

Tears erupted in her eyes.

"Go chase those rainbows," I said.

My rainbows were sitting at a table, cheering me on. And the newest one was better than any pot of gold.

CHAPTER FIFTY-FIVE

Peyton

"Let's sit outside for a while," Lachlan said, leading me to the bench after we parked in the carport. The drive home had been filled with light conversation about his performance and the night. He straddled the bench so he was facing me. I followed suit.

He took my hands. "I'm sorry, Peyton. I was so scared you were going to leave us that I pushed you away."

I took a deep breath. "I didn't do much to ease your mind. Instead, I just retreated into myself."

He rubbed my hands with his thumbs. "I don't want you to ever think you don't have a voice in this family."

I nodded.

"I know you felt you didn't. All I did was steamroll you."

I closed my eyes and took a breath. He knew everything about me. There was nothing I could or should hide.

"I never wanted to hide my life in Boston from you. I

didn't talk about it much because I didn't want it to taint what I have here, with you."

"That life made you who you are today. It can't take what we have away."

I nodded. "I've spoken to my mother. I told her that until she can respect my decisions and our relationship, I don't want to speak to her."

"I don't know how you survived so long."

"The accident gave me clarity about a lot of things. And it showed me how much strength I have."

He leant forward and brushed his lips against mine. "You give me strength every day. I never knew so much was possible."

"Neither did I. You have made me feel loved, wanted, respected. I can never thank you enough for that."

He leaned in close, releasing my hand and kissing me while cupping the back of my head. It was like that kiss so many months ago. And it left me breathless like that kiss had.

"I've found a home here with you," I said. "I never want to leave."

He needed to know that. He needed to know that he gave me everything I needed.

His eyes glistened. I raised my palm to his face, and he rested his cheek against it. My heart opened as this man of strength and integrity laid his heart in my hand.

"Let's go to bed," he said.

We hopped up.

"Are you disappointed you didn't win?" I asked.

"I am a little. But I got what I wanted." He squeezed my hand. "Stacy needed it more than me."

When we got to the bedroom, I said, "I don't have my PJs."

He smirked. "You don't need them."

"Is that so?"

"Maybe we can test out another one of your sex facts."

I giggled. "This could be fun. Keep your smartwatch on."

"Why?"

"It's said that the heart beats 110 bpm during an orgasm."

"How many sex facts did you learn during medical school?"

"Not many. I looked that one up," I admitted.

He strode toward me, his gaze roving across my body. "You look beautiful tonight."

His fingers found the straps of my dress and made their way to the skin beneath, touching the scarred skin of my right shoulder. He traced the hem to the top of my breasts, cupping them and pushing them up so the soft skin was exposed above the hemline.

"Nice," he said before he drew his tongue across them. "The dress needs to come off though."

I lifted my arms up, and he pulled the dress over my head.

"Everything needs to come off."

"You first."

His eyes never left mine as he undressed. As his shirt bared his chest and stomach, I licked my lips. His belt came off next, and his jeans dropped ever so slightly, showing the hair rising to his navel. The bulge in his jeans told me exactly how much he wanted me.

If he had touched me right then the wetness between my legs would have told him how much I wanted him.

I reached out, my hands eager and shaking, and undid his jeans. I slipped them off his waist. Then I took the top of his underwear and pulled them down. I bent before him, pulling everything down so he could step out. As I stood up, I took his dick in my hand and pumped it.

He closed his eyes and moaned.

My panties were soaked. I guided his hand to them. He rubbed his fingers between my legs.

"You're so fucking wet."

He reached behind me, unclasping my bra. Then he looked at each of my breasts. "Perfect."

He pulled down my panties, and there was nothing left separating his fingers from my wetness. As he rubbed and explored, he guided me to the bed.

"Lie down," he said.

I let go of him and did as he asked. He lay on top of me, nestled between my legs, his gaze trapped with mine.

"I love you, Lachlan."

I opened my legs wider, waiting.

He pushed himself inside, moving with measured strokes.

"I love you too, Peyton."

He rested on his elbows. His harsh breath brushed against my neck. Tingles spread through me.

"We're going to test every sex fact you can find," he said into my ear.

My hips met his with every stroke. "I'm sure I can find plenty."

"I hope so." His voice was no longer smooth and fluid.

He moved faster now, low grunts escaping. Tightness formed between my legs. I latched onto Lachlan's shoulders and lifted myself to meet him. He slammed into me. I threw my head back and gripped his shoulders tighter. I wasn't ready. I wanted more.

His legs tensed next to mine. "Peyton."

He came undone. I came undone. I clenched around his dick. I held tighter, crying out.

"Don't stop," I pleaded.

He slammed into me again and again. I let go of him, laying my palms flat on the bed. My back arched. My whole body pulsated. I moaned as I let my body relax into the mattress below me.

Lachlan lay his sweaty body on mine.

I loved the feeling of his weight on me. We lay there, letting our breaths slow and our heart rates return to normal.

"What was your heart rate?" I asked.

"I forgot to check."

"We'll have to do it again." I smiled. "I never knew fraternising would be so good."

He chuckled and rolled off me.

"We should fraternise until the day we die."

EPILOGUE

Peyton

LACHLAN, Scarlet, Thomas and I sat together in the front row of seats. Lachlan—my husband—and our children. Just thinking the words lifted my heart, even six months after our marriage. My palms were sweaty even though the air in the room was cold. The two seats I'd reserved for my parents beside me were empty.

"Do you think they'll come?" Lachlan asked.

"I don't know."

The last time I'd spoken to my mother was the night I told her not to call if she couldn't respect Lachlan's and my relationship. That was seven months ago. We'd invited them to the wedding but only received a polite reply saying they couldn't make it.

I wiped my hands on my emerald green dress.

"Do you feel this nervous before a performance?" I asked.

He leaned in close and whispered in my ear. "Depends on the performance."

The sly remark sent tingles across my skin.

Scarlet turned around and scanned the room. "It's full."

Butterflies took flight in my stomach, and I took a few steadying breaths. Lachlan wrapped his hand around mine. There was movement beside me, and I turned to see my mother and father taking their seats, both dressed in tailored suits.

They'd come.

"Hi, Mom, Dad," I said.

Mom leant over to kiss my cheek. Dad smiled.

"This is my husband, Lachlan."

He stood up to shake their hands. "And our children, Thomas and Scarlet."

Mom's eyebrows raised ever so slightly. Lachlan sat down, and Scarlet and Thomas approached. They were much more reserved than the day I'd met them.

"Nice to meet you," Scarlet said, shaking their hands.

"Thank you, Scarlet," my mother said. "That's a lovely dress you're wearing. A very pretty blue."

"It's my pop's favourite colour."

Thomas shook their hands and promptly returned to his seat. Lachlan patted his leg to tell him he'd done a good job.

The mayor took to the stage and sent a broad smile around the room.

"Thank you all for joining us today to celebrate the heroes in our community. They have made an enormous difference to the city of Boston. They will tell you they did what any normal citizen would, but I beg to differ. These heroes have put others first, which is a rare occurrence today. Their actions inspire us to be better people. As mayor of Boston, I'm proud of every one of them."

I shifted in my seat. Lachlan took my hand again. I was aware of my parents' straight, stiff postures beside me.

Thomas, on the other hand, oozed excitement. Scarlet took his hand.

"We will celebrate heroes from all walks of life. Some of those put their lives on the line to save others. Some have put a lifetime of work into changing people's lives."

Applause from the crowd.

"Let's get the ceremony started."

I sat listening while names were called and others received recognition for what they had done. Each and everyone received a rousing applause. They were presented with their medal and then made their way off stage.

"Next, we have Peyton Carter."

I stood up and made my way to the stage.

"Peyton was involved in a serious car accident two years ago. She didn't hesitate to save the family in the other car regardless of the danger she found herself in."

I was at the stairs now, hoping that I wouldn't make an idiot of myself by falling up them.

"She sustained significant burn injuries during the rescue. To this day, she maintains her actions were driven by instinct."

I approached the mayor and shook his hand. Camera flashes went off.

"Thank you, Peyton." He hung the bronze medal with the Boston skyline around my neck and handed me the velvet box. Applause rang out. The cheers from my family were distinct. I smiled at the mayor and made my way back to my seat.

Lachlan kissed me. "Congratulations."

Thomas leant over him. "Why did he say, Peyton Carter? You're Peyton Harris."

"That was my name before I married Daddy."

He nodded and sat back.

"Congratulations, Peyton," Mom said.

"Well done, honey." Dad sent a smile my way.

We listened and applauded the remaining recipients. I was amazed and humbled to be included with such smart, driven and brave people. When the ceremony was over, we all stood together. Refreshments were going to be served in the foyer, but we hadn't headed that way yet. Mom and Dad would know many of the people out there, important people. It surprised me that they didn't make their way out there immediately.

"Shall we go to dinner tonight to celebrate?" Mom asked. "I'm sure we could get a reservation at Lloyds."

"I'd prefer somewhere closer to the hotel, please. That way, if the children get tired, Lachlan can take them back to our room."

I knew my mother wouldn't have intended for the children to join us. It would have been an adult invitation where the children were expected to have a sitter. But in *my* family, we always included the children in special occasions.

"Yes, OK. We will arrange something," Mom said.

I would let her do that, at least. It would allow her to have a sense of control. I watched as they walked off together.

Three people approached us next. The family from the car—Zoe, Megan and their mother. The mother came straight up and hugged me. She held me tight as if I was a lifeline.

"Thank you for saving my children," she said, letting go of me. Tears rolled down her cheeks. "I'm sorry you were hurt."

I took her hands in mine. "I never blamed you for my injuries. What happened was an accident."

I glanced at my family. I wouldn't have them if it weren't for that accident.

Zoe, the youngest, approached next. "Thank you, Miss Peyton. I say a prayer for you every night."

I crouched down. "You must have prayed really hard. I'm all better now."

She gave me a hug.

Megan smiled at me. "Thank you for saving us, Miss Peyton." She came and stood in front of me and spoke quietly. "I have nightmares sometimes. But you're always there to save me."

I gave her a hug. "I will save you every time."

"How is your arm?"

"It doesn't hurt much anymore."

"That's good. Mommy said you can't be a doctor anymore because it was hurt so bad."

"I had to stop being a surgeon, but I'm still a doctor. I work near my home in Australia now."

She nodded, giving me another smile and then walked away with her family.

"Ready to leave, Dr Harris?" Lachlan asked as he came to my side.

"Bloody oath."

THANK you for reading Take the Bull by the Horns. If you would like to join Peyton and Lachlan on their wedding day please click here for the bonus epilogue or alternatively type in https://dl.bookfunnel.com/nnh56c4hfc.

THE NEXT BOOK in the Love Down Under series is Seal of Approval, a small town, workplace romance.

JASMINE

The boss from hell has arrived. Well, he thinks he's my boss, but I have news for him. I will not bow down to his superior marine biologist ways. Even if he has come from the most reputable marine center in America.

I know these waters and the seals who call it home. I will protect them like I protect my two children. What I don't expect is how Ethan protects us when the past comes calling.

Now I see him in a whole new light, and that could be dangerous...especially for my heart.

The same heart I vowed never to open to a man again.

ETHAN

When they said small Australian town, they should have said non-existent town. There is nothing here, even the phone signal comes and goes.

And when they said I'd have a house to live in, they neglected to mention I'd be sharing with Jasmine and her two children. Her two wild children.

I don't have much choice; I've committed to this position for a year. Working with the seals here will catapult my career. It's worth one year of my life.

Soon, my career isn't the only thing on my mind.

Jasmine invades it.

All. The. Time.
Love doesn't align with my career plans.
When my twelve months is up a sacrifice will need to be made.

KEEP IN TOUCH

To be notified of future releases, and to keep up to date with other news, please join my newsletter.
https://www.subscribepage.com/p9p9yo

OTHER books available in the Love Down Under Series are:

The Cat's Out of the Bag

She's started a new life. He's escaping his. Can two tortured souls find a future together?

Evie's a survivor. After rebuilding herself and her life, she's feeling the one thing she never thought she would – happy.

Until Jesse...

When she meets Jesse while volunteering at a cat shelter, dark memories of her past return. She is stronger now and wants to trust him, but after all she's been through, is trust even possible?

Jesse's a self-made billionaire yearning to get away from his empty life and the money-hungry parasites who inhabit it.

The plan?

Go to sunny Australia, leaving his old life behind, to find himself. But instead of finding just himself, he finds Evie, who is everything anyone should aspire to be. Now, what he aspires to be, is hers.

But to be hers, he needs to tell her everything and putting his heart on the line is hard.

The quest to find a cat a forever home leads them to travel across the country together. Will they find the strength to confide in each other? Or will the close quarters drive them apart?

When she left him…

…Tara couldn't explain why.

After five years, did she still have feelings for Shepherd?

Her brother's passing hit Tara hard and it left a scar. That night, at the party, when she saw Shepherd high, Tara had no choice, it was over. It brought up too many painful memories and she wouldn't go through it again. The decision was simple.

She had to leave.

No goodbye.

For Shepherd, losing Tara broke his heart. Not knowing why she left, well that pain he addressed with drugs, alcohol, and meaningless relationships. After he hit rock bottom, he cleaned up and came up with a plan to get her back. Could it work?

It was his only shot.

Would a desperate ruse, with the best intentions, but costing a fortune, give him the chance to win her heart for good? Or would it ruin him?

Will she be brave enough to be loved?

When two opposites collide will their differences ignite a spark?

Frankie and Sebastian live totally different lives. Lives that are entwined through polo, the sport of kings. How entangled will they become?

Australian farmgirl, Frankie, has no interest in high society or the rich, arrogant riders she has to deal with, especially Sebastian. Her heart may be softening to his kindness and love of horses, but her brain won't be convinced. She's looking forward to her summer break on the farm, away from him...

...until her parents invite Sebastian to stay.

Sebastian never felt comfortable in his role as the Crown Prince of Oleander. He'd rather spend his days working with horses, playing polo and being with Frankie, whose fiery spirit has set his heart aflame.

But pressure from his mother, the Queen, to return to his royal duties is mounting. Everything he desires is in danger of being ripped away.

Can Sebastian convince Frankie that his hopes and dreams aren't so different from hers, or is he destined to return to a life he doesn't want, alone?

Love and secrets are a tricky combination

For Emily, going home isn't easy, especially when her small town never felt like home in the first place. She escaped Alma seven years ago when she went to university, but now her estranged father needs her help. At least returning means spending time with the only good thing in town—her best friend, Luke.

Luke always knew Emily needed to be free of their hometown, so he withheld his true feelings. Even though she has returned, he knows she will never stay. He tries hard to respect the boundaries of their friendship but every moment they spend together makes it harder to deny their connection. Self-control dissipates. One kiss turns into two...

But is Luke really the man Emily remembers? When Emily discovers Luke has betrayed her trust, they could lose the most precious thing of all—each other.

A Bird in the Hand

She yearns for the past. He wants a better future. Can they learn to love the present together?

When thirty-something Makayla's long-term boyfriend breaks it off, she is left broken hearted. Her best friends seize the opportunity and book a bus tour up the west coast of Australia. They hope distance will give her perspective, but she can't see past what she's lost.

Tyler needs a break from work and seeks something more fulfilling, even if he has no idea what that is. When his mates plan the trip of a lifetime he decides to tag along. He's sure it will get him out of his rut, and in turn, help him set a course for his future.

No one is prepared for the planning mishap that finds Makayla and Tyler sharing a room. They are opposites in just about every way and are definitely not interested in each other. Add a fouled mouthed cockatoo to the equation and the perfect trip is not so perfect. Or is it?

Eight years apart hasn't made her heart grow fonder...

Clare Walker is a third-generation company woman. *Hart Apples* saved her family from destitution and now it's her turn to return the favour. Work is her one true love, leaving no room for anything – or anyone – else. She knows what the company needs to survive another generation, and it's not the owner's son—her ex-best friend, the annoying and attractive, Beau Hart.

Beau returns to his family orchard after eight years away. He's stronger now and has his mental illness under control. He wants to prove his worth to his family. Most of all, though, he wants to reunite with the only woman he has ever loved, Clare Walker. The first task is difficult, but the second is near impossible, especially as Clare's attitude toward him goes beyond the cold shoulder.

When Beau's father elects them as the company's saviours, Clare's plans of keeping Beau at a distance are thwarted. Now she just needs to keep it all about business...if only those pesky feelings would stay away.

ACKNOWLEDGMENTS

Cover by Amanda Walker
Edited by Empowered Writing
Proofread by Half Caff Press
And thanks to my amazing beta readers

ABOUT THE AUTHOR

Cynthia is a project officer by day and a writer by night. She enjoys writing about places she visited with her daughter while they travelled around Australia. She says that travel and reading are the best educators. Still, to this day, they both enjoy travelling and reading. A love of animals sees them feature in her books, some have small parts, others larger.

Find her online: http://cynthiaterelst.com/

All of her social links can be found here, Linktree: https://linktr.ee/cynthiaterelst